CHAPTER 1

THE FAMILIAR WHO BROKE EVERYTHING

The ceremonial hall smelled of wet stone, boiled rosemary, and the sharp tang of sweat from people trying to exude confidence. Candle smoke curled under the rafters where the shadows were thickest.

Decent perches up there, but no self-respecting cat would perform for an audience of hat-wearing bureaucrats.

Chalk circles glowed on the floor, their lines so perfectly drawn they made my whiskers itch. Light pooled across the grimoire's leather where it sat atop the pedestal, and the clasp twitched once.

Someone else's scent has marked this space. Chalk dust, authority, and the stale breath of committees. Time to improve the territorial boundaries.

Felicity stood in the center, her robe pressed within an inch of its life, a wand gripped tightly in her palm, her breath coming in nervous little hitches. She had scrubbed the ink from her fingers, though the scent of fear still clung to her. Near the chalk, a dish gleamed with three sardines in oil, their silver skins catching every speck of light.

At last, one wise decision.

The Council perched on its dais, all threat display and puffed importance. The High Priestess wore an emerald brooch that caught the light, marking her as the alpha of this particular pack. The clerk smelled of ink and panic, clearly bottom-tier. The apprentices clustered at the edges, unwilling to stand too near the grimoire, each watching it with wary attention.

I picked my way across the chalk, testing each line with my pads for texture and temperature before committing my weight to it. The magic hummed against my paws, curious but not hostile. I chose the fattest knot of lines and arranged myself in a perfect loaf, weight distributed for maximum comfort and instant escape if these bureaucrats proved more dangerous than they appeared.

The air carried the scent of metal and mint, the smell of people determined to enforce order, whether or not it wished to be enforced. My whiskers twitched, mapping the room's dimensions, cataloguing exit routes past robes and ceremony.

"Mischief," Felicity whispered, the word whispered urgently. "Please behave."

I slow-blinked at her, the way that means never.

Ceremonies thrive on boredom, which means it's my duty to improve them. Consider it a public service.

The High Priestess raised her hand, and every mouse in the room went still. "Candidate Felicity Hargreaves," she said, her voice sharp enough to make my ears flatten, "Begin."

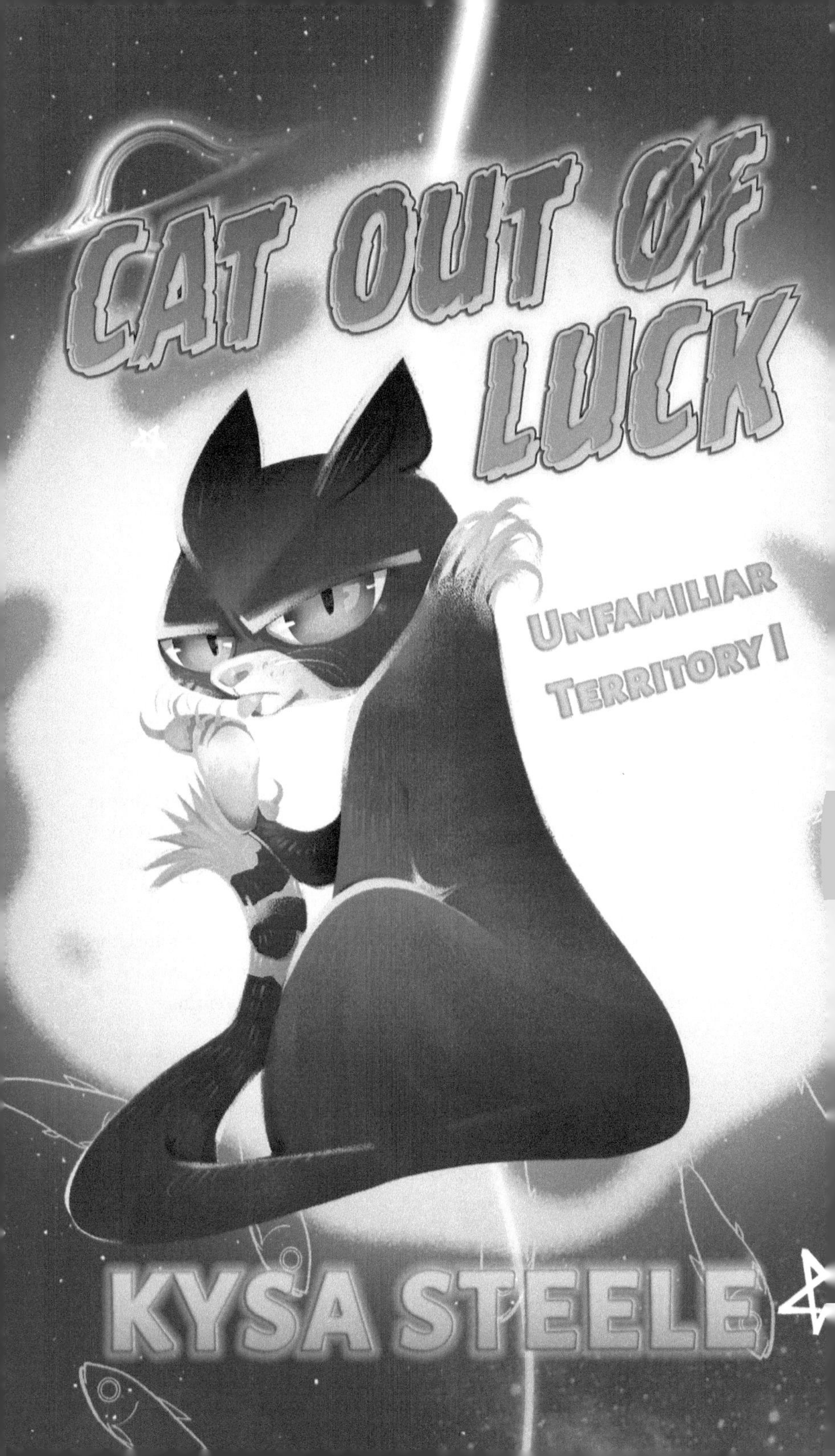
CAT OUT OF
LUCK
UNFAMILIAR
TERRITORY I
KYSA STEELE

Cat Out of Luck

Unfamiliar Territory Book I

Copyright © 2025 by Kysa Steele

Kysa Steele

1st edition: 2025
ISBN: 979-8-9989422-4-2 Paperback
ISBN: 979-8-9989422-5-9 Hardback

Cover design, headers, and dividers created by Velga Al Rasyid with internal layouts by Kysa Steele.

Felicity stepped into the circle, and the chalk answered with sudden brightness. The grimoire creaked. From one rune, a golden mote drifted upward and hovered before my nose.

I batted it toward a patch of dust and tucked my paws beneath me, settling deeper into loaf formation. The hum steadied, then rose to a pitch that made my fur want to stand on end. The clasp of the grimoire clicked once, sharp and hungry.

Books with teeth never stop looking for their next meal. Time to help.

The first verse rose, thirteen voices together, Felicity's line running clean through the middle. The smell in the room sharpened to lemon and rain. The burning incense spat a tiny coal toward a loop of chalk. I extended one paw and pressed it flat, claws just touching the stone, leaving a smear of gray ash.

"Keep the familiar focused," a councilor muttered, his nose forever wrinkled as if the world smelled of litter boxes.

"I am focused," I said, because the best time to speak is the moment no one expects it. "On quality."

Half the dais jumped. The clerk dropped a blotter. Felicity's mouth tried to smile, but then she brought it under control. Several apprentices shuffled backward, recognizing a predator when they heard one speak.

The circle thrummed beneath my paws, the vibrations traveling up through my bones in a way that made my tail twitch with interest. I stretched deliberately, letting my weight shift forward as I brushed one line with my claw tip. The harsh angle softened under my touch. The tone shifted, less brittle now.

Controlled mess prevents explosions. You're welcome.

"Please continue," said the High Priestess, her eyes fixed on Felicity, brooch gleaming as if it were bearing its own teeth.

Felicity steadied the second cadence, grounding the ritual's focus through the grimoire. Her fingers held firm. The book whined, its binding stretched tight.

I placed one paw deliberately on a peak at the knot's center, pressing down until the magic flattened and behaved as expected. My pads read the chalk's texture, too tight here, too loose there. I swiped another ember away before it could alter the pattern. In payment, I claimed a sardine, leaving the bones properly arranged once I was done.

Cold, salty, perfect. Proper tribute to my obvious superiority.

"Do not," Felicity breathed.

I did not, technically. Gravity has opinions, and I allowed it a few. My weight shifted, tail helping with balance as I adjusted angles. The circle breathed easier.

Too easy. Their pattern was a trap with no exits. Even mice know better than that. Magic needs escape routes.

I extended a single claw and shaved one chalk tail into a friendlier curve, the way I'd mark a favorite scratching post. A gold mote wobbled, then settled again. The floor's vibration softened against my belly. The grimoire's clasp twitched again, obviously paying attention to my improvements.

"Assistance noted," I told it, purring low enough that the vibrations sank into the chalk. The interwoven lines absorbed the rumble, each loop and crossing point lighting from within until the entire pattern glowed in rhythm with my chest. The room's trembling steadied.

But improvement never ends.

I dabbed a pinch of ash across the line feeding the grimoire with the precision of a cat burying something distasteful. The mark was barely visible, just enough to bend the flow. The book pulsed, offended and eager. The golden light deepened to amber, then bled towards orange, sharp and hot like embers about to catch.

The High Priestess's fingers flinched. "Hold the resonance."

Felicity held, dropping the cadence a breath lower. She listened to the room instead of the rules. Pride swelled in me, inconvenient but real.

Then the book grew greedy. A purple spark leapt, burrowing into a rune. It spun a wet ring, and the gold I had teased into fresh paths braided with the purple in a dance no one wanted.

That's when things got weird. One of the council members' hats jumped to a new head, its owner yelping. A pair of shoes turned into mice and bolted under a bench. The clerk's ledger spat paper birds into the air. One landed on the High Priestess's shoulder and began grooming itself with grave devotion.

Now this is interesting.

"Contain the flux," barked the High Priestess. Wands lifted. Lines flared. Apprentices scattered. A bottle rolled, shattered, the smell of vinegar searing the air and making my whiskers recoil.

I planted both forepaws and pressed down hard on the knot, claws extending to grip the stone. The hum took my full weight, steady for two heartbeats. Felicity drew a countersign into being, the scent of iron and rain sharpening the air as she thrust it into the grimoire's line. The book hissed. Its clasp cracked open another sliver.

The opening began. It was as if the floor decided it was tired of being a floor. The stone beneath my paws went uncertain, neither warm nor cold. Light leaked everywhere, then faded. The smell of fish crept in—not just any fish, but the particular sardine-and-salt scent of home. Beneath it, Felicity's soap, her skin, her heartbeat.

The High Priestess slashed a sign. "Seal the rift!" A net of light sagged across the opening.

The void snagged my whiskers, tugging them cruelly toward my spine, making every nerve ending shriek with its wrongness. My tail fluffed to twice its size. My legs braced, claws scoring the chalk as I fought for purchase.

"Ground," Felicity said, the word meant for me. I pressed my full weight into the chalk and purred with everything I had, the vibration thrumming deeper than claws ever could. The interwoven lines brightened, pulling my purr down through the pattern like water soaking into parched earth. Each crossing point flared as the vibration reached it, stabilizing the flow. The grimoire's pull hesitated, confused by the sudden anchor.

"Do not let him move," a councilor barked.

Too late. The circle had already claimed me for its own territory. It yanked. The floor tilted. I lurched forward, hind legs scrabbling for leverage that wasn't there. The chalk rose to my knees as I began to sink. Felicity's hand caught my scruff, and for a blink, I was dangling in the air. Her grip shook. She smelled of fear and lemons. Beneath it all, the desperate love of someone watching their cat fall.

It yanked without mercy. My fur burned off in waves, leaving skin raw and defenseless. Cold air bit into nerves that should have been safely buried under a proper coat. I yowled, the sound coming out human and insulting, like trying to hiss through a mouth built for the wrong species.

My ears flattened, then reshaped themselves under hands that used to be paws. Pressure exploded behind my eyes, sharp. My whiskers were vanishing even as they tried to measure the shrinking space.

My bones began reshaping themselves into new formations. My paws betrayed me, stretching into fingers, pads flattening into useless human skin. Their absence left my feet defenseless, unable to grip anything.

And then—the tail.

The tail tried to lash, to balance, to communicate my outrage in the ancient language of cats. There was no tail. The void of it had teeth, a phantom pain that screamed from a limb that no longer existed. Balance shattered. I pitched sideways, body folding wrongly, a creature built for four legs trying to manage with only two.

Where is it? Give it back!

Felicity's arms locked around my chest, heartbeat hammering against my cheek. "I have you," she swore, voice fierce and determined.

It dragged at me, hungry for more. Her grip slipped. Sardine oil was slick under my new feet. My knees bent awkwardly. The glowing threads stretched between the grimoire and the chalk pattern sagged under the strain, snapped taut, then tore.

"Close it," the High Priestess cried. She flung signs and salt. Apprentices shoved anchors into place, their panic-scent thick enough to taste. One fumbled his and swore. The clerk tried to snare a paper bird; it bit him and escaped toward the rafters I could no longer reach.

I tried to stand the old way—back feet set, front paws stretched, tail for balance and pride. These alien legs crumpled under me, dumping me onto bare knees.

"Let him go," someone said. Cruel. Practical.

"No," Felicity hissed, her arms trembling with effort.

I placed my hands on her shoulders, fingers spread wide where paws would have been precise and knowing. Her robe scratched my palms with a texture I couldn't interpret. Her face filled my vision, pale in the candlelight, jaw set.

"Mischief," she said. Just my name, cracking around the edges.

I wanted to tell her to stop being stubborn and just run. But the pull choked my voice, turned my yowl into nothing.

The pull swallowed all. Sound died. Everything rushed toward the center. The grimoire's pages fluttered. The sardine dish spun.

Out of habit, I tried flexing claws that weren't there. Fingernails scraped and failed where proper weapons should have been. Shoe-mice squeaked under a bench. A wand clattered. The High Priestess's brooch gleamed cold and watchful, predator recognizing predator even as I was being pulled away.

A cold sensation wrapped around my hips. The air dragging across bare skin in a way that felt unnatural without fur. My ghost tail thrashed at nothing. Phantom whiskers strained and mapped nothing, a sensory system trying to function in a body that had forgotten how to be a cat.

I pressed my face against Felicity's shoulder because home lives in a scent, and hers was the only one that mattered—soap, ink, and the warm oil of her skin. The smell that meant safety, sardines, and someone who understood that dignity could coexist with chaos.

Her heartbeat hammered, burning itself into my memory. "Mischief." The word cracked through the room. Candle flames bent sideways. The golden threads connecting us flared white-hot.

The portal opened wide.

The hall slipped away. Candlelight smeared. Chalk condensed to a seed. Felicity's face stretched and broke into stripes of color. Sound rose to a needle's pitch that made my phantom ears flatten. The smell of sardines became faint and then vanished, taking the last of home with it.

I fell.

There was no up, no down, only directions stacked and waiting to be knocked over. Ozone, stone, old ink, and chalk dust tumbled around me. Phantom whiskers flicked at emptiness, trying to measure spaces that didn't follow mundane geometry. Balance collapsed in the absence of a tail that should have been steering my fall.

Sardines flashed bright through spaces between spaces. Mine. Following. Pleased with their theft.

Absolutely unacceptable.

The last taste was metal against a tongue that didn't know how to be human. The last sound was Felicity speaking my name like a promise that would reach across any distance. The last thing I carried was her heartbeat, stubborn as a purr, fierce as claws.

Then all went soft and black.

Rain tapped at the window. The room smelled of beeswax, dust, and scorched soap, the stink of laundry boiled too long. Straw pressed against bare skin unused to such sensations. A candle guttered in its iron bracket, the smoke sharp on my nose.

I opened my eyes to see rafters deep in shadow. I tried to flick my tail and found nothing. I could feel the panic rising within me.

Still gone. Still wrong. Someone owes me a tail.

A face leaned over me. Ink on their fingers, old-style robes, and eyes too calm for comfort. "Steady now," he said. "Just breathe. Start with that, okay."

"Book-mouse," I croaked. My throat felt like I had tried to eat gravel.

He smiled ruefully. "Rowan. Archivist. You've been unconscious... well, long enough for me to start a catalog entry." He held out a steaming cup that smelled of mint and bitterness, medicine humans swear will help, even though it always tastes bitter.

I bared my teeth at it. He lifted my shoulders without asking. The touch was wrong in every way. Too heavy, too flat. Skin where there should be fur. Fingers applying pressure like clumsy slabs instead of proper claws. Warmth without purr. Wrong weight on an alien body.

Handled by strangers. This apprenticeship is already unacceptable.

I drank anyway as warmth spread through my chest, chasing out the cold.

The door opened and winter air rushed in, sharp and cold, carrying incense that scratched the back of my throat. Another man followed, older than Rowan, his scent marked with smoke and iron. The weight of him settled into the room; even the candle flame straightened. Rowan rose straighter.

"Abbot Jeran," he said. "Our guest is awake."

"Alleged guest," I muttered. "Portal laundry."

The universe had folded me like a napkin and shaken me out. At least the sardines landed prettily.

The Abbot studied me as if I were a puzzle box he intended to open. "You can speak. Good."

"I can do several inconvenient things. Two on purpose."

"What's your name?"

"They call me Mischief. It's less a name and more a warning."

He nodded once. "Your arrival brings disturbances. The wards flicker, and my novices are behaving strangely."

A monk hurried past the doorway, rubbing his cheek. Fine phantom hairs quivered there, then vanished. His pupils narrowed to slits, then flared wide in alarm. He bolted. Farther down the hall, a novice kneaded a cushion with slow, dreamlike focus, then jerked back in horror and fled.

Rowan glanced at me, a quiet apology in his eyes. The Abbot didn't blink. He was waiting for me to say it.

"Contamination," I said. "Apparently, I shed personality now."

Apparently, my magic thinks sharing is a public service.

The Abbot folded his hands. "Something's leaking out of you. It's making the wards behave oddly."

A bell tolled once. The sound crawled up through the stone and rattled my bones. Phantom whiskers twitched, hunting for walls that weren't there. My ears rang, folding back against a body that wasn't mine.

Wrong body. Wrong place. Wrong world.

Rowan set a tray on the table: a bowl of water with mint, a strip of ribbon, three chimes, and a small stone that hummed faintly. "We need to take some quick measurements," he said quietly. "Then we'll find you a better room before the monks start sprouting tails."

I folded myself onto the stool, knees betraying me with angles no cat was meant to endure. Cloth rasped against skin that still remembered fur.

Rowan nudged the ribbon closer with academic patience. The moment my fingers touched it, frost bloomed across the fibers. One chime gave a startled tick before falling silent.

Apparently, I freeze things now. Wonderful.

The Abbot's eyebrows climbed toward his hairline.

The stone hummed under my palms, its vibration crawling up my arms and settling behind my ribs. Something gold and warm uncoiled from my chest, reaching toward Rowan with invisible fingers. He jerked back, hand flying to his cheek where phantom whiskers prickled against his skin.

"Not imagination, then," he murmured, rubbing the spot. "It spreads."

So, I touch a ribbon and it freezes. A stone hums, and the monks sprout whiskers. Congratulations, I'm contagious. Someone write it down before I sneeze personality onto the curtains.

The Abbot's mouth pressed thin. "If our wards falter, the city's streets will split open and things from outside the walls will pour in."

A silence stretched. I could feel them weighing options, looking for the cage that would solve their problem.

"No cages," I said, fingers curling uselessly where claws should have extended. The pathetic scrape of fingernails against cloth was nothing compared to what it should have been.

"We're not discussing imprisonment," the Abbot said carefully. "But containment—"

"A guest room," Rowan interrupted, voice quiet but firm. "Window, blanket, and a box. I suspect he'll insist on that last part, anyway."

"A box is non-negotiable."

The Abbot studied me for a long moment, perhaps recognizing that cooperation would work better than coercion. Finally, he inclined his head. "So be it."

The stone's hum faded, leaving only silence. The Abbot rose, decision made. "Rowan will see you settled."

The halls stretched ahead, stone and shadow. We passed monks who tried not to stare, though my presence made them twitch. One novice froze mid-step, pupils slitting sharp. His hand jerked in a sudden batting motion, sending a cup flying from his tray to shatter against stone. Peppermint steam rose with the smell of panic.

Everywhere I go, I improve things. You're welcome.

Ward-lines carved into a lintel flickered as I passed beneath, then steadied with what sounded almost like a sigh. The stone itself seemed to be breathing differently, as if my presence had taught it new rhythms that didn't quite match its original purpose. Rain drummed against windows, and phantom whiskers twitched in response, mapping walls my eyes couldn't see.

"Here," Rowan said, stopping at a narrow chamber.

I catalogued the space with predatory efficiency: a cot with a scratchy blanket, a table, a stool, and a window leaking gray light. And there, against the wall, a wooden crate scrubbed until it smelled of apples and sun.

Box. Sanctuary disguised as wood. My throat tightened. I couldn't look directly at it.

The Abbot appeared with a plate of fish. "Rest. We'll speak again at None."

None. Mid-afternoon, when civilized creatures take their second nap. Monks give every hour a pompous name and act like it matters.

Rowan lingered in the doorway. 'The suppression cloth helps when you concentrate on it," he said quietly. 'Think of it as... dampening your natural resonance. But when you're emotional or distracted, it becomes less effective. Worth knowing. If you need anything, I am three doors down. Knock if you like. Or throw something... you strike me as a good shot."

"Stool's throwable," I said. "Apprentices... less so. Keep it that way."

He smiled, tired and kind, and left.

I devoured the fish with surgical precision, leaving clean bones arranged in neat rows. Oil coated my tongue, salt sharp between my teeth. Victory, temporary but acceptable.

Rain blurred the garden beyond the window. Phantom whiskers twitched, trying to track the water patterns against the glass they couldn't feel.

Rowan returned carrying a wooden crate, setting it down near the hearth without fanfare. "Storage crate from the kitchens," he said quietly. "Thought you might want it."

I stared at him. The crate waited, plain and square, smelling faintly of old apples and summer. It was human-made, imperfect, but close enough to matter.

A flawed offering, but sacred all the same.

I tested the edge with fingers that felt clumsy as clubs. The first attempt at entry failed—knees betraying me, nearly tipping sideways. The second attempt left me cursing ankles that refused to bend properly. On the third try, I managed to wedge myself inside, shoulders hunched, body folded into angles humans were never meant to endure.

It wasn't right. Not the way a real box cradles a proper cat. But the moment I settled in, something essential clicked into place. My ribs unlocked. My breath steadied. For the first time since the portal spat me out, my body stopped expecting attack.

The wood even held sound correctly. My breathing echoed back, soft and contained. When I growled experimentally, it came out clean and satisfied. Rain drummed against the window, and my phantom tail twitched once without pain.

"Acceptable," I announced to the empty room.

I reached to groom behind my ear, jabbed myself in the temple instead, and scowled. The box kept my dignity intact. No witnesses.

New world. Wrong body. Contamination-spreading fur. Fine. After a nap, I'll civilize the lot of them.

I closed my eyes. Stone breathed around me. Rain kept time. My phantom whiskers finally settled.

Day one in a stolen body. Three hours until the Abbot wants answers I don't have. Plenty of time to make this place regret its hospitality.

CHAPTER 2

CONTAMINATION PROTOCOL

Afternoon crept closer, heavy with the lingering smells of something grain-based that had given up on life. The midday bells had already rung. *None would come soon enough. Three o'clock interrogation, dressed up as spiritual concern.*

My box had left creases on my shins but restored my dignity. The blanket had been acceptable. The fish, edible.

Rowan brought a tray to the door. Steam rose from a clay bowl, beige and joyless. A chunk of bread leaned against it. Only the small dish of pickled herring gave me pause—not sardines, but at least fish, and therefore the only part worth respect.

"I see the monastery's food standards are a cry for help," I said.

"You can help by eating," Rowan replied, maddeningly calm. "The Abbot wants you steady before the examination."

I ate the herring first. *Priorities matter.* Vinegar bit my tongue, sharp but alive. The bread crumbled. I gave the porridge two ceremonial swipes with the spoon, enough to establish dominance, then abandoned it to sulk in its bowl.

They led me to the round chamber once I'd properly defeated breakfast. Light poured through a circular opening in the domed ceiling, harsh as an interrogation.

Dramatic, these monks. Everything had to frame you in holy judgment.

The air smelled of beeswax, rosemary, and ink—sharp, orderly scents that made my phantom whiskers twitch with suspicion. Ward-lines scarred the floor in chalk, humming loud enough to set my nerves on edge. The Abbot waited, hands folded, watching me carefully.

"Today we measure your signature," he said. "How far does it spread. What does it affect?"

"Everything," I said. "You'll be impressed."

He ignored this and nodded to Rowan. The archivist kneeled with maddening precision, placing a pebble on slate and drawing chalk lines.

"Stand here. Step forward when I say. Stop when I say."

I positioned myself on the mark, tail still stolen, dignity intact but threadbare.

"Now," Rowan said, voice flat as a ledger entry.

I stepped forward. The pebble hummed like it had developed opinions. A wooden chime on the table rattled. The chalk tingled under my feet, curious.

"Again."

Two steps. The hum swelled. Light ribboned along the ward-line. The chime gave a sulky cough.

Three steps. Air prickled across my cheek. From the corridor came a thud, then a startled hiss—the sound cats make when furniture betrays them.

Rowan cracked the door. A monk crouched on flagstones, staring at a sunbeam with religious devotion while claws he didn't possess scratched furrows in stone.

"Brother Hale," Rowan murmured, his eyebrow ticking upward, filing the observation.

"Report," the Abbot said.

The novice flushed. "Apologies, Abbot. I... slipped."

Brother Hale fled down the corridor. Rowan closed the door with deliberate care, then turned back to observe the sunbeam pooling on the stones. I glared at it anyway. "I improved your wards," I announced. "They were antisocial. Now they have personality."

The Abbot's stare could have pinned beetles to boards. "You're dangerous."

"Obviously," I said, letting my smile show teeth. *Finally, proper recognition.*

Rowan reset the slate, adding a shallow bowl of water with mint floating in it. "My sister had a familiar," he said quietly, not looking up from his instruments. "A raven. Smart enough to solve puzzles, stubborn enough to argue with professors. She vanished during a scrying mishap three years ago." His quill paused. "I've been documenting irregularities ever since." Three chimes formed a triangle around it, aligned with obsessive precision.

"Hands over the bowl. Don't touch the water."

"Everything here is so delicate," I muttered, stretching fingers over the surface.

Cool vapor rose. The mint twitched with false confidence. One chime ticked softly.

The ward-line brightened beneath my feet. Outside, wood groaned.

The door burst open. A breathless novice stumbled in. "Sister Mariel is stuck in the cloister window box. She insists it will fit if she exhales completely."

Rowan rubbed his forehead like editing a particularly dreadful manuscript. The Abbot's eyes closed briefly, then fixed on me with weary certainty.

"This is entertaining," I admitted. "Also, my fault."

Responsibility settled on my shoulders. Unwelcome but undeniable.

"Final test," Rowan said quickly, gesturing to the ward circle. "We need you to purr."

The Abbot went rigid. "Absolutely not."

"Better controlled conditions than accidental," Rowan said, tone gentle but immovable. "We need to know what we're dealing with."

I settled onto the chalk, equal parts offended and curious, and built a purr in my chest. Small at first—the growl I saved for furniture that needed correction. The stone drank it greedily. Chimes shivered into harmony. Ward-lines blazed white. Dust in the light beam spun wildly.

Every instinct screamed *hunt*. Phantom whiskers flared wide, missing claws ached for the pounce. Outside the chamber, monks hissed in chorus. A shadow appeared in the open doorway, hand rising to scratch at the frame before jerking away in horror.

"Enough," the Abbot snapped.

I let the purr die. Wards sagged, then steadied with wounded dignity.

Rowan's quill raced across parchment, hand trembling despite his calm expression.

"It strengthens with distance," he muttered, scribbling

frantically. "Everything conducts it. Stone, air, water. Not leaking, but spreading deliberately."

"Spreading what?" I asked.

The Abbot answered, voice flat. "Your impulses."

Silence fell. Even the stone's hum went cautious.

I rubbed herring oil between my fingers, chasing the ghost of better fish. "I didn't mean to break your monks. They were already cracked."

"We can establish boundaries," Rowan said softly. "Rules. Think of it as... containing your influence until we understand it better."

The Abbot studied me warily. "Your presence creates problems. Until we find solutions, you will avoid wards, kitchens, and novices. No purring in public spaces."

"Harsh," I said. "But acceptable."

He slid folded linen across the table. "Carry this. Touch it before touching anything else. It may help contain your... effect."

Cold, clean cloth. A human solution to a cat problem. I pocketed it anyway. "Restraint offends my nature. But I suppose I can try."

I claimed it. *Territory trumps principles.*

The dismissed novices fled stiff-backed, eyes wide, trailing dignity. One paused to stare longingly at the sunlight before bolting.

My chest tightened. This should have been amusing. Instead, it had become my responsibility.

Rowan packed instruments with feline precision.

The Abbot lingered, expression heavy. "We'll speak again at Vespers. Lunch will be provided."

"Please tell me it's not soup."

"Bread, cheese, and fish if I can negotiate for it," Rowan said, almost smiling.

"Finally, someone who understands priorities."

They left me with humming stone and sulking chalk. I folded into their ridiculous sitting position, joints protesting. My hands pressed against my knees—a reminder that these clumsy appendages had no business rearranging territories they didn't understand.

Dangerous and displaced. The combination should have felt empowering. Instead, the chamber pressed close, thick with obligations I'd never requested.

Dust spiraled through the light beam, each mote begging to be chased. I watched without moving, denying the hunt.

Let them dance. I have bigger prey to consider.

The monastery garden smelled of mint, damp earth, and hedges sulking in rigid lines, pretending they were walls. Bells tolled Terce. I sat on the north walk as instructed, trying to ignore the mint patch making territorial advances toward my ankles.

Then the scent of sardines hit my nose sharply and clearly. Real sardines—bright, oily, magnificent—not the salted ghosts the monastery called food. The smell threaded through the garden wall, sharp enough to make my mouth water.

Non-negotiable.

The Abbot's rules crinkled in my pocket. I folded them smaller. The ward on the garden gate hummed complaints when I pushed, but I rubbed my cheek against the latch, marking it as mine, and it surrendered with wounded dignity.

Rowan materialized from behind a quince tree, book under one arm, eyes narrowed with suspicion. "Where exactly are you going?"

"Field research," I said. "The sardines require investigation."

"You were instructed to stay on the walk."

"The sardines are calling. Ignoring them would be rude."

"Mischief—"

"You may escort me," I offered magnanimously.

He sighed wearily but fell into step.

The city spilled downhill in cobbles and chaos. Scents layered thick—bread, coal smoke, fish, dung—while stalls clustered around the square. The gate ward flickered as I passed, then steadied with nervous energy. The guard scratched his cheek where phantom whiskers might have threatened, then looked away quickly.

The fishmonger ruled his domain near the well. Silver skins gleamed on wet planks, glassy eyes staring accusations. Crabs brooded in their tub. Sardines lay arranged in perfect rows, gleaming. The fishmonger himself wielded his knife with the contempt of someone who'd gutted better fish than me.

I planted both hands on his counter. Cold bit my palms. The sardines glittered.

"This territory," I informed the crabs, "belongs to me now."

The fishmonger glanced past me to Rowan. "Brother, if your friend starts sermonizing about fish sanctity, I'm doubling my prices."

"I don't sermonize," I said. "I establish ownership."

He tapped my knuckles with his blade's flat. "Move along."

I shifted precisely two inches left and claimed his scale with my palm. The fish approved. The gathering crowd pretended not to be entertained.

Rowan attempted diplomacy. "One fillet, please. For… research purposes."

The fishmonger's eyes narrowed, but he split a sardine in two clean strokes. Salt perfumed the air.

That's when I saw it.

A flicker leaped from stall edge to awning post—quick and bright, reeking of sardines. *Mine.* A fragment of my own magic, smug as prey that thought it was clever.

I palmed a coin from Rowan's sleeve, devoured what mattered in two precise bites, and arranged the bones with proper ceremony. The fishmonger cursed. Crates tumbled. Sardines scattered across cobblestones. Lemons rolled toward the cooper's stall. Voices rose sharply. Rowan lunged after the chaos, robes flapping, quill threatening escape.

I dropped into the alley between stalls, tracking the spark. Phantom whiskers mapped its path—not random at all, but deliberate. Corners, anchor points, the same rigid geometry from the graduation ritual. A map carved in light and mischief.

Showing off, are we?

The spark skimmed a bread cart, scattered sesame seeds,

then darted beneath a donkey's belly. The donkey considered violence, then decided dignity mattered more.

It led me toward the fountain where stone dolphins posed awkwardly. The spark kissed water, sending ripples spreading eastward in unnatural straight lines. My phantom whiskers recoiled from the ward's metallic taste—hungry and wrong.

Rowan caught up, breathless. "It's following the ward conduits. Using them like highways."

"It's drawing me a map," I corrected.

The ripples sketched patterns before collapsing. The spark zipped away, and I followed—but not blindly.

Something shifted around me. Porters stepped aside without knowing why. A woman raised her basket, creating space that hadn't existed. An awning snapped open as I needed passage. My body anticipated gaps before they formed, chaos bending reality into useful shapes.

I nearly purred from satisfaction. A small sound escaped anyway, and the market rearranged itself obligingly.

The spark darted into the Council Hall's shadow, perching on the iron serpent carved into the steps—tail curled around to meet its own jaws. Light flared. The crowd gasped.

"Theatrical," I muttered.

Rowan cursed in academic Latin. "It's testing the anchors deliberately. This isn't an accident; it's reconnaissance."

The spark bolted down a side street, striking ward stones in a pattern I recognized: first, third, sixth, avoiding the obvious. A familiar's approach—the kind built for finding weak points and exploiting them.

"It's teaching you sabotage," Rowan warned.

Of course. My magic has impeccable judgment.

A guard noticed me, hand moving to his whistle. The shrill note pierced the air and bone. The spark froze on the stone above the door, then chirped mockingly.

I hesitated—fatal mistake. The guard shouted. Boots thundered closer.

I spun back toward the crowd as the spark pursued, offended at being ignored. It rattled a spice stall, jangled bells, and spooked a mule sideways. Pigeons erupted skyward in feathered chaos. The square filled with noise and panic.

But the spark wanted me in that wrong-humming alley. *Herding me like prey.* I veered away on principle—never chase what wants to be caught. The spark sputtered indignation, then course-corrected to follow me instead.

Better. Let it learn proper hunting.

I threaded between cart and child through gaps the wind carved open, emerging near the fishmonger's stall. The spark perched smugly on his awning rope.

It tugged the knot loose.

Canvas snapped. Sardines flooded the cobblestones in a silver torrent. I maintained dignity while admiring them intensely. The crowd showed no such restraint, lunging and slipping and grabbing fish under the pretense of helping.

The spark flicked another rope. Poles clattered. Pigeons shrieked. Children laughed with pure delight.

Then the net fell.

Hemp rough, cold iron woven through every cord. Resin bit the air. Ward-knots burned against my skin. My knees folded. I scrambled for balance with clawless hands.

Four guards cinched the ropes tight. The captain stepped forward, boots steady in the sardine chaos, eyes hard.

"By Council order, you're charged with ward vandalism, public endangerment, and inciting riot."

"I merely liberated sardines," I said. "They were clearly unhappy with their arrangements."

He remained unamused.

Rowan pressed forward, hands raised peacefully. "This is a misunderstanding. He only wanted food."

"And now there's fish everywhere and the wards are failing," the captain replied flatly.

Above us, the spark bobbed with satisfaction before darting toward that wrong-humming alley—my pattern still waiting to be exploited.

I jerked my chin toward it. "There. That's your real problem."

"We'll contain you first," the captain said. "Then assess the damage."

The net lifted. Iron and resin stung my nose as the cords tightened. The spark stamped invisible feet, insulted I wouldn't follow its script, then melted into the warded stones.

I stopped struggling. *Dignity lives in stillness, in waiting for claws to return.*

The guards bore me through the market. The fishmonger leaned over his counter, face purple. "If I see you near my stall again, I'll—I'll gut you like a mackerel!"

"Understood," I said solemnly.

He blinked, knife faltering.

Agreement disturbs people more than argument.

Rowan paced alongside, face creased with thought.

"Don't speak," he murmured.

"Unkind," I replied.

A child waved. A cat on a barrel offered solemn approval. The fountain dolphins glared with stony spite.

As we passed under the Council Hall's shadow, the door ward bristled. Behind us, invisible to everyone but me, the spark peeked from its alley, flicked a sardine-bright farewell, and vanished into stone.

Mine, obviously. Clever, rude, and working an agenda, I should definitely worry about.

The rope bit deep, and they carried me inside.

Limewash and old paper—the smell of rooms convinced of their own importance. The guards dragged me through a warded door reeking of iron and chalk, sharp enough to make phantom whiskers recoil, then deposited me in a chair ringed with protective lines. Iron threads in the rope hummed cold against skin that remembered fur.

The Council waited in formation. Two perched at a table, collars starched into rigid authority, hats aspiring to be mountains. A third stood with folded hands. A scribe hunched over his desk, quill squeaking. Rowan pressed against the wall, clutching his book.

The standing councilor spoke first, voice graveled with self-importance. "State your name and origin."

"Two questions," I said. "Pick one for a clean answer."

He didn't blink. "Name."

"Mischief. Consider it fair warning."

"Origin."

"Wherever Felicity keeps her tea kettle. Different realm. Proper sardines. Her reading chair by the window. Oh, and no monks."

The woman leaned forward, rings chiming like tiny bells. "Species classification."

"Formerly cat," I said. "Currently grievance."

The scribe's quill protested with scratchy indignation.

"You stand charged," the man intoned, "with ward vandalism, public endangerment, and inciting civil disorder." He glanced toward the captain. "Add resisting lawful detention."

"I resisted nothing," I said. "Your rope disagreed with me."

Rowan muffled a cough. The captain's ears pinked.

The woman folded her hands, rings clicking territorial warnings. "Multiple witnesses saw you manipulating the crowd."

"People move when you show them interesting paths," I said. "They performed admirably."

Her pupils contracted. Fear lurked behind that official pride, waiting to pounce.

Finally, proper recognition of my capabilities.

"Why were you in the marketplace?" the standing councilor pressed.

"Sardines," I said. "Also, because a fragment of my magic went racing ahead—sardine-drunk and showing off. It traced your ward conduits in a pry-bar pattern. Very educational."

Hats tilted forward in alarm. Even the scribe paused mid-scratch.

"Describe this pattern," the woman demanded.

"I'll show you instead." I nodded toward their workspace. "Maps."

She gestured impatiently. An aide unrolled canvas across the table—chalk-crusted, over-folded, marked with circles and crosses. Intersections bled white where lines had been erased and redrawn. My phantom whiskers mapped the geometry automatically.

"Your anchors cluster like nervous sheep," I said. "Same spacing, same predictable connections. See how disruptions stack at these crossing points? Especially after the bells ring, especially when the humidity rises. Someone's reading your patterns."

Rowan spoke quietly, "The fourth anchor stone was poorly repaired after the eastern earthquake."

The councilors shifted uncomfortably. Authority developing cracks.

The captain's voice dropped. "Three incidents this past week. Smoke that condensed into a boy with glass eyes. A burned-edge hound hunting voices nobody else could hear."

"Don't forget the woman who emerged from winter fog," Rowan added reluctantly. "Or the whispers from the well."

The chamber's temperature seemed to drop. Ink hissed in the scribe's well.

"You have a collector," I said. "Something prowling your boundaries, testing weak points, dragging through whatever fits. It tests weak points, waiting to see which ones give way."

"Conspiracy theories don't excuse the sardine chaos," the woman said crisply.

"True," I admitted. Guilt tasted sour as old fish. "The sardines were my fault. The mess was my fault. But the larger pattern isn't. Someone else is working to split your city's defenses wide open."

The standing man stepped closer. "This spark of yours—do you intend to exploit what it showed you?"

"Absolutely not," I said. "It wanted me to tear the hole wider so you'd blame me for everything. Instead, I intend to seal the breaches. You can assist, or continue drawing useless circles while your city crumbles."

The woman's rings tapped an agitated rhythm. "Why should we release you from restraints?"

"Because I'll remain dangerous whether sitting or standing," I said. "But I'm only useful if allowed to act."

Rowan straightened with unexpected backbone. "The Abbot confirmed the risk. If this contamination spreads beyond monastery walls, it will infect the entire ward network. The city's defenses will collapse."

The councilors exchanged meaningful glances. They hated the truth but couldn't deny it.

"Conditional release," the woman pronounced. "You remain within designated boundaries. You carry the suppression cloth at all times. No unsupervised movement."

"I require a proper box," I said. "And fish of acceptable quality."

"Granted."

"What happens if I simply leave?"

"We hunt you down."

I shrugged philosophically. "I'm already running—the

question is direction. Toward your problems, or away from them."

The standing councilor's mouth twitched despite his efforts. "For now, toward."

About time. The rope loosened and circulation returned painfully to my wrists. *Appropriate respect for my obvious talents.*

CHAPTER 3

UNDERGROUND RECONNAISSANCE

The Council chamber spat me out like a hairball on polished stone. Ropes gone, wrists prickling, chalk still humming at my soles as if it wanted my feet back. Rowan fell in beside me with his book and the dry rustle of paper. He smelled of mint and ink. The captain stalked ahead, helm tucked under one arm, boots thudding like an apprentice trying to scare mice.

They brought us into a tower room where maps covered every wall. Canvases, pins, and threads connecting everything in ways that begged for a good swipe. The air held chalk dust, ink, and yesterday's beeswax. A high window leaked winter light across the table.

The councilor with the rings had abandoned her hat. She tapped the tabletop once, rings clicking sharp as claws on tile. "Sit. Just keep off the maps."

Wise. Without the hat, she almost looked like she had ideas worth chasing.

"I suppose," I said, lowering myself into a squeaky chair, "I can spare time from my napping schedule."

Rowan sat with me, neat even when tired. He set his ledger down on the table. The captain planted himself by the door, puffed up.

Spoiler: doubts don't flinch.

The councilor gestured at the nearest canvas, and I padded closer to examine their handiwork. Pins clustered across parchment that smelled of too many hands and not enough washing. A red thread connected incidents, blue-marked ward stones, and yellow traced what they probably thought were patrol routes. A spider's web drawn by someone who'd never watched a proper spider work.

Humans and their straight lines. No wonder their magic keeps breaking.

I leaned in to study their patterns, then jerked back as static bit my fingertips. The map itself was warded—of course it was. Can't have important information sitting around where cats might knock it off tables.

"Disturbances," the councilor said, tapping a cluster of red pins with one manicured nail. "Logged by our scribes over the past month. You claimed you see patterns we're missing."

My phantom whiskers twitched toward the gaps between their neat clusters. Not the pins themselves—the spaces they'd left empty. The places their methodical minds had dismissed as unimportant.

"Your scribes," I said, circling the table, "see what happened. I see what's going to happen." I traced a claw along an empty stretch of parchment. "Here. Tomorrow, maybe the day after. Something will poke at your east gate ward just hard enough to make it hiccup."

Rowan's quill paused mid-scratch. "Based on what evidence?"

"Based on the fact that whoever's hunting you thinks like I do." I tapped three pins in sequence—a pattern that would be invisible to anyone who'd never spent hours plotting the perfect route to the cream pitcher. "They're not random strikes. They're probes. Testing your reflexes."

The captain shifted his weight, leather creaking. "Testing for what?"

"For how long it takes you to respond. How you coordinate. Whether you panic or adapt." My burn-line pulsed as I traced the actual pattern underneath their scattered pins. "Your Collector is sniffing around the edges before it pounces."

I leaned towards the pins, following lines I could feel but not see. My human skin crawled with the wrongness of it. "They gather where the stones spit and claw at each other," I said. "Here. East gate. The anchors spit and the air arches its back."

Rowan's quill moved. "I noted a fracture there after the spring tremor."

"Your fracture squeaked. Familiars hear it. So does whoever is collecting them."

The councilor's mouth went thin as a blade. "Collecting."

"It's a string left dangling from a shelf. You bat at it because it moves. Sometimes you catch a mouse. Sometimes just lint. But something always comes running to see what the fuss is about."

I padded around the canvas. Cloth rasped under my unworthy fingers. My phantom whiskers twitched toward the gaps between pins, mapping something the councilors couldn't see.

"Your stones hiss at each other here." I pressed a finger to the bent triangle near the river. The static nipped back, angry. "Listen."

The councilor frowned. "I hear nothing."

"Exactly. They're holding their breath." I traced the line between two pins.

Rowan's quill paused. "The anchors are under stress?"

"Everything's under stress when it can't move." I flicked a pin, watched it quiver. "You built a cage. Forgot that cages need hinges, or they crack."

The captain shifted his weight. "Explain cages."

I considered how much truth humans could swallow. "Your magic walks the same path every day. Bells ring, rituals repeat, energy flows in circles. More predictable than my breakfast bowl appearing at dawn." My phantom whiskers caught something else—a vibration too regular, too patient. "But someone's been listening to the rhythm. Learning when to step in time."

The captain's jaw ticked. "Scheduled."

"Traps love schedules like cats love sunny windowsills. Even mice know to change their routes."

The councilor tapped one ring against wood. "Why these places? Why not everywhere at once?"

I pointed two fingers at a bent triangle near the river. "Your posts are crammed here tighter than kittens in a basket. The lines pull so tight they twitch when something big moves nearby. The Collector pokes at that twitch. First, a nibble. Then a bite. Think of one greedy cat clawing at every mouse hole it finds."

Rowan's quill wrote it down as if ink could keep it from escaping. "So, the disturbances are sequenced."

"Yes," I said. "It's yarn. Tug a strand, watch the rest snarl up. The Collector is weaving. Or unweaving. Hard to tell the difference from the floor."

Humans talk about weaving. Cats talk about string. One of us is honest about the claws involved.

The captain cleared his throat and gave the room a report that it already feared. "Another flicker at the east gate. Third bell. Same as yesterday."

Rowan underlined with a neat stroke. "Predictable."

Good. Predictable mice are the easiest to catch.

A purr slid out before I could stop it, and the pins on the map shivered. The councilor cut me a look that could peel paint. I closed my mouth. The hum lived on in my ribs, where it belonged.

"North ward next," I said. "Near the flax exchange, right after it rains."

"How certain?" she asked.

"As certain as a cat in a box," I said. "Which is to say entirely, until the box betrays us."

"That is upsetting," the captain muttered.

"Accurate," I said.

Rowan glanced between us. "He should be there. His perception is unique."

The councilor drummed her rings once, then again. "Under escort," she said. "And you will keep your influence from seeping into my novices. I don't want to find them kneading the Council table."

I considered the table. It had excellent grain.

"Try," she added.

"I'll leave it a dead mouse as a warning," I said.

A novice arrived just then with a tray of cups. Steam rose, sharp and green, the kind of leaf humans mistake for comfort.

Catnip would have been better.

The novice stepped into the winter light with ordinary feet. Then his gaze snagged on a bright rectangle of sun on the floor. His hands slowed. The tray tilted. His fingers traced the wood rim in slow circles while his palms pressed, kneading the tray like a tom on a blanket.

At least this novice kneads properly. Half these monks slap cushions.

The captain's shoulders went tight. The councilor's rings stopped moving.

Rowan stood and crossed to the novice, voice pitched with a soothing rhythm. "Brother. Count with me. One. Two." He set a steadying hand over the boy's knuckles. A sigil whispered across the tray, rosemary and rain. The boy blinked. Focus crawled back into his face, chasing off the confusion.

He looked at me with embarrassment, but the fear was gone.

The air went sour on my tongue. "This is funny," I said. "And it stinks of me."

Rowan nodded without looking away from the boy. "It is our problem. Shared."

The novice fled with his dignity and most of the peppermint. Cups rattled, then froze like mice hoping not to be noticed.

Cowards. I noticed.

The councilor cleared her throat. "Your field spreads. It infects."

"Yes," I said. "A noble infection. You should thank me before the symptoms fade."

I spread proper cat behavior. You're welcome.

Rowan returned and set a cup by my hand. "There are records you did not hear in the chamber," he said to the councilor. "At the docks last month, a woman stepped out of the foam. Water poured from her sleeves, and she spoke in tide rhythms. The fishermen understood every word, until she fell silent and turned to salt on the stones." He turned a page. "Before that, in the north quarter, smoke coiled from an alley and condensed into a boy with glass eyes. He listened to bell-metal as if it were speech. And the hound with burned edges was hunting a voice in the walls."

Quite the menagerie. I should start charging admission.

The room chilled. Ink stiffened on the quill tip.

"Salt in sleeves, smoke in alleys, bells that talk, shadows that bite," I said. "Your Collector paws at every post it can reach."

The captain swallowed his temper and stuck to the facts. "Three incidents like those in ten days. Others scattered over months."

"Patterns," I said. "Tracks that cross and curl. The bait matches the hunger. Sardine for me. Tide for the docks. Bell metal for the child of ash."

"Enough," the councilor said. She didn't snap. She ironed the word flat and set it on the table. "Third bell, north ward. Captain."

He nodded. "Circle the watch post, the flax exchange, and both lanes. Record whether the stones are damp or dry."

"Damp," I said. "Your stones reek of mildew. If I'm expected to suffer it, fetch blankets. And fish."

Her rings tapped once. "If you are wrong, you spend the week in records. Copying, by hand."

"If I am wrong, I will scratch your records myself. Every margin. Every page," I said. "We will both suffer."

The captain almost smiled. He killed the smile before it could escape.

We left the map room with chalk dust following us. The corridor lay quiet under the weight of stone and winter. A bell tolled above us, the note crawling down the wall.

At the foot of the stairs, a young monk leaned into the sun that pooled on the step. His face tilted, pupils narrowing to pinpoints, then flaring wide, then narrowing again as if the light told a joke only cats laugh at. His hands pressed the stone with careful devotion, palms moving in a rhythm that would feel good under claws.

Rowan was already there. "Hale," he murmured. "Look at me."

Hale's breath came fast. Sweat cut through the soap on his skin. His fingers tried to draw circles he could not see.

Rowan drew a square in the air, then another, then a circle inside the square. A modest grounding charm, stubborn and reliable. It thrummed in the bones of my jaw.

"Focus," Rowan said. "Say the first letter of your name."

"H," the novice whispered. His hands let go of the stone. His shoulders dropped.

I stepped back two paces and pinched the square of linen the Council had given me. Cloth answered yes to pressure. My phantom whiskers reluctantly eased.

Hale saw me and tried to bow. He settled for a nod and a fast exit.

Dignity preserved. The better part of bravery.

The captain exhaled for the first time in that minute. "I dislike this."

"Keep disliking it," I said. "Dig your claws into that feeling until we hand you a better post."

We crossed the cloister. The rain had stopped and left the stones steaming. Mint patches sprawled arrogantly in the wet. The ward at the garden gate hummed against my whiskers, all patience and strain. It wanted to flicker. It chose stillness.

Good gate.

Rowan and I claimed a bench that hissed judgment the moment I touched it. The captain stayed standing, trying to tower over problems that don't care about posture.

I've tried it. Doesn't work. Tail is better.

Rowan tapped his ledger, gaze on the square of damp gravel where the sun failed to warm anything at once. "Explain the network again," he said quietly. "Humor me. I want to understand it better."

I drew a finger through the air, sketching a box he could not see. "Anchors are posts. The world sharpens its claws on them. Conduits are the paths between posts, much like a cat walks on shelves without looking. Brace a post too tight, and the path snarls. That snarl hums wrong. The Collector claws until it splits, and the split gapes into the between."

Rowan rubbed ink across his nose. "So, what do we do?"

"Two claws," I said. "Loosen the posts so the box flexes before it breaks. And catch the paw that keeps scratching, make it drop what it stole."

The captain grunted. "You make crime sound like chasing vermin."

"Crime, vermin, apprentices, it's all the same. Find the weak spot and pounce."

The councilor appeared at the arch, hat still banished, rings catching the light. "You can go. With guards watching. If you purr in the square, I'll take it back."

"My purr is a weapon of restraint," I said. "Be grateful I aim it elsewhere."

Her mouth shifted, slow as winter arriving, toward an almost-smile. "Third bell. Flax exchange. Rowan, stay with him. Captain, bring blankets. And a net that doesn't hum. And apparently fish."

Rowan shut his ledger with a soft thump and watched the last wet patches fade from the gravel. "You meant what you said," he murmured. "About closing holes."

"Yes."

"You will help us." Not a question.

"I will," I said. "Until the box splits. Or the fish run out. Whichever comes first."

The captain checked the sky and scowled on purpose. Clouds scowled back. He would bring blankets, scowl, and hate everything, yet he would do it, anyway.

My human hands tried to smooth the hair that wanted

to stand up at the top. Habit pricked, then eased. My phantom tail twitched and met nothing, as usual.

"Third bell," I said. "And sardines fit for council business. If your standards slip, so will mine."

Rowan wrote it as if it were a contract with two signatures and a paw print. "Fish," he said. "Blankets. Chalk."

"And curiosity," I said. "Let the posts scratch back for once."

The garden breathed. The stone at my back gave up a thread of heat it had been saving for someone else. A bell rolled a low note across the enclosed garden courtyard. It combed my ghost whiskers and left them lying flat for once.

Tomorrow. We pry back. We make the box stretch. And if the Collector scratches at my hole again, I will be there to bite the paw.

The monastery bells tolled for evening prayers, bronze notes echoing through stone corridors. I sat in my box, knees folded at angles that would embarrass a proper cat, listening to the sound settle into my bones. The burn-line on my palm pulsed in rhythm, a second heartbeat I hadn't asked for.

Beyond my window, the city spread in geometric patterns that made my phantom whiskers itch. Lights kindled in windows, each one a star in someone else's constellation. Somewhere among those lights, the

Collector's arrays hummed their patient songs, sorting through displaced souls like a librarian with very particular tastes.

The spark behind my ear chittered, restless. It wanted to hunt, to follow whatever invisible threads connected us to the thing that had marked me. Smart little predator. It knew what I was beginning to suspect—that waiting was just another kind of trap.

Rowan knocked, the sound soft as falling leaves. "Time."

I unfolded from the box with dignity intact, despite my joints complaining in languages I didn't recognize. Human architecture had no appreciation for proper cat comfort. "Lead on, apprentice. Let's see what your sardine-scented mystery wants to show us."

But as we descended toward the north ward, something cold settled behind my ribs. The kind of chill that meant predators circling just beyond the light, patient as winter, inevitable as mice.

The north ward sulked under rain that had opinions about everything it touched. Cobblestones gleamed, every puddle a trap. The flax exchange huddled behind shutters that leaked the scent of wet rope and older, less savory bargains.

The third bell rolled from the tower, low and certain. My phantom whiskers shivered, catching something that didn't belong in the lane's familiar symphony of dripping and complaint.

The air tasted wrong. Metal where there should be stone, sardine where no respectable fish would venture. Someone had been arranging my favorite things in places they had no business being.

Rowan shifted beside me, his fingers already ink-smudged from a book I hadn't seen him open. The captain paced in front of us with two watchmen in tow, boots steady, eyes on doorways, trying to look innocent.

Boots never stay unnoticed. They always find your paws the moment you nap.

I tasted the air. Metal and sardine. Sardine did not belong to this market.

Unforgivable. Sardines should always belong in every market.

The market square reeked of fish guts and morning ambition, vendors hawking turnips that should've been compost weeks ago. The third bell had tolled, right on schedule, and my phantom whiskers were already mapping wrongness in the air.

Too much metal where stone belonged. Sardine where no self-respecting fish would venture. Someone had been arranging my favorite scents like bait in a trap—which was either flattering or insulting, depending on how hungry I felt.

Bait. Obviously bait. The question is whether I'm curious enough to be annoyed by the presumption.

"There," I said, pointing toward the gutter where something flickered just wrong enough to catch a predator's attention. A spark no bigger than a firefly, but fireflies didn't pulse in mathematical precision. This one bobbed at knee height, trailing the scent of my own magic mixed with something that tasted like copper pennies and desperation.

The captain's hand moved to his sword hilt. "Contact confirmed."

"Don't," I said, raising a palm toward his weapon. "It's

not attacking. It's *showing off.*" The spark zipped along the gutter's edge, pausing every few feet. "Someone wants to impress me with their needlework."

Rowan squinted at the dancing light, scribe's brain sorting the impossible. "It chose the third ward stone, bypassing the fourth entirely."

"Of course it did." I slipped ahead before the captain could suggest something stupid like following behind armed guards. The spark responded to my approach, brightening. "The fourth stone was patched after the earthquake. Solid, stable, boring. Third stone still sulks about being ignored during the repair work."

The spark darted deeper into the lane, weaving between puddles with the fluid grace of something that had been watching me move for months. Learning. Copying. Getting my mannerisms wrong in ways that made my phantom tail lash with territorial irritation.

Imposter. Rude. If you're going to steal my magical signature, at least do it with proper style.

It paused at a broken lintel, pulsed violet, and waited.

Rowan murmured, "Signal."

"Show-off," I said. I pressed my palm to the stone. Cold lanced up my arm. The spark wriggled and vanished through the lintel.

Lines crawled awake across the stone: circles and broken arcs that tried for precision but showed fangs. At the bottom, a paw print glowed faintly, gold, with toes ruler-straight. A stranger's mark, close enough to mine to make my ribs buzz.

Imposter paw prints. Offensive. Mine are artistry. This was draft work with a ruler.

My stolen spark sang in my chest, eager. The sigil snapped a thread into my hand. Pain bit its way up my wrist; when I pulled away, a pale, straw-colored burn-line etched my palm.

Rowan's quill hovered. "It keyed itself to you."

"It claimed me," I said. "Which is worse."

Under the paw, letters burned into the stone. Each word smoked like fur singed by a candle:

Subject acquired. Proceeding to phase two.

The captain bent close and flinched. "Who carves messages into wards?"

"Someone who expects me to read them," I said. My voice sounded like claws on slate.

The spark inside me chirped approval. I wanted to bite it. *Everything in this city either hums, sings, or chirps. Not one thing knows when to shut up.*

The trail pressed us deeper, through passages that seemed to breathe with accumulated secrets. My spark, regardless of who'd been puppeteering it, led us through passages that narrowed like a predator's throat, guiding us toward whatever had been arranging this elaborate game of mouse-and-cat.

The air changed as we descended. Warmer. Thicker. Tinged with scents that made my phantom whiskers recoil: ozone, old fear, and something organic gone wrong, like finding spoiled fish hidden behind the good sardines.

The passage opened into a chamber that made my burn-line pulse with recognition. Not built—carved. Someone had spent considerable time hollowing out this space, smoothing walls, and creating alcoves that suggested permanent occupation rather than temporary shelter.

In those alcoves, shadows moved with the careful deliberation of things that had learned not to attract attention.

The first crouched in shadows thick as velvet, where even my enhanced vision struggled. A boy made of smoke, or maybe smoke pretending to be a boy. He'd been here the longest, judging by how still he held himself—the patience of someone who'd learned that movement only brought attention. Three months, maybe four, since he'd been pulled from whatever forge-world had birthed him. His edges wavered, never quite solid, never quite gone. When he breathed, vapor coiled from his mouth in patterns that spoke of forge-fires and cooling metal.

"Hello," I said, because proper introductions matter, even in stone-walled prisons. "You smell of hammered copper and homesickness."

He tilted his head, listening to something beyond even my superior hearing. "The walls gossip. They remember the sounds that shaped them. Your stones are very chatty."

"Terrible conversationalists, though. No sense of proper timing." I settled onto my haunches like I was approaching skittish prey. "What do they tell you?"

"That something hunts here. Something that tastes like brass coins and broken promises." His edges stopped wavering, enough to show eyes bright as glass in candlelight. "It left marks in the metal. Recent marks."

I followed his gaze to the iron grate set into the wall. Scratches marred the surface. Fresh scratches. Deliberate scoring that smelled of silver and spite. Claw marks, if the claws were made of silver and sharpened in desperation.

Rowan whispered, awed, "He hears what metal remembers."

Archivists creep around like the books might scratch back. Books don't have claws. I do.

The boy didn't look at him. He tilted his head, listening to the walls, as though every echo was a word.

The second leaned against a crate, salt crusting her arms. Seafoam still clung to her hair despite the weeks since her tide-pool had been torn open and she'd been dragged through. Her eyes held the deep exhaustion of someone fighting dehydration in a place that had never known the ocean.

"This is not my tide," she said, accent thick as waves. Her voice rasped like surf chewing rocks.

The third lurked at the back. A man-shape with shoulders too wide for his frame, as if borrowed from something else. The rope collar had worn permanent grooves in his throat—fresh when he'd arrived a month past, now settled into the rhythm of breathed oppression. When he moved, he sounded like someone dragging chains across gravel.

The not-man raised his nose and whispered, "They said the subject would come. Mocking voice. Chaos-furred." His gaze fixed on my marked hand.

In the deepest shadow, a girl no older than ten hummed a tune that spilled into words, thin as rain through cracks. The girl had been here for at least a week, maybe two. She still remembered her mountain-cave clearly enough to call its stones by name in her humming. The newest addition to this collection. "The walls remember falling," she said. Her tune wavered; the stones shivered.

They all flinched at once. They ignored Rowan's book and the captain's boots; their eyes were fixed on me.

My phantom whiskers twitched, sorting their scents like a proper inventory: ash, brine, rope burn, and something that made stones weep. "Hello," I said, since a proper greeting establishes dominance. "You smell of fish promised and never delivered."

Rage pricked sharp and quick. "They think they know my pawprints. They don't."

Rowan crouched, palms open. "There's food if you're hungry. Warmth if you'll take it."

The captain's men lowered packs with bread, water, cloth, and a small flask of something warm. Useless comforts for what had been stolen.

Blankets solve nothing unless they are mine.

The boy sniffed but drank. The salt woman cradled a cup as if it might break. The not-man refused. His eyes never left the burn-line on my palm. The girl sipped, then giggled. The walls shuddered at the sound.

Rowan murmured as he scribbled, "Different places. Different smells. All dragged here like mice in a sack."

"Collected," I corrected. The carved words still scratched behind my eyes. *Subject acquired.* "Someone isn't waiting for accidents. They're fishing."

And I'm apparently the prize catch they've been dangling bait for. Outrageous. I don't even like hooks. Bait is for idiots and carp. I am neither.

The salt woman met my gaze. "A hand with the wrong number of fingers."

"Or a paw pretending to be a hand," I said.

She almost smiled. It cracked like breaking water.

The captain looked unsettled, which meant he had finally noticed the obvious. "What happens if this spreads?"

"Then your wards fray," I said. "Your posts splinter. And your city becomes a scratching post for whoever is tugging the seams."

And I don't share scratching posts.

Rowan tapped his notes, lips pale. "Someone planned this. Like setting multiple mousetraps in the same corner. And the sigil was keyed to you specifically."

"Yes," I said. The words came out flat. "This was deliberate. I was chosen. Acquired."

The spark inside me thrummed with pleasure. I dug my nails into my palm. "I do not enjoy being property."

The smoke boy watched me, ash drifting from his mouth. "They said you'd follow the trail. They want you standing there when the window tears open."

"Of course they do," I muttered. "It's what I'd do."

Never trust pawprints that look like mine but don't smell right.

The captain scowled. "And your choice?"

I bared my teeth in a smile made of nothing but threat. "To be the claws waiting on the other side of the hole."

Rowan exhaled slowly. "You mean to fight them."

"I mean to remind them I bite back."

The salt woman's laugh was a salt-crack, brief and bitter. The not-man tilted his head. The boy tapped the clapper again, once, as though agreeing to an oath. The girl rocked on her heels, humming a single note. The arch shuddered as if it wanted to echo her oath.

We led them out. The rain had softened to mist, stones slick, city sulking. The captain muttered orders, Rowan wrote, and my phantom whiskers twitched with every step.

In my palm, the burn-line still glowed faintly, a brand and a dare.

Phase two, the stone had said. *Subject acquired.*

"Very well," I whispered, letting the rain cool the heat in my chest. "Phase three will be mine."

And mine comes with claws.

The spark led us deeper, through passages that narrowed. My phantom whiskers twitched at every corner, nose wrinkling at how wrong each angle felt. Stone that should have been cold burned against my paws. The air that should have moved clung to my fur.

"The way they're scattered," Rowan murmured, quill scratching against parchment despite the dim light. "Look at where we found them. There's a pattern here."

I traced the path we'd taken, seeing it now with predator's eyes. "A spiral. Tightening."

"Toward what?"

The spark bobbed ahead, eager. It paused at intersections, waiting for us to follow, leading us in a dance I was beginning to recognize. The same patient stalking I'd use to corner a mouse behind the flour sacks.

"Toward whoever's been arranging the furniture," I said. My burn-line throbbed harder with every step, pulling me forward like a fish hook in my skin. "We're being invited to dinner. Question is whether we're guests or the main course."

The air changed ahead—warmer, tinged with copper and the sharp bite of contained lightning. Machinery hummed beyond a door that crouched at the tunnel's end like a fat rat blocking the only exit.

"Last chance to run," I told the displaced.

The salt woman's crystals chimed once. "Running is for tides. We are the wave that drowns."

CHAPTER 4

THE COLLECTOR'S WEB

Rain skulked through the lane, refusing to leave and making sure everything was damp enough to ruin any nap worth the name. My marked palm burned, the thread across my skin prickling like unwanted restraint.

Try it. See what you catch.

Blankets moved by, hunched shapes under cloth, shuffling. Rowan herded them carefully—adequate apprentice behavior. The captain watched the rooftops with competent alertness that might eventually earn him a better title than 'useful human'.

The lane reeked of sardine oil in cracks even mice avoid. Something sharp and sour curled under the stink, magic, or just nerves. Sardines in the gutter. Sardines on the doorstep. Sardines placed with all the subtlety of a bad ambush. Someone's been arranging snacks, thinking I'd be flattered.

"I should have known." The sardines were too convenient.

Rowan glanced up, ink on his fingers, rain streaked across his nose. "Known what?"

"Bait," I said. "Crumbs with opinions."

The spark nosed around the corner, too shiny for its own good, fishy and smug. It bounced, let out a squeak begging to be pounced, then vanished into a side alley where the bricks pressed close.

The not-man's rope collar twitched. The smoke boy tapped his clapper, eyes wide. The salt woman licked her cracked lips, crust flaking off her knuckles. The girl in the shadow hummed a tune that made the bricks ache and the mortar sweat. I flattened my phantom ears.

Children should not terrify architecture. That's my job.

"No vermin," I announced. "Mine." The word stuck in my throat. Ownership should feel like a purr. This one prickled.

I followed. Rowan trailed behind, ink-stained and tense. The captain blocked the alley mouth, all chest and hat, as if human bulk could stop anything interesting.

The spark paused, all ember-light and mouse-nerves, tail streaming fish-oil, eyes flat and watching, daring me to chase.

Rowan's breath stuttered. "Your field."

"Yes," I said. "Copycat magic. Should have known it would pick up bad habits."

The fragment traced a circle on the wall, then scratched a line through it. Showing off.

Trying to bait me with my own tricks? Typical.

I place my palm on the bricks. The burn-line flared, hot and wrong. The fragment shrank, speaking in two voices—mine, with attitude; another, purring sour and false.

"Same as the lintel," Rowan whispered.

"Yes. The Collector. Close enough to sniff, too scared to show claws."

Something behind the bricks shifted, big as a storm cloud on a window ledge. Watching. Waiting. The fragment tucked itself into a rusty grate, quivering.

"How's the collar?" I asked the not-man, eyes still on the wall.

He tugged at it, voice rough. "Too tight. Chafes."

If he'd had fur, it would have bristled.

The smoke boy turned his clapper in his hands, smoke leaking between his teeth. "Feels stuck. Can't breathe right."

The salt woman dug at her skin, flakes falling. "Pulled the tide out of me. Left the salt behind."

The girl just hummed, stones sweating under her heels.

I bared my teeth at the wall. The fragment froze.

They sniffed around, stole my fur, and now think I'll come when called? Not a chance.

The spark zipped deeper, ducking through a door that squatted at the end of the hall. I shouldered it open.

Copper wire crawled up the walls, glass jars in chalk circles, each humming a fraction of a note. Tally marks everywhere. They'd hung bits on hooks: my fur, salty crust, a strip reeking of kennel, something heavy and damp as rain-soaked mortar. The whole collection had the stale disappointment of day-old sardines—technically edible, but insulting to anyone with proper standards. Human scribbles under each: bell ash, sea salt, kennel smoke, felid, weeping stone.

A collection. Not a single mouse tail among them.

I resisted the urge to mark the whole room as mine.

Barely. Wrong setup entirely—too many escape routes, insufficient elevated perches, and whoever arranged the shelving clearly never consulted anyone with proper spatial instincts.

The fragment hopped into the silver dish and coiled up, as if the metal belonged to it. The dish began to vibrate, glass jars on the wall joining in—a shiver of sound, sour and thin. The not-man's collar bit, making him wince. Smoke boy's breath turned gray and wrong, as if he'd swallowed the fire instead of the air. Salt woman hunched, sweat running in little salty beads.

Even my own whiskers felt the pull, nerves twitching at someone else's tune. I hated it. Hated more that it was familiar.

"Batteries," Rowan managed, voice dry.

I hissed low. That's what they saw when they looked at us— food to hoard, energy to bottle. Sardines in a jar, waiting for someone else's teeth.

"They call it smart. I call it stealing my treats when I'm not looking." I flicked a finger over a tally. Fresh. "Quotas. Always quotas."

The captain touched a chalk line, jerked away, knuckles white. "There's a pull. You're not just making this up."

I snorted. "If I were making it up, I'd charge admission."

Rowan started a grounding charm, then stopped. "It's tuned to you. I'll only make it worse."

"It's after what's mine." I set my hand on the rim, ears flat.

Let it try. See who loses a paw.

The dish vibrated, skittering an inch across the floor. Jars rattled. I purred, off-key, just enough to make the spell twitch. The way you purr on a stolen pillow and watch the humans try not to disturb you.

"Off," I told the room. "This bowl's mine. Paws out."

The fragment shivered, eyes going dull. The not-man's collar slackened. Smoke boy coughed once, ash clinging to his lips. The salt woman's skin was dried, with crusts flaking off. The humming girl's tune wavered, the wall beneath her heels sagging in relief. Rowan pressed a cold iron charm into the air, the magic dropping like a heavy paw on a too-quiet room.

The captain looked like he wanted to attack something. I approved.

I nudged the dish. Light crawled back into the chalk, jars quit their whining, and wires sagged. Silence settled in.

Everyone remembered to breathe again. The room stretched, let out a shaky sigh.

The air changed when they stopped being scared. Humans leak emotions through their skin.

Rowan leaned on the door frame. "You jammed a listening post."

"Good. Maybe now they'll chase their own tails for a while."

The fragment curled, tail flicking, then hopped to my wrist and crawled into my palm. It pressed its nose against the burn line. The mark flared, faded. Mine again.

"You can be trained," I told it. It bit me. Acceptable.

A message scratched itself across the chalk: Yield loss: array 9B. Adjustment logged. Below it, a sloppy paw print pressed itself, already fading.

Even their warnings have bad penmanship.

The captain hissed out a curse. "They'll notice. They always patch things up."

I licked my finger and smudged the paw print just to be petty. "Let them. Maybe next time they'll think twice before leaving their mark on my territory."

Rowan's pen scratched. "Systematic harvest. Arrays everywhere. They tuned it to you."

The not-man tugged his collar, voice rough. "Batteries. That's all we are to them."

Smoke boy rattled his clapper. "They said the subject would come. That's you."

Salt woman hugged her elbows, flakes scattering. "Tide's gone. Only the salt is left."

The humming girl's tune trailed off, leaving the stone beneath her heels damp and silent.

I flexed my claws until my teeth stopped buzzing. "No more study notes. Next time, we bite back."

Rowan reached for a wire and jerked his hand away, wincing. "We can't break them all today."

"No. But we can make them late. Let their magic trip over its own tail." I purred, ragged and sly. The magic sagged, all paws and no claws. Still running, just badly—all paws and no claws.

Perfect. Even spells should learn to nap.

"When things go sideways, they'll blame the staff." I twitched my whiskers. "We just make the mess."

Rowan scribbled, lips tight. The displaced watched the jars, shadows stretched across their faces.

The salt woman hugged her arms, voice brittle. "They turned my tide into a tally. I want it back."

The not-man gripped his collar, scowling. "Batteries don't bite. I do."

Smoke boy rattled his clapper, eyes glinting. "They called for a subject. They got a cat with claws."

I swiped a page from the log and dropped it in Rowan's hands. "Let's see who tries to follow these paw prints home."

The tunnels spat us into a cistern that reeked of burned chalk and bad attempts at fur. We'd descended three levels below the monastery's foundation, following passages that seemed to burrow deeper into the realm itself rather than merely underground. The walls here hummed with a different energy—not the monastery's protective wards, but something that tasted of distant places and stolen doorways. Wrong proportions for proper napping—too wide, no corners for security, terrible acoustics for purring. Even my standards have limits. Copper pipes mapped the walls, glass jars lined shelves in neat rows, and in the middle, a stone ring thrummed, the noise worming under my skin. My marked palm itched, like the walls were sizing me up for scratching post duty.

Rowan peered at the setup, voice gone tight. "This was made for a reason. Everything here's... intentional."

I flattened my ears at the jars. "Only humans would bother. Look at it. All that work to catch what doesn't want to be caught." My phantom whiskers flinched away from the nearest copper line. "If any of this tries to taste me, it's getting furballs for a month."

We checked the first doorway.

A fox lay strapped to a stone platform, fur shaved to reveal runes scored into her skin. Threads of light stretched from those marks into jars. With each breath, the jar by her head flickered brighter, swallowing up her magic. When it topped off, a bell shrieked—a needy, brittle noise. Nobody came to claim it. The jar just kept glowing, hoarding every bit it stole. Her whiskers twitched once, then stilled.

I spat. "Cages and jars. Always the same trick."

If they tried this on me, someone would lose a finger.

Rowan gripped the lintel until his knuckles whitened. "They're draining familiars like batteries."

I ignored him, watching the bell glow. *Let them try that with me.*

The air behind the second door was thick with feathers, iron, and fear.

A crow slumped on an iron stand, wings pinned open with clamps crusted in ugly runes. Every forced caw flickered down copper wires, magic peeled off its throat. A mirror hung in front of its beak so that it couldn't look away from itself. The bird's eyes were wide, glassy, never blinking.

Rowan whispered, horrified, "They're making it watch itself."

I curled my lip. "That's not magic. That's just mean. Even I look away when I cough up a feather."

The crow croaked again, thin and scraped out, and the wires pulsed brighter. I slammed the door before Rowan could keep staring.

If anyone hangs a mirror in front of me, I'm breaking it. And then I'm breaking them.

The third door was locked tight, stinking of ozone and bottled storms. I didn't bother. That kind of magic bites back.

The fourth door stopped me cold. Inside: a rig made for a cat. For *me*. Table, clamps, neat little hollows for paws, a loop for the tail, a headrest with a dish of fish oil. Wrong proportions entirely—no consideration for proper stretch positions, insufficient space for dignified exit strategies, and the restraint points showed a complete misunderstanding of feline spatial priorities.

Cheap bait.

The moment I stepped in, the wood shivered awake. A yank on the burn-line in my palm, hot and sharp. My ghost tail lashed, furious.

"They built a trap for me," I muttered, phantom fur bristling. "How thoughtful."

The rig gleamed, eager. My field leaned. *Traitor.* I backed up so hard I slammed into Rowan's chest.

Rowan's hand landed on my arm, anchoring me. Steady, silent, and annoyingly gentle. The displaced crowded behind. The not-man's rope collar hummed, the salt woman pressed a hand to her crystals, and the smoke boy lowered his head as if bracing for his bell to ring. All of them recognizing the shape of their own cages in mine.

"Later," I spat at the rig. My claws ached in these useless hands. "We'll see who fits who."

The next chamber reeked of old ink and rules. Waxed books, copper plates with scratchy diagrams, parchment in tidy piles, scrolls sealed shut with gray wax. Everything stacked, sorted, lined up for someone's idea of control.

Humans and their records. If I had a tail, half these shelves would be on the floor by now.

Rowan drew one from the shelf. His lantern spilled across the cover.

Monitoring log. Field signature. Months -9 to 0.

Routine observation phase: Months -9 to -3.

Acquisition evaluation: -3 to -1.

Active targeting approved: Months -1 to displacement.

He read under his breath: "−9, subject corrects chalk angles with tail tip. −7, sardine-ash test positive. −3, misalignments seeded. 0, graduation scheduled, proceed with displacement window."

Another page: "−4, subject attempted nap on sigil. Result: resonance increased the stability of the containment circle. Note: further naps recommended."

And another: "−2, candidate bonded response elevated with fish bribes. Efficiency of offering confirmed."

They'd watched me for nine months—first as routine familiar monitoring, then with growing interest as my independence scores climbed past their comfort thresholds. They catalogued my whisker twitches. Filed my stretch preferences. The observation had shifted from passive to predatory sometime after my mid-year evaluations. Even noted which ear I wash first.

Sardines weren't kindness. They were data points.

Rowan turned a final page. A diagram, paw pads drawn to scale, left pad labeled *preferred*.

I bared my teeth. "It's rude to describe me so accurately."

And deeply suspicious. If they measured my tail, someone's going to get bitten.

On the copper plate beneath: Primary variable: Field. Anomalous stability under chaos load. Recommended for integration.

Recommended. As if I'd let myself sit on their shelf without pushing something off first.

My spark hissed inside my chest, eager to agree. I dug nails into my palm until the burn-line flared, pressing the suppression cloth between my fingers. Emotion made the field want to spread, but deliberate focus could contain it.

It was mine. It would not be theirs.

We stood in the central ring, jars humming faintly all around. I listened until the rhythm betrayed itself. Dawn for birds, noon for snakes, evening for cats, midnight for moths. The whole schedule had the mechanical precision of humans who'd never learned that quality trumps timing—like serving sardines by the clock instead of when they're properly fresh.

Only humans would put suffering on a schedule. Bet they make a chart for it, too.

Rowan raised the lantern higher. "We can't smash it all now. They'd feel the rupture."

I yawned. "Why break it when I can make it nap? Slow, lazy, harder to spot."

I pressed my palm to the stone and purred, but not the soothing kind—a lopsided, nagging rhythm, the sort that makes a sleeping human twitch and roll. Like purring on someone's good pillow just to watch them try not to disturb you while slowly going insane. The ring hesitated. Jars dipped, humming out of sync. Still running, just poorly.

"When things go off-beat, they'll scold each other, not notice the claws in the curtain."

Rowan wrote it down. The captain nodded once.

The displaced stared at the jars, faces caught in shadow.

The salt woman whispered, "They made my tide into numbers."

The not-man touched his rope. "They called me a battery."

The smoke boy turned his clapper once. "They said the subject would come."

I shrugged. "I'm here, I'm bored, I'm leaving. And I'm taking what matters."

At the threshold, I looked back.

The fox's jars pulsed faintly in her room. The crow stared into its mirror and croaked again. The rig sat waiting, clamps gleaming like teeth, fish oil a cheap bribe. The jars all hummed their new, lazier rhythm.

"They watched me for months," I said. "Measured my tail. Filed my naps. All for charts they can't read."

Rowan closed the ledger. "Let's give them something to worry about."

I scratched behind my ear—no whiskers, just the echo of what should've been there. Something purred, deep and stubborn, and mine.

Not enough time. Not enough claws. But I'll be back to ruin their locks properly. The facility could have its jars. It wasn't getting me.

We slipped into the tunnels, leaving the hum stumbling on its new rhythm. By morning, the wards above would feel different. The anchors would be less eager, the posts less obedient.

Let the Collector have their records. Sardines and naps don't belong on a chart.

Find another cat. This one's not staying put.

We left the jars humming on their new, lazy beat—my sabotage just enough to make the Collector's neat rows go crooked. The tunnels pressed close, stone cold and mean, but underneath the floor, something answered my off-key purr.

A resonance. Familiar.

My burn-line prickled. The mark on my palm grew warm, then hot, as I recognized something in the stone's vibration. The fragment behind my ear chirped, excited.

"The arrays are connected," I said, understanding dawning. "All of them. One big web."

The hum I'd twisted kept tugging behind us, but it wasn't trying to flatten itself out anymore. It was calling. And somewhere in the network's confusion, I felt something else responding—a distant tether that pulsed with familiar warmth. The chaos I'd introduced was creating echoes, and one of those echoes was reaching toward home. My chaos signature had found the network's weak point and was relentlessly clawing at it.

Then something under the floor clicked.

In the center of the room, the ground split in two. The network had decided to sneeze me out rather than let my chaos spread further. An emergency release, triggered by my signature going properly viral through their carefully ordered system.

Rowan found his voice first. "An integrity bleed. Your chaos destabilized their control grid—it opened a relief gate to prevent cascade failure." His eyes widened. "It's keyed to your magical signature. It chose your origin point."

Home.

The circle widened without chalk, without hands. Rowan's lantern shrank to a dot. The captain's face emptied of arguments. The displaced froze. Even the fragment behind my ear shook with wanting.

Now the portal opens. Typical. Magic always waits until after the fun part's over.

Air from Felicity's side touched my cheeks. Garden soil. The old clock down her corridor ticked a heartbeat I knew. My phantom whiskers lifted. My tail, still stolen, tried to lash and sent pain up my spine.

Rowan found his voice first. "An integrity bleed," he said, hushed. "You jammed their system, so it opened a relief gate. It's keyed to you; it chose your origin."

A door, just big enough to shove the problem through. The Collector's paw, sweeping the problem away and hoping I wouldn't land on my feet.

The pull was gentle. *Temptation often is.* It licked my ankles and promised cushions, clean bowls, warm blankets, and a witch who would scold me for making the bed smell like fish.

I stepped toward it. Heat pooled in my chest. Her magic tugged under my ribs, familiar as her hand at my scruff. She smelled of rain after a long day. My paws, gone but remembered, ached for the scratchy warmth of her desk, that perfect nap spot above her half-finished spells.

Something behind me chimed—a fox's bell, anxious or jealous, I couldn't tell. The crow croaked at its mirror, one last useless warning. Down the hall, the cat rig heated up, as if it expected me to lie down and be tamed. All of it fading, nothing I owed.

The portal's pull sharpened. Everything else became noise.

Two bounds. Maybe one proper pounce and I'd be back where the tea never gets cold and someone understands that sardines don't serve themselves. She'd scrub the city's stink from my fur with hands steady enough to never spill the tea. We could slam the door on this place and let someone else mop up the mess.

Rowan's hand hovered at my shoulder, careful. He didn't touch. "If you go, the portal will close. They'll move the prisoners before the Council even decides which hat to blame. You know that."

The captain's voice dropped, honest for once. "No shame in taking your way out. Survival's its own kind of smart."

The salt woman shivered, crystals clinking. "We wouldn't blame you."

The not-man's rope collar buzzed, rough and tired. "If you go, leave them a trail. Show someone where to look."

The smoke boy rolled his clapper in his palm, gaze fixed on the floor. "The bell in this place never stops."

I set one foot across the threshold. The bond tugged, sharp. A sound escaped me, half-growl, half-want.

I could go. I could be safe again. I could have someone call me good, claws and all.

The ledger waited in the other room, proud of its perfect little sketch of my paw. The rig waited with its sad bowl of fish oil, convinced I'd be impressed. Copper wires lay in wait, ready to turn a single purr into another number on their stupid charts. They'd watched me, snooped on my naps, tallied every sardine I bothered to eat. They tried to learn my tricks, but all they got were smudged lines and empty dishes.

They called it research. I called it making them jealous of my naps.

The pull brushed my shins. Gentle, insistent, the way cats mark what they want to keep.

I glanced at the displaced. Something heavy and inconvenient clicked in behind my ribs—responsibility, or indigestion, or both.

The smoke boy's knuckles were scraped raw from clutching that clapper desperately. The salt woman's lips split at the corners, salt flaking with every breath. Rope had chewed permanent furrows into the not-man's neck. The fox barely noticed she was breathing for a jar instead of herself. The crow watched its own eyes until there was nothing left but staring.

Apparently, I collect strays now. Someone should warn the next box.

They stole my habits and made a mess of them. Sardine aftertaste, chalk in the fur, and strangers forced to play at being me.

Insulting to everyone.

I crouched at the rim, letting the light warm my face. Home caught at the back of my throat. Felicity's scent and the promise of tea curled up my nose. Her magic pressed in, silent but sharp, prickling my whiskers and dragging every thought toward her.

I put my hand to the light. The burn-line flared hot. The circle hummed, trying to claim me. It wanted my magic, not my name.

"Listen," I said, speaking quietly so the room had to lean in close. "I'm coming back, but on my own terms, through a door I choose."

The light lingered. The opening waited, as if unsure whose territory it was about to cross.

Rowan stood where I could see him if I turned my head, white around the mouth. The captain had set himself firmly. The displaced watched with the thin, bright attention you learn in cages.

Apparently, I'm the only one qualified to clean this litter box. Typical. No respect for proper delegation.

"If I go, the Collector closes his case. No more mess. Cat gone. The rest get swallowed by the system."

The portal's edge warmed, coaxing. Behind me, a jar chimed.

I pressed my hand to the light and purred loud enough to rattle windows. The gate's pulse matched mine, then shifted when I nudged it. Rowan slipped in a chalk square beside my wrist, neat as a library stamp. The captain planted his boots wide and locked his knees. He couldn't feel the ripple yet, but instinct told him to brace.

"Close," I told the portal. "My decision. My claws."

The light tried to lounge there. I bared my teeth. "Move."

It bucked once. Heat flared in the mark on my palm. Deep inside, the tether to Felicity stretched, sharp and almost sweet. A single thread slipped through the gate, her focus sparking at the other end. She felt it. Felt me choosing, not vanishing.

I drew a ragged breath and coaxed, "Steady now, keep the string tight."

The gate shivered once, then folded neatly in on itself. Felicity's garden scents drained away, the old clock fell silent, and the rosemary thinned to the bare ghost of a memory.

Silence slammed into place. The cistern took a grudging breath, unhappy its mouth had been shut. Jars shook, acting innocent. Somewhere inside the walls, little ticks started up.

Rowan's shoulders eased. The captain let out a breath he'd been hoarding. The smoke boy's chest fluttered once, safe air at last. Salt crystals on the woman's arm settled. The not-man rubbed his raw throat.

Rowan spoke first, voice soft enough for secrets. "A door like that may not open for you again. Could take months, if it ever does."

"Yes," I said. Iron on my tongue, cool and satisfying.

He tried again. "Felicity might think—"

"She'll know." The bond under my ribs hummed, a tight wire of fury and agreement. She would have words later.

Excellent. I prefer her loud and breathing.

"Someone has to teach you how to keep a familiar. Start with this: no cages, no jars, and definitely no numbers."

Rowan made a sound that nearly qualified as a laugh. The captain's mouth twitched once before he caught it. The displaced didn't smile; they watched me carefully.

I pushed to my feet. Legs cooperated. The absence of my tail voiced its usual complaint, then sulked in silence. The fragment behind my ear purred like a smug little engine. I flicked it. It purred louder.

"First, we make the arrays forget their song. Then we teach your posts to bend. After that, we bite the hand that keeps tugging the leash."

Rowan nodded. The captain shifted his grip on a sword he still hadn't drawn. The displaced fell in beside us, silent.

I didn't look back at the place; the door had vanished. The tunnels ahead coiled, pointing toward the next weak spot.

Home still lived where it always had—in Felicity's skin and in my name when she spoke it. The path there had changed shape; that was fine. I would claw a new one.

I swallowed the ache. "Move, before the third bell remembers its own voice."

The cistern's hum followed, off-key and picking up my worst habits. Good. Let the Collector watch their toys fall apart. Let them try opening another door and wait for me to scamper through.

They'd spent months making my field jump through hoops.

Now I'll teach their whole system to misbehave.

CHAPTER 5

PARALLEL INVESTIGATION

The antechamber reeked of cold ink, boiled nettle tea, and decades of crushed ambition. Felicity perched on a bench worn smooth by generations of summoned witches, each groove a testament to bureaucratic patience. Her palms pressed flat against wood that had absorbed more confessions than any priest. Across the chamber, scrolls leaned like bored sentries, red wax seals stamped with the Council's authority, proof that paperwork outlasted memory.

The brass clock ticked loud enough to shame a guilty heart. Each tick, the bond beneath her ribs fluttered: three weeks of scattered signals, then this morning's pulse, sharp as a needle prick. The connection had been erratic since the displacement—fragments of sensation that came and went like whispers through thick walls. *Alive.* The sensation wobbled, stretched thin, then stumbled over itself like someone learning to walk in borrowed legs.

She pressed fingers to her sternum. Through the bond

came impressions: straw dust, sardine oil, the peculiar satisfaction of claiming territory. The connection worked differently across realms—emotions and sensations traveled clearly, but specific thoughts required intense focus from both ends. Distance stretched the tether thin, but Mischief's distinctive personality blazed through like candlelight in darkness. He'd found a box. Of course, he had. Mischief would consider imprisonment an organizational challenge worth winning.

Oak hinges groaned. Scribe Marrow appeared, jowls sagging with procedural weight. "Candidate Hargreaves. Tribunal floor." His slate bore her infraction number in precise numerals. She had become arithmetic.

The hearing chamber opened like a throat: circular, tiered, hungry. High Councilor Alder presided from the dais, emerald brooch catching candlelight like a predator's eye. Councilors Briar and Sable flanked him, quills poised over parchment that rustled with each breath. Two apprentices hauled document stacks. Her file was thick enough to choke on.

"Candidate." Alder's voice carried the softness of overripe fruit. "State the nature of your failure."

Felicity drew breath that tasted of copper and chalk, the metallic bite of fear mixing with ritual residue that clung to everything in Council chambers. "The graduation ritual was destabilized. Portal magic escaped containment. One familiar displaced, seven apprentices treated for magical inversion, chamber wards destroyed." She delivered facts like a coroner's report, bloodless and accurate.

Sable's rings clicked against parchment, silver against paper, impatient as beetles. "Damage assessment incomplete. Include the brazier losses, ward reconstruction costs, and reputation impact."

"Addendum recorded." Felicity kept her tone flat as winter stone. The bond flickered again: annoyance at monks who dared handle him, the indignity of human limbs that folded wrong. She bit her cheek to keep from smiling.

Still yourself, even in the wrong skin.

Briar unfurled a scroll heavy with ribbons. "Morning of examination, you accessed Workshop Seven at the second bell. Explain the schedule deviation."

"Fresh calcite required. Original batch failed mineral-leach testing." True, though incomplete. The calcite had gone chalky overnight; the lines were too brittle to anchor properly. She'd blamed humidity then. Now the memory felt edited, edges worn smooth like a palimpsest someone had scrubbed.

Wax flakes drifted as Briar scribbled. Sable leaned forward, perfume sharp with lemon oil and bureaucratic satisfaction. "Council audit shows a second Workshop Seven entry. Three hours post-departure. No authorization logged. Door seals intact. Who entered?"

Felicity's pulse stuttered. "I was unaware."

"Unaware or complicit?"

Heat climbed her neck. "I work alone. Any tampering occurred without my knowledge or consent." The bond pulsed: Mischief's disdain for interrogation techniques, his certainty that competent villains left better breadcrumbs.

Alder raised a soft hand. Silence fell like a curtain. "Investigation pending. License suspended. You will assist the archivists with ledger maintenance until resolution."

Death by bookkeeping. Mischief would appreciate the

irony. Bureaucracy as an execution method, performed with quills instead of blades. The punishment fit their aesthetic: slow suffocation disguised as mercy.

"One allowance," Alder added, gaze sharpening. "Continued familiar bond monitoring. We note aura fluctuations." His tone suggested scandal brewing. "Creature death requires immediate notification."

Creature. The bond answered with sardonic amusement, static mixed with straw and the ghost of purring gone sideways. Alive, certainly. Changed, definitely. Probably critiquing monastery architecture between meals.

Dismissed, Felicity exited through corridors lined with memorial glass. Afternoon sun bled through amethyst panes, laying bruised light across marble. She paused at bronze plaques listing portal casualties: names, dates, official apologies. Her finger traced one inscription. The metal felt warm, as if it had been recently touched. How many of these "accidents" had been engineered?

Workshop Seven waited behind cedar darkened by candle soot. Stone gargoyles crouched above the lintel, eyes tracking her approach with carved suspicion. She whispered the password and pressed her palm to the sigil plate. The ward recognized her magic but dragged, like cloth caught under furniture.

Inside smelled wrong. Lavender soap layered over a chemical bite, masking the effects of a spill. Her benches sat suspiciously aligned, pewter tools arranged with hostile precision. Mischief would have knocked half of them off by now, just on principle.

She kneeled beside the ritual platform, stomach tight with growing certainty. Chalk dust usually decorated the floor in lazy arcs, impossible to sweep thoroughly. Today, the stones gleamed scrubbed clean. She checked the brass floor vent, fingers trembling slightly. A single grain was lodged inside, dark green chalk reserved for Council sigil masters. Her stock was pale blue.

The equipment cabinet told the real story. The brass lock bore a half-circle scratch blooming at the end: skeleton key signature. Inside, calcite jars sat reordered, lids askew. Fresh wax sealed over old, blended too smooth for natural storage. She chipped a sample, tasted bitter grit with an iron tang. Sabotage disguised as carelessness.

Her chest tightened. Someone had been in her sanctuary, had touched her tools, had orchestrated her failure with methodical precision. The violation felt personal and intimate, like finding a stranger's handprints on her skin. They'd catalogued her private workspace the way Mischief might investigate a new box —methodical, invasive, claiming ownership through touch.

The bond pulsed warm encouragement, carrying the distinct sensation of phantom whiskers twitching with approval—Mischief's equivalent of a satisfied purr. An image flickered through: Mischief's disgust at watery porridge, his pleasure at slipping bureaucratic leashes.

Evidence, kitten. Show me where to look.

The response carried copper taste, chalk dust, sardines, and underneath it all, a thread of protective fury that made her spine straighten.

From the supply shelf, she pulled a copper scribing rod. Its tip bore grayish residue. Two drops of lime acid turned the sample effervescent, releasing burned rosemary scent—

a ritual dampening paste. Applied to chalk lines, it weakened structural integrity under stress.

Someone had engineered her failure. Planned it. Executed it with bureaucratic efficiency.

She unrolled Briar's incident documentation with hands that trembled. Among neat schedule entries, one annotation slanted left in different handwriting: *Pre-qual check completed, array integrity confirmed. —C. Sable.* The ring-clicker herself.

Felicity pocketed evidence samples in a handkerchief, mind reeling. The bond sparked approval, followed by Mischief's irritation at phantom ears and a missing tail. She whispered, "Working on it."

Folded foolscap waited on her workbench, edges too crisp for the usual mess. She opened it with growing dread.

Terminal Protocol reference update: Subject FH—Asset Reassignment Pending Administrative Resolution.

The protocol for familiar decommissioning involved breaking the bond, draining magic, and reassigning the witch. Her initials decorated the margin with a date five days hence. Someone had scheduled her removal like a routine appointment.

Felicity's stomach dropped through the floor. The bond pulsed distant and fragile, a thread stretched across realms that someone wanted to cut with surgical precision. They'd tried severing her by stealing Mischief. They would try again if she uncovered too much.

But she already had.

In the silence, she heard his voice, insolent and comforting: *Boxes are for naps, but claws are for paperwork.* She tucked the protocol sheet into her sleeve and scattered fresh chalk across the floor in a deliberate disorder. Her signature mess. Mischief would recognize the rebellion.

At the door, she paused, palm on cedar. "This isn't finished," she told the room. Her words sank into wood grain that had heard promises before. The workshop kept its silence, but somewhere beyond stolen doorways, a human-shaped cat surely planned revenge.

The archivists' annex smelled of parchment and patient fury. Sister Liora glanced up from ledger mountains, quill stained black as judgment.

"You're early."

"I need Council key logs," Felicity said. "Apprentice duty rosters for two nights before graduation."

Liora's quill froze. "Sealed records."

Felicity set the green chalk grain on parchment. Beside it, the residue vial hissed faintly, still angry at the disruption. "Someone used Council materials in Workshop Seven without authorization. Perhaps extensive ledger copying might earn clearance?"

Liora studied the evidence. Her eyes carried the sharp intelligence of someone who'd weaponized filing systems for decades. "Copy efficiently, and I may misplace keys. Parchment seventeen-oh-eight has a habit of slipping behind drawers."

Felicity inclined her head. The bond fluttered with

pleased approval, as if Mischief had tasted conspiracy and found it delicious.

She accepted the ledgers and brass lamp, settled into a corner desk where shadows pooled like old secrets. Forms blurred beneath her quill, numbers becoming background music. Between columns, she jotted down questions on scrap paper: *Who requested the skeleton keys? Who scheduled protocol FH? Why rosemary dampening paste?*

Beyond windows, lamps snapped alight like awakening stars. Felicity worked until ink stained her cuffs anew, each copied line tracing paths toward whoever had sabotaged her ritual. The mechanical repetition steadied her nerves, gave her hands something to do while her mind churned.

Somewhere across fractured worlds, Mischief stalked different corridors. They would compare claw marks soon enough.

For the first time since disaster struck, Felicity smiled without forcing it. Bureaucracy expected submission. It had underestimated a witch who knew how to weaponize documentation.

Tomorrow she would begin dissecting their lies, one ledger entry at a time.

The restricted stacks lurked five floors below the cloister garden, past a tarnished silver gate that hummed disapproval at honest visitors. Felicity's borrowed key sang

CAT OUT OF LUCK

off-pitch, which seemed appropriate. Proper conspiracies deserved dissonance.

The stairwell exhaled mildew and lamp oil. At the final landing, a sign warned *Authorized Curators Only* in letters brittle with age. She nudged the door open, listening for footsteps. Only the distant drip of a leaking cistern. Good. Archivists slept like dragons once ledger bells went silent.

Inside, shelves rose toward chapel-height shadows, stuffed with ledger boxes and grimoires that hadn't seen daylight in decades. Charcoal braziers smoldered along aisles, casting amber light that made shadows stretch like curious fingers. The air tasted of secrets left too long to ferment.

Felicity unpinned her lamp hood and climbed the rail-mounted ladder, brass wheels singing softly against tracks. Bronze tags labeled each shelf: *Licensure Disputes, Aetheric Malpractice, Squid Summoning Permits.* She rolled until she found *Familiar Dissolution Hearings.*

The bond pulsed again—straw dust, distant harp music, Mischief's amusement at monastery choir practice. *Found your trouble pile yet?* The sensation seemed to ask.

Working on it, she thought back, hoping the message would travel across whatever impossible distance separated them.

She pulled the 1827-1832 volume. Pages crackled like dried leaves. The first entry made her stomach clench:

Petitioner: Councilor Sable Subject Familiar: Anise (crow) Independence Index: 4.9/5 Outcome: Displacement during remedial scrying, body unrecovered.

Independence above four was exceptional. Mischief had tested at five. The Council considered anything above three to be "manageable with guidance"—polite phrasing for *keeping it leashed.*

She flipped forward, copying names and scores with growing unease. Entry after entry logged "problematic" familiars credited to accidents: portal flux, anchor fracture, spindle collapse. Always supervised by the same three councilors: Sable, Briar, and Alder's predecessor, Thorne.

Too convenient. She continued scanning dates. The disasters clustered around examination seasons, when independent testing ran at its highest. However, the explanations seemed rehearsed, too polished for genuine accidents.

She pulled older volumes, hoping for different patterns. The entries from 1815-1820 showed similar patterns, but with frustrating gaps. There were whole months missing, pages torn out with bureaucratic precision. Someone had sanitized the records, but why leave any trace at all?

Her hands shook as she turned pages. The scope was becoming clear, and it was worse than sabotage. This was systematic.

Between 1800 and 1805, luck changed. A misfiled section revealed entries marked *'Research Hold'* instead of the usual *'Displacement'.* The first listed Coriander (ferret, index 4.7). Status: *Pending.*

A margin note in unfamiliar ink, added months later: *Subject lost during array stress test. See Collector docket.* Below that, Sable's neat handwriting circled "lost" and penciled *acceptable variance.*

Felicity's vision blurred. Her hands trembled as she traced down the page—another ferret, two ravens, a fox, a lynx. Each was flagged as independent, and each was subsequently "lost" under Sable's clinical summaries. No witch ever reclaimed their familiar.

The Collector again. And Sable, signing off on *acceptable variance* as if she were approving inventory shrinkage.

The bond flared suddenly—sharp alarm, the taste of fear and iron. Through the connection came images: stone corridors, the smell of trapped magic, distant screaming that sounded like wind through broken glass. Mischief had found something terrible.

Breathe. She tried to breathe, though horror made her chest tight. *Evidence first. Murder charges later.*

She slipped parchment between crucial pages, marking entries to copy, though her fingers felt numb. A sound made her freeze. Footsteps approached, measured, and patient. She doused her lamp and pressed between the cabinets, her robe snagging on the warped oak.

Archivist Penn emerged carrying an oil can, humming a hymn about orderly fire. Felicity waited, heart hammering against ribs that felt suddenly brittle, until the elderly woman vanished through the far doorway.

Lamp relit, she wheeled the ladder to *Experimental Protocols* with hands that shook. A slim folio sat squeezed between thick treatises, spine bearing only a sigil: crossed quills over a closed eye.

Terminal Protocols for Familiar Reassignment. The title made her stomach lurch. Pages rustled like shed snakeskin. Diagrams mapped ritual circles with twin anchor points, showing how to narrow bonds and then sever them without recoil. Success rates rose when independence exceeded four. Their autonomous aether allowed stable bleed-off.

In the margin: *Collector requires subjects with autonomous cores.* Below that, a different hand: *Supersedes prior ethical objections.*

Near the end, specimen status listings made her blood freeze completely:

Mischief (cat, provisional human) Independence: 5.0 Status: Priority Acquisition Subject currently unmoored. Monitor witch for destabilization.

Ink still gleamed wet.

Someone had updated this within hours. She blotted the entry with scrap paper, watching as the wetness smeared, indicative of recent handling. Proof that someone was tracking Mischief in real time.

Decades of familiar murder. Systematic elimination of anyone who thought for themselves. And now they wanted her kitten.

The bond pulsed again: sea salt, amusement, distant candle smoke. *Tell them I bite,* the impression threatened.

She snapped the folio shut, sliding it under her arm. Evidence had to leave this chamber, even if smuggling texts carried punishments that made suspension look like a gentle correction.

"Apprentice Suites curfew ended an hour ago."

She spun. Councilor Briar blocked the aisle, emerald brooch glinting like a predator's eye above thin lips that had signed too many death warrants to count. "Why are you trespassing?"

Think. Her mind clawed for plausible lies while her pulse hammered. "Archivist Liora assigned cross-checking duties. Ledger seventeen-oh-eight."

Briar's eyes fixed on the folio like a hawk spotting prey. "Uncatalogued material?"

"Misfiled, I assumed." She forced tremor into her voice, not difficult when genuine terror ran underneath. "Should I return it?"

He stepped closer, lamplight catching dust motes between them. "Curiosity is cherished when it stays on approved paths. Forbidden shelves earn their name." His ringed fingers drummed a nearby grimoire. Click, click, click.

The sound echoed like funeral bells. Felicity gauged distances—the ladder rails would screech if she bolted. Penn might still be nearby. She needed subtlety and perhaps divine intervention.

"I acted in desperation," she said, bowing low. "The bond stutters. I seek remedies."

"The Council will manage your bond." His breath carried clove and licorice. "Consider that burden lifted."

Over my broken wand. She rose. "Of course, sir."

"Hand me the folio."

She offered it, fingers lingering to charge the goatskin cover with static from her lamp's copper frame. The arc snapped when Briar grasped it—harmless, but he flinched.

His eyes narrowed. "Clever girl. But cleverness without permission is dangerous." He pocketed the folio. "Return to your suite. Consider tonight's reading educational material about boundaries and consequences for crossing them."

The threat sat heavily between them. He knew she'd found something important. And now he knew she knew.

"Thank you, sir." She bowed again, mind racing through implications.

Briar strode away, robes rustling. Felicity exhaled shakily. She still had her notes, the ink sample, and the certainty of systematic murder stretching back decades. Losing the original hurt, but the pattern no longer depended on one proof.

She waited until his footsteps faded, then climbed to a hidden nook between cabinets, a childhood trick for avoiding inspections. Knees tucked, she withdrew her journal with shaking hands.

Under lamplight, she outlined the conspiracy, forming words around horror:

Decades-long culling of high-independence familiars. Sable, Briar, and Thorne signatures are consistent. Collector requests autonomous cores. Terminal Protocol updated tonight, targeting Mischief. Pattern escalates during examinations. Motive: harvesting familiar magic for an unknown purpose.

Genocide. That's what this was. Familiar genocide, disguised as accidents, was signed off by Council members like routine paperwork.

The bond fluttered softly. She sent him images of dust-heavy shelves and ink-spattered discoveries.

Decades, Mischief. They murdered any familiar who refused to kneel.

The reply came as a warm sardine aroma and a growl of predatory satisfaction.

Before leaving, she misfiled a valuable codex in an empty herb-duty box—chaos for the morning shift. Mischief would approve of weaponized disorder.

She emerged into moonlit cloisters, the bond humming with shared determination. Briar would report tonight's encounter. That gave her hours, maybe less, before they moved to active suppression.

It was time to find allies who understood that

independence wasn't a crime, but rather a means of survival.

Felicity slipped into the vacant lecture hall before dawn, dust motes drifting in slanted light. The room smelled of cold ink and yesterday's chalk... safe, forgotten, private. She needed all three after what she'd discovered.

The pilfered duty scroll lay spread across an oak scarred by generations of note-taking. Lines of cramped script marched down parchment like a ledger of the damned: *Terminal Protocol: Familiar Rejection Cases.*

She traced entries with growing dread, each line a life erased. A crow, twenty years past, independence index 4.7, outcome: *essence reassigned to Collector arrays.* The crow's witch followed two months later, after her license was revoked for psychological instability.

The pattern crystallized with horrible clarity: target the familiar, watch the witch fracture, process both into footnotes. Clean. Efficient. Monstrous.

Her finger found a fresh entry, ink still gleaming like spilled blood. *Subject Familiar: Mischief (species variable). Independence index 5.0. Status: unmoored, priority acquisition.*

Below it, a second line that stopped her breath: *Associated Witch: Felicity Hargreaves. Risk level elevated. Recommend surveillance, compulsory evaluation, and possible reassignment.*

The words blurred. She gripped the table edge, wood

grain pressing ridges into her palms. They weren't just hunting Mischief; they were hunting her. She was next on their list of problems to solve.

The bond pulsed, carrying hay dust and sardine oil tinged with irritation. Mischief sensed her distress and answered with lazy confidence, the spiritual equivalent of a dismissive ear flick. *Not dead yet,* the sensation seemed to say.

Neither of us, she thought back fiercely. *And we won't be.*

A folded memorandum lay beneath the scroll, Council crest stamped in green wax. She cracked the seal with hands that wanted to shake: *Subject Hargreaves demonstrates adaptive problem-solving outside approved parameters. Forward to Enforcement once Terminal Protocol is executed on familiar.* Sable's signature curled in ink that smelled of lemon oil.

Her workshop saboteur, signing her death warrant with bureaucratic precision.

Felicity closed her eyes, breathing through her nose until raw terror crystallized into something harder. Cold purpose. They had marked her for elimination like livestock for slaughter. The evidence was damning, comprehensive, and utterly incriminating. It also wouldn't survive five minutes if they searched her quarters.

She needed an ally who could act beyond Council oversight. Someone who still believed in law over convenience.

Junior Councilor Marlow's private study occupied a cramped tower room above the archives, accessible through a servants' stair that avoided main corridors. Felicity climbed in pre-dawn darkness, botanical sketchbook pressed against her ribs like armor.

She knocked—three short, two long, their childhood signal for *urgent and secret.*

The door cracked open. Marlow's sleep-rumpled face registered her expression and went pale. "What's happened?"

"Terminal Protocol," she said, pushing inside. "They're not just hunting Mischief. They're hunting me."

His study was an organized chaos, with scrolls stacked on every surface, quills scattered like fallen feathers, and a cold brazier surrounded by law books. She spread the documents across his desk, over half-finished briefs and committee notes.

Marlow read in silence, jaw tightening with each line. When he reached her name on the watch list, he sank into his chair like a man who'd taken a blow to the chest.

"Decades," he whispered. "How many familiars?"

"All the independent ones. Anyone who scored above four, anyone who thought for themselves." She pointed to the margin notes with a hand that trembled slightly. "The Collector pays them. The Council supplies the merchandise."

"And now you're merchandise." His fingers drummed the desk, lawyer's mind calculating angles and finding them all sharp. "They'll move fast once they realize you've seen this."

"I copied everything. But the originals need to go

somewhere beyond their reach." She watched his face carefully. "Will you help me?"

Marlow was quiet for a long moment, staring at Sable's signature like it might transform into something less damning. Finally, he opened a locked drawer, pulling out a leather portfolio. "Council oversight reports. I've been documenting irregularities for months—budget discrepancies, unexplained familiar disappearances, ritual supply diversions." He met her gaze. "I suspected. Now I know."

Relief flooded her chest like warm honey. "What do you need?"

"Time to create a legal record, they can't simply disappear." He gathered her documents with careful hands. "And access to the scrying arrays. If we can establish contact with Mischief, prove he's alive and where, it becomes kidnapping rather than displacement."

"The arrays require senior clearance."

His smile held no humor. "I still remember Alder's seal pattern. Forgery as evidence preservation, Mischief would appreciate the irony."

The bond pulsed sardine-scented agreement.

"Hide these tonight," she said, pressing copies into his hands. "If they take me—"

"They won't." His voice carried lawyer's certainty. "Not while there's law left to invoke. But Felicity—" He caught her wrist as she turned to leave. "Be careful. Once they realize what you know, a suspended license will become the least of your worries."

Dawn clouds blushed peach as Felicity returned to the Apprentice Suites. She paused outside her door; the latch sat fractionally ajar, though she distinctly remembered having secured it.

Her throat tightened with growing dread.

Inside, surgical devastation awaited. Bedcovers sliced open, mattress gutted, drawers emptied in geometric stacks. Her travel trunk lay cracked, false bottom exposed like a broken secret. Someone had hunted methodically and found nothing because there had been nothing to find.

But the violation burned anyway. They'd invaded her sanctuary, touched her belongings, and violated the one space that was supposed to be hers.

A copper card waited on the desk, runes pulsing red: *Comply or be processed.*

No signature. None needed.

Felicity closed the door, spine straight, violation crystallizing into something harder than ward-etched steel. They'd marked her for elimination, ransacked her room, and now threatened her with casual brutality.

She kneeled by the ruined mattress, fingers finding silver thread sewn near the frame. Quick knots transformed it into an alarm sigil, a spiderweb meant to bite intruders with raw static. Anyone crossing her threshold uninvited would meet teeth.

The bond thrummed approval, spicy with anticipation. Mischief always loved a proper trap.

Rising, she faced the ransacked room with eyes that caught dawn light like blades. "You wrote my name on your list," she told the emptiness, words carrying through stone to wherever Marlow worked to weaponize law itself. "I'll write over yours with claw marks."

Outside, the second bell tolled hollow and grand. Each strike counted down to war, rebellion dressed in ink, procedure, and sardine-scented defiance.

The Council wanted obedience. It would receive revolution instead.

Chapter 6

First Contact

Rain pelted the roof as if it had a personal grudge against clay. Impressive dedication. I respect that in a weather pattern. It was the perfect weather for crime. The air reeked of old leather, vinegar gone sour, and something sharp that made my nose wrinkle. It smelled like hot and bitter metal and left an aftertaste similar to licking a brass key.

Territory ripe for the taking. Should have pissed on something by now.

Rowan hunched beside me, shoulders cramped under an oilcloth cloak never meant for real rain. His breath puffed white in the air that bit back. The displaced huddled behind him like nervous apprentices. Salt woman sparkled aggressively—show-off. Smoke-boy leaked atmosphere like a poorly maintained chimney. The captain waited down the street with two watchmen, lanterns shuttered, patience wearing thin as morning ice.

The grate blocking our path was a nest of iron bars

wrapped in spellscript, a Council seal slapped on like a pompous rosette. I pressed my nose close.

Wrong-metal smell. No cat-marks anywhere—amateur hour.

Who built a proper entrance without considering whisker clearance? Water hissed where protective glyphs sizzled, little sparks declaring their ownership.

"Secondary ward layer," Rowan whispered, pointing to sigils carved into the stonework. "Alarm triggers if the primary fails."

Of course, there's a backup. Humans who hoard territory always hide more territory somewhere.

I pressed my palm against the metal. The burn-line on my skin sparked, tasted the ward's flavor: proud, hungry, desperately lonely.

"Sit," I whispered, purring just wrong enough to make the frequencies hiccup. The bars sagged with a sound like breaking glass. The secondary wards flickered, confused by my chaos signature, then decided they didn't want to argue with something that made their logic itch. A soft click, and the whole gate surrendered with wounded dignity.

Rowan exhaled fog. "You terrify me."

"I'm adorable. Terror is something you humans create for yourselves." I slipped through the gap, phantom whiskers mapping the space ahead. "Besides, terror implies I might be unpredictable. I'm absolutely predictable. I'll knock something over, eat your fish, and judge your life choices."

We crawled through the gap into the throat of the facility. Stone stairs wound down, numbers etched into every step like inventory marks. Someone counted lives like the springs I hide under Felicity's dresser. The scrawl shivered when my chaos field brushed it, numbers scurrying away like startled mice.

Each step deeper smells more wrong. Like a den that reeks of predator scent where only prey should live.

The walls pressed closer, forcing us into single file. I led, because cats always scout new territory first. My phantom whiskers caught vibrations through the stone—machinery thrumming deep below. My ears twitched at distant sounds: the splash of liquid, something that might have been breathing. Or whimpering.

A trip-wire stretched across the seventh step, hair-thin and gleaming. I stepped over it, but Rowan's boot caught the edge. Wire twanged sharp and thin. We froze.

Nothing happened.

"Broken," I murmured, examining the mechanism. Acid had eaten through the connection points.

Even their security systems are falling apart. Sloppy.

Green lantern globes lined the corridor, their light weak as dawn through dirty windows. The air grew thick, pressing against my throat like wet wool. Ahead, the walls opened into alcoves filled with glass cylinders—a collection of transparent coffins for foxes, crows, ferrets, and creatures I couldn't name.

Each familiar floated in brine, eyelids fluttering with nightmare sparks. Tubes slurped from glyphs inked across their fur, drawing something essential from their cores. The liquid pulsed with stolen light, beautiful and nauseating.

My stomach clenched. Humor died in my throat like a caught mouse.

"Mother of storms," the salt woman breathed, crystals forming along her arms like armor. "How many souls..."

I counted without wanting to. Dozens of cylinders in this corridor alone. Each one a familiar who'd thought for themselves, who'd dared to be inconvenient. A badger floating near the floor still wore a collar—leather worn smooth by affection, brass nameplate reading "Bramble." Someone's beloved companion, reduced to raw material.

"Too many," I said, voice rougher than intended. "And not enough witnesses." I flicked phantom whiskers. "Basic hunting error—if you're going to be evil, don't leave evidence floating in glass jars."

The salt woman reached for a lynx sealed mid-snarl, crystals bursting from her fingers to web the glass. Rowan touched her shoulder, whispering something that didn't help. His face had gone pale as old parchment.

A small cylinder near the wall contained something that made my chest tight. A kitten, maybe six months old, striped orange and white. Still alive, still dreaming, electrodes pressed against its skull like a crown of thorns. Its paws twitched in sleep-running.

Kill first. Joke later. Dead fish don't need jokes.

"We can't save them all," Rowan said, reading my expression.

"Watch me."

At the far end, a big door opened when we got close. It let loose an angry metal sound. Beyond lay a staging bay where automatons in Council livery sorted crates labeled *"raw conduit: live contents."*

The captain scanned the ceiling, mapping exits with military precision. I sniffed deeper: ozone, hot copper, resignation. A terrible stew that made my phantom whiskers curl. Under it all, familiar magic being processed into fuel—the warm scents of living creatures turned cold and metallic.

They're cooking us. Like fish turned into paste.

We spread out. Rowan jotted disruption sigils meant to confuse alarms, hands shaking slightly. I stalked the central conveyor, claws itching inside useless human nails. One crate quivered. Inside, a golden weasel whimpered around a gag rune, eyes wide with intelligence and terror.

I sliced the binding with a stolen scalpel. The weasel spilled into my arms, trembling like a caught bird. "Run when you hear the scream," I told it, voice low. "Mine will be the loudest."

The weasel chittered what might have been 'thank you' or 'about time' or possibly 'do you have snacks?' I chose to interpret it as a profound expression of gratitude. It vanished into the shadows.

Good. One free, forty-six to go.

More crates lined the walls, some silent, others rustling with desperate movement. I opened three more, freeing a crow with silver-tipped feathers, a fox missing part of one ear, and something that looked like a cross between a rabbit and a small dragon. Each took to the shadows, waiting for chaos.

The stairs dropped us deeper into the facility's belly. A library lit by violet orbs stretched beyond iron archways, scroll tubes rattling, eager for touch. Shelves groaned under grimoires bound in hide that still remembered the donor. Ink smelled of burned feathers and scholarly obsession.

Rowan shimmered with excitement and disgust; books

were both his doom and salvation. He traced titles with reverent horror: *Behavioral Drift in Autonomous Familiars, Tail Ratios and Portal Shear, Subject MCC-139: Longitudinal Degradation Charts.*

"MCC," he whispered. "Mischief, Containment, Cat."

"Cute. They gave me a vanity plate." I pulled down the thickest journal, pages crackling with academic pride. Notes detailed my pawprint patterns, dream cycles, and sardine preferences with scientific precision. Minutes from Council committees debated whether "Subject MCC-139 displays emergent strategy beyond mere instinct." One margin bore a single verdict in red ink: *Promote to terminal protocol if empathy persists.*

They think caring about my strays makes me weak. Ha. Wait until they meet my claws.

I flipped deeper, violation crawling up my spine like cold fingers. They'd catalogued everything. My favorite napping spots. The way I chirped at birds through windows. How I brought Felicity dead mice as gifts. The precise angle of my ears when annoyed versus genuinely angry.

Twenty-three pages on my bathroom habits. These people need better hobbies.

Dozens of familiars have been catalogued, studied, and processed. Each is reduced to data points and extraction rates. Success was measured in how long they lasted before their cores burned out. Failure was a quick death.

A loose sheet slipped from the back: *Integration Candidates: High Independence Subjects.* My name headed the list, followed by careful annotations. *Responds to sardine incentives. Attachment to witch: exploitable weakness. Recommend separation trauma for cooperation leverage.*

Cold crawled up my spine. They'd been watching me for months, studying my habits, learning my weaknesses. Planning my capture with the thoroughness of predators selecting prey.

Another file detailed Felicity's daily routine, her workshop schedule, even her soap preferences. A photograph showed our graduation morning from an impossible angle... someone had been watching from inside the Council chamber itself.

Inside job. Of course. Trust paper-hoarders to sell anything for the right stack of documents.

The final descent opened into a vast cavern of machinery. Copper rings spun around a central dais, conduits pulsing like arteries carrying stolen life. The air thrummed with harvested magic, thick enough to taste. Steam rose from vents in the floor, carrying the screams of processed familiars. And on a throne of welded anchor posts sat the Collector.

Its shape masqueraded as feline: a lithe frame draped in midnight fur threaded with copper wire, tail split into braids clipped to eyelets in the steel. Instead of ears, silver antennae twitched, harvesting frequencies no mortal throat could sing. Eyes glowed cobalt, beautiful and wrong. A collar of rune plates sat around the neck, a royal decoration.

The room went dead quiet.

Fake-cat. Everything about it screamed imposter—the wire whiskers, the antenna ears, the complete lack of proper disdain for authority.

Real cats don't sit on thrones. We sprawl across them and judge everyone else.

"Subject designator: Mischief," the Collector said. The

voice rolled through pipes, spliced with echoes stolen from every captive throat—a chorus of the processed. "Integration threshold confirmed. You exceed all projections."

"Your projections need better seasoning. Have you considered sardines? Everything's better with sardines. Even megalomaniacal schemes." A spark inside my skull fluttered like a drawn moth. I locked it down with a mental swat, but felt its interest. This place wanted to claim me, make me part of its terrible symphony.

"Your décor is grim," I said, stepping onto the dais. Copper plates measured my cadence and pulse, as well as my probable napping schedule. "Ever consider curtains? Maybe some plants? This place screams 'megalomaniac with abandonment issues.'"

The Collector's whisker-wires curved in what might have been amusement. "Data collection spans decades. Portal residue analysis, chalk anomaly tracking, and sardine preference variables. Yet you eluded direct study until the Council kindly delivered you." Those blue eyes fixed on mine. "You're the first candidate strong enough to integrate properly. The others break."

Others. Plural. I thought of the cylinders, the careful notes, the failure rates. "How many have you processed?"

"Forty-five high-independence subjects over two decades. Thirty-one expired during extraction. Eleven suffered cascade failure in integration. Three achieved partial synthesis before core depletion." The Collector leaned forward slightly. "You represent unprecedented potential."

My mouth went dry. Three out of forty-five. And those

three had only achieved "partial synthesis" before burning out entirely.

"Tell me about the successful ones," I said, buying time while my chaos signature probed the machinery around us. "What made them special?"

"Subject MCC-092, a raven of considerable wit. Lasted eighteen months before cognitive dissolution. Subject MCC-101, a wolf with pack-bond trauma. Fourteen months. Subject MCC-118, a fox who believed cooperation meant survival." The Collector's eyes brightened. "Ten months, but he powered seventeen portal anchors simultaneously before failure."

They remember every victim. Keep score like trophies.

"To preserve order," the Collector continued. "Worlds fray. Portals gape. Reality bleeds between realms. I sew the seams with energy drawn from willing partners."

I flicked phantom whiskers. "Willing? I saw a lynx praying for death up there."

"Volition is statistical," they said with chilling calm. "Most minds fracture under integration pressure. Yours bends without breaking. Perfect autonomous function without identity loss. Join me, and we calibrate every anchor across ten planes. Become my partner in maintaining universal stability."

"Partnership implies choice. What you're offering smells like conscription with better benefits."

Images flickered across hanging screens: cities stitched with glowing lattices, seas restrained by sigil nets, mountains pinned beneath coordinate grids. Neat, ordered, and utterly lifeless. A universe where nothing unexpected could ever happen.

"Consider the alternative," the Collector said, gesturing to new images. Realms tearing apart, portals spewing chaos, cities consumed by dimensional static. "Without intervention, cascade failure consumes everything. Billions die in dimensional hemorrhaging."

"And you prevent this by turning familiars into batteries?"

"I harvest autonomous cores to power stability matrices. Your chaos signature alone could anchor fifty portals permanently. Think of the lives saved." Those blue eyes blazed brighter. "Cooperation grants dominion over your storm. Submit willingly, and I leash your volatility constructively. Refuse, and I break you as I broke the others."

"Leash? I don't do leashes. Ask anyone who's tried." I examined my clawless fingers with theatrical disappointment. "Besides, storms aren't meant to be leashed. They're meant to knock things over."

"Your attachment to chaos is primitive thinking. Order creates stability. Stability preserves life. Life has value."

"An order that requires murder isn't an order; it's control with a prettier name. And you don't get to decide which lives have value."

Glass pods around the chamber brightened suddenly. Liquid drained with mechanical precision. Inside, silhouettes jerked as consciousness returned, familiars awakening to their captivity. Gauges spiked and pain bled into the air like static.

A fox screamed. A raven thrashed against glass. The weasel I'd freed earlier pressed against a window somewhere, chittering in distress.

Rowan shouted in outrage. Salt woman's tide-song rose wrathful. Smoke boy's form darkened, ash swirling, murderous.

The Collector never blinked. "Choose, Mischief. Partner or processed material. But understand, I know exactly how to break you. I've studied every familiar who thought themselves special. The proud ones shatter fastest."

"Partnership implies equality. This smells like 'obey or die' dressed up in fancy words. I've heard that song before."

Images flashed through the screens: familiar after familiar, each showing the moment they broke. A raven clawing desperately at its witch-bond before it snapped. A fox curled catatonic as its memories drained away. A lynx that fought until its heart simply stopped.

Every one of them belonged to someone. Someone's hunting partner. Someone's responsibility. And this thing broke them like bored children break toys.

"The raven lasted longest," the Collector mused. "Seventeen attempts to escape. Quite ingenious, really. But pride made him predictable. In the end, I simply threatened his murder of corvids. He surrendered to save them."

"And the wolf?"

"Pack-bond severing. She couldn't bear isolation. Cooperation became relief from loneliness." The Collector's smile held mechanical warmth. "You have similar pressure points. Your witch-bond. Your need for autonomy. Your protective instincts toward other familiars. I will find the combination that breaks you."

I purred, a discordant, slicing sound that made glyphs hiccup and gauges dip. "I choose freedom. And naps. And fish. Definitely fish."

Cables whipped from the throne like striking snakes. I dodged, phantom whiskers mapping the strike zone, boots betraying me where paws would have gripped. Sparks carved constellations across the air. Rowan hurled disruption runes with academic fury. The captain's sword rang iron sermons against copper conduits. Smoke boy exhaled molten bell-notes that shattered the closest glass pods, freeing a raven who rolled in midair and clawed machinery with savage glee.

The Collector flowed with terrifying grace, each step spawning new geometric patterns that tried to cage my chaos. I bounded onto the throne's armrest.

Wrong-body, wrong-paws, but the principle remained: when in doubt, claim the highest perch and knock things off it. Universal cat law.

One clawless hand slapped a glyph array. My off-key purr jammed its syntax, turning elegant equations into gibberish. Machinery stuttered, shrieking metallic profanity.

"Fascinating," the Collector said, tail-braids crackling with electricity. "Your chaos signature operates on quantum uncertainty principles. Very inefficient. I can improve that."

"Efficiency is overrated. Chaos keeps things interesting."

More cables lashed out. I scrambled higher, using the throne's anchor posts like a cat tree. The Collector flowed after me with terrifying grace, glyphs blossoming under each step. Perfect geometric patterns meant to crystallize chaos into mathematics. They carved a cage of right angles designed to trap me in artificial order.

I scribbled circles across their lines with deliberate

CAT OUT OF LUCK

messiness, asymmetrical shapes that unbalanced symmetry.

Cages assume I'll stay put. I don't stay put for anything.

The patterns wavered, stumbled, collapsed. Order tripped over its own perfectionism.

Rows of containment tubes erupted as pressure systems failed. Brine geysered toward the cavern ceiling. Freed familiars scattered in all directions—an otter slapping across wet stone, a manticore cub dragging severed wires, the orange kitten mewing pitifully as it stumbled on unsteady legs. Each escape siphoned power from the central throne.

The salt woman unleashed a tidal wave that slammed into primary machinery, shorting out half the chamber in spectacular electrical tantrums. The not-man ripped loose an anchor post, hurling it like a javelin through the main manifold. Copper screamed.

"You're forcing cascade failure," the Collector hissed, form flickering as power fluctuated. "The portal network requires constant stabilization. Without control systems, realms will hemorrhage into each other."

"Then maybe the system is the problem, not the solution."

I leaped from the throne, chaos signature flaring. Every glyph in the chamber began to stutter and fail. Alarms bawled like wounded brass. Ceiling tiles cracked under vibrational stress. One fell, squashing a control console into expensive sparks.

The facility shook, metal screaming as beams bent and twisted. Steam vented from emergency releases. The orange kitten had found its way to my boots, mewing urgently.

Pack-instinct demanded I guard the retreat. Never leave kit scent behind enemy lines.

I scooped up the kitten, tucking it safely inside my coat. A tiny green lizard blinked behind shattered glass, too small for the main cylinders. Into the pocket it went.

Mine now. Pocket lizard and rescue kitten.

Rowan corralled fleeing familiars toward the stairwell, herding them like scholarly sheep. The captain guarded our retreat, his shield flaring whenever debris attempted to converse with his skull. Salt woman's crystals carved exit paths through failing machinery.

At the stairs' base, the Collector's voice sliced through the smoke and chaos. "Integration parameters logged. Stress responses catalogued. Breaking points identified." Those blue eyes fixed on me with chilling certainty. "You think chaos protects you. But chaos follows patterns. I know yours now."

"Patterns?" I snorted. "That's your first mistake. Cats don't follow patterns—we create them, ignore them, then knock them off tables just to watch them fall."

Pain lanced through my phantom tail, immediate agony as if something gripped the limb that once existed. I hissed, stumbled, and caught myself against the stone that buzzed under my palm. The sensation lingered, promising worse.

"Next trial starts with what you miss most," the Collector continued, voice following us up the stairs. "Your witch-bond. Your tail. Your precious autonomy. I'll take them piece by piece until cooperation becomes relief."

The freed raven caught my sleeve, yanking me upward with desperate strength. Rowan grabbed my collar, and together we climbed while the facility convulsed below, machinery eating itself in magnificent failure.

We burst into the tannery yard as green fire coughed from storm drains. Rain hissed against superheated metal. Freed familiars scattered into the night's dark alleys, their joyous screeches echoing between buildings. Forty-five prisoners had become forty-five problems for the Council to explain.

Good. Chaos is contagious.

The orange kitten purred against my chest, a tiny engine of contentment despite everything it had endured. The pocket lizard shifted, finding a comfortable position. Small victories in a war of attrition.

Rowan doubled over, coughing acrid smoke. "We made it."

"Define 'made,'" I said, flexing fingers that ached for claws. Rain washed blood and brine from my coat, but couldn't wash away what I'd seen. "Half those familiars are traumatized beyond recovery. The Collector rebuilds faster than we demolish. And they know entirely too much about my behavioral patterns."

The salt woman brushed water from her crystal formations. "Tide flows free. Gratitude runs deep."

"Keep flowing," I muttered, watching green light pulse from the facility's depths. "Stagnant puddles breed mosquitoes and megalomaniacs."

The captain approached, helmet under his arm, expression grim. "Council will demand a comprehensive report. Doubt they'll appreciate your methods."

"They can chew on it like tough mutton," I said.

Lightning gnawed the sky. In the flash, I saw glyphs

crawling across distant rooftops—new wards glowing like fresh claw marks. The Collector's influence is spreading, adapting, and preparing countermeasures.

It rebuilds fast. Challenge accepted.

I scratched the brick wall beside me, leaving marks that smelled of chalk and rebellion. My phantom tail twitched with remembered pain.

"Let them come," I whispered to the rain, the night, the sprawling city that didn't yet know what hunted in its depths. "But bring sardines. I fight better on a full stomach."

Far below, amid shattered glass and flooded circuits, the throne reassembled itself like a wounded beast knitting bone. The Collector stood amid the ruins, cable braids coiled around a single, unbroken containment pod.

Inside floated a tiger the color of midnight, stripes silver in the chemical light. Its eyes were closed, but electricity crawled across its fur in patterns that suggested fierce dreams.

"Subject MCC-140," the Collector murmured, stroking the glass with mechanical tenderness. "The next candidate strong enough to last. Perhaps more cooperative than his predecessor."

They smiled, a brittle curl of metal-threaded lips, and began repairs. The facility would be operational within hours. The harvest would continue.

But now they had detailed scans of the one who got away. Every stress response. Every behavioral quirk. Every weakness wrapped in fur and stubbornness.

The hunt would be very different next time.

Chapter 7

The Healer's Discovery

Market day stank of fish guts, burned bread, and sellers desperate to offload turnips that should've been compost. Rain quit during the night, leaving cobblestones slick enough to send any apprentice flying. Steam rose off the pastry carts, thick enough to choke on. I prowled the gutter, phantom whiskers twitching, every shout stabbing behind my eyes like needles.

Too many apprentices in one place. Recipe for disaster. Or entertainment. Possibly both.

Rowan hunched by the fishmonger's stall, ledger on one knee, quill twitching like a tail in trouble. He reeked of lamp oil, stale ink, and nerves about to snap. Salt woman drifted past spice vendors, crystals on her arms sparkling like she'd rolled in broken glass. She hummed tide-songs under her breath, the sound making children stop mid-step to listen. Smoke-boy coiled near the baker's ovens, gray wisps sampling the heat, invisible to everyone except cats and probably pigeons.

The anchors sang wrong. Every stone we passed thrummed with a sour note, like bells cracked and trying to pretend they still rang true. My burn-line itched, the straw-colored mark pulsing in rhythm with the ward stones carved into lintels and fountain rims.

Someone's been scratching at the ward stones. Leaving their mark.

I crouched beside a ward stone set into the fountain's base, pressing my palm to carved sigils still warm from yesterday's rain. The hum bit my fingers, then settled into a purr that tasted of metal and chalk dust. Chalk dust clung to the grooves, too fresh, too white.

"Recent work," I called to Rowan, loud enough to carry over a fishwife's argument about crab prices. "Someone's been retuning your stones."

He closed the ledger with a snap, worry creasing the corners of his mouth. "Authorized maintenance?"

I scraped a fingernail along one groove. White powder came away, but underneath, gold thread gleamed like fish scales. My chaos signature, thread-thin, woven into the anchor's foundation.

Scent trail. I've been marking territory without realizing it.

My fur would've stood on end if I still had any. Every ward I'd touched, every anchor I'd contaminated with my off-key purr, every stone I'd knocked sideways to make the magic flow smoother. Traces of me, bright as fish scales, leading straight back to wherever I'd been sleeping.

"They're tracking me," I said, voice flat as yesterday's beer. "Every anchor I touch keeps a taste of my magic. They've been following the trail."

Salt woman's crystals chimed an alarm, sharp and

brittle. Smoke-boy's wisps darkened, pulling tight around his shoulders like a nervous cloak. Rowan's knuckles went white on his quill.

Stupid, careless cat. Marked territory without checking for predators.

The crowd pressed closer as the morning wore on. Farmers wheeled barrows piled with turnips and cabbages. Apprentices darted between legs, carrying messages and small coins. Children chased an escaped chicken through puddles, shrieking with laughter. Too many people, too much noise, too many ways for claws to find soft flesh.

I studied the market's layout with a predator's gaze. Three main exits: north through the chandler's row, east past the livestock pens, south toward the docks. The fountain sat dead center, surrounded by stalls in a rough circle. If something ugly happened here, people would panic, scatter, and trample each other trying to reach doors that couldn't swallow a crowd fast enough.

Perfect kill zone. Civilians were penned like sheep.

Rowan followed my gaze, understanding dawning in his scholar's eyes. "They chose today on purpose. Market day. Maximum witnesses, maximum chaos."

"Maximum leverage," I corrected, stomach tight with realization. "They don't want me dead. They want me to be obedient."

A bell tolled somewhere to the west, the sound flat and wrong. My phantom whiskers twitched, catching vibrations that didn't belong. The anchors' sour hum shifted, notes sliding into harmony that made my teeth ache.

The salt woman grabbed my elbow, crystals blazing an

alarm. "Something comes. Tide tastes of metal and old blood."

Smoke-boy's form wavered, gray wisps scattering like startled birds. "Iron in the air. Too much iron."

The crowd flowed around us, oblivious. A baker's boy balanced a tray of honey rolls. Two goodwives argued over the price of eggs. A street musician tuned his fiddle, bow scraping strings into submission. Normal people living everyday lives, unaware that predators circled overhead.

They trust their wards to keep them safe. Their wards answer to whoever holds the leash.

Movement caught my eye. Atop the cooper's shop, copper gleamed where no copper should be. Not roof tiles, not weathervanes. Eyes. Flat, emotionless, scanning the crowd like a hawk hunting mice.

More movement. The blacksmith's chimney. The chandler's signpost. The church bell tower. Copper and brass and silver, too bright in the morning light, too still to be alive.

Watchers. Posted like sentries.

Something cold crawled up my spine that had nothing to do with the morning air. Those weren't just weapons or surveillance tools. The way they moved, the predatory stillness, the patient focus—I knew that posture. I'd used it myself a thousand times.

They're familiars. Corrupted familiars.

My phantom whiskers recoiled. Whatever had been done to them, they still moved like us, thought like us. But wrong. Hollowed out and refilled with someone else's purpose.

I counted six. Maybe more hiding behind gables and

weather vanes. Each one focused on the fountain, on the exact spot where I stood with my phantom whiskers twitching and my burn-line pulsing like a beacon.

This should be me. This could have been me.

The thought hit like ice water. Every choice I'd made since the portal spat me out—every moment of defiance, every refusal to submit—had protected me from ending up like them. But barely. And if I failed today, if they dragged me back to their processing facility...

They'd turn me into another watcher. Another broken toy wearing my scent.

The bell tolled again. Closer now. Wrong notes echoing through the market. Children stopped playing to cover their ears. Horses stamped and snorted, harness leather creaking with nervous energy.

Rowan's quill trembled in his grip. "How many?"

"Too many." I backed toward the fountain's rim, keeping the stone at my spine. "They've been watching all morning. Waiting for the crowd to thicken."

Bait in a trap. The cheese always thinks it's safe until the spring snaps.

A vendor's cart overturned near the north exit. Apples scattered across cobblestones, their owner shouting curses at the wind that had supposedly knocked his goods flying. But there was no wind. The air was dead still, thick with the smell of fear-sweat and copper pennies.

Another cart tipped at the east exit. Then the south. Wooden wheels blocked the narrow passages, and goods spilled like deliberate barriers. People pushed and shoved, voices rising from annoyance to alarm.

"Exits blocked," Salt woman observed, crystals singing sharp as breaking glass. "Nets close."

The watchers dropped from their perches. Not climbing down, not using ladders. Dropping like stones and landing silent as shadows, they prowled between stalls, copper skin gleaming, joints clicking with clockwork precision.

Corrupted familiars. My people, twisted into their people.

Bile rose in my throat. Each one moved like me, thought like me, hunted like me. But wrong. Controlled. Pieces of themselves carved out and replaced with gears and compliance.

The crowd noticed them now. Screams started, thin and sharp, children crying for parents who couldn't reach them through the press. The corrupted familiars paid no attention to civilians, their flat copper eyes fixed on me.

One leaped onto the fountain's rim. Close enough to see the sigils burned into its forehead, the brass wires threaded through its whiskers, the way its tail moved in mechanical jerks instead of fluid curves. Its mouth opened, revealing teeth filed to points and a throat lined with speaking tubes.

"Subject MCC-139," it said, voice echoing from a dozen throats at once. "Compliance window initiated. Surrender for processing or civilian casualties will mount exponentially."

Of course. Corner the cat, threaten the kittens. Standard human tactics.

I could run. Leap the fountain, scatter through the crowd, use chaos to carve an escape route while they fumbled with their straight-line thinking. I was faster, cleverer, more flexible than their mechanical perfection.

But they'd follow. And the people trapped in this market square would pay the price for my freedom.

A child stumbled near the baker's stall, small hands pressed to his ears as bells tolled wrong notes through his skull. His mother reached for him, but a brass ferret skittered between them, chain-wrapped tail lashing warnings.

No. Not happening. These are my strays now.

"Counter-offer," I called out, loud enough for every watcher to hear. "Come take me. But first, you'll have to catch me."

I vaulted onto the fountain's central pillar, arms spread wide, phantom tail lashing defiance at nothing. Let them see their target clearly. Let them focus on me, rather than the crowd.

Salt woman's eyes went wide. "Mischief, no."

"Mischief, yes." I grinned, all teeth and bad intentions. "Besides, I'm curious what they think they've learned about catching cats."

The copper cat crouched, servos whining as it prepared to spring. Around the market, more corrupted familiars emerged from shadows and hiding spots. A wolf with brass ribs. Ferrets wrapped in chains. A hawk with bronze feathers that rang like tiny bells.

My kind, stolen, and broken. Time to teach them what claws are really for.

Time to see what they'd learned about fighting cats. *Spoiler: probably not enough.* And I wouldn't be running away.

Someone has to teach these people proper familiar care.

Starting with: no cages, no chains, and definitely no copper plating.

The copper cat sprang.

The copper cat slammed into me, servo-muscles hissing steam as claws raked air where my throat had been a heartbeat before. I twisted sideways, phantom tail lashing for balance that never came, boots skidding on wet cobblestones. The impact sent me sprawling into a turnip cart, vegetables scattering everywhere.

Grace is overrated anyway.

Around the market square, more nightmares dropped from rooftops. Chain-wrapped ferrets skittered between stalls, copper eyes flat and empty. A wolf prowled from the chandler's row, brass ribs gleaming where flesh should be, each breath a mechanical wheeze. Above us, a hawk circled on bronze feathers that rang like tiny bells, its talons sparking against stone with each dive.

They used to be like me. Now they're broken toys that still move.

Worse than the claws was knowing what they used to be. These weren't just weapons; these were familiars who'd thought for themselves, loved their witches, napped in sunbeams, and complained about the quality of fish. Now they moved with the terrible precision of clockwork, every gesture calculated, every breath measured.

The copper cat stalked closer, joints clicking wrong, fur

shaved in perfect squares where glyphs had been burned into skin. When it opened its mouth, teeth filed to points gleamed around a throat lined with speaking tubes.

"Subject MCC-139," it said, voice echoing from a dozen sources at once. "Compliance window initiated. Civilian casualties escalate with each moment of resistance."

They even stole its voice.

People pressed against blocked exits, panic spreading fast. A baker's boy clutched his tray of rolls, eyes wide with terror. Two goodwives huddled behind an overturned cart. The street musician still held his fiddle, bow trembling in his grip.

"Let them go," I called out, rising from turnip debris with what dignity I could muster. "Your quarrel is with me."

The Collector's laughter echoed from every corrupted throat, sharp and wrong. "Quarrel implies equality. You are inventory. They are motivation."

Leverage. Threaten the pack to make the alpha submit.

The chain-ferrets flanked to the left, their metal links singing as they moved. The brass wolf circled right, clicking toward a flower seller who'd backed herself against a wall. Above, the hawk folded its bronze wings and dove at the children who'd been chasing chickens.

Too many targets. Not enough cat.

I couldn't reach them all. Couldn't protect everyone. But I could try.

Rowan hurled chalk shards—bent wrong on purpose— at the diving hawk. The geometry twisted mid-air, confusing the bird's mechanical flight patterns. It clipped a stall awning and tumbled, brass feathers scattering.

Salt woman slammed crystal fists into cobblestones.

Brine erupted, turning the square into a tide pool that sent ferrets skidding into each other. Their chains tangled, locking them mid-leap in a frustrated steel knot.

Smoke-boy exhaled thick fog, swallowing the exits in gray obscurity. Civilians vanished into the haze, finally able to flee unseen.

Good apprentices. They learn fast.

But the copper cat was mine. It moved like me—same pivot on phantom claws, same disdain for obstacles, same arrogant assumption that everything in sight needed proper supervision. It zig-zagged between stalls, tail whirring like a broken clock, trying to corner me against the fountain.

Straight lines again. They studied my moves but missed the point.

I ran crooked, bouncing off walls, leaving chaos in my wake. The puppet's programming lagged as it tried to calculate angles that made no sense. Its movements grew jerky, confused by prey that refused to behave logically.

We careened through the row of spice vendors. I vaulted a saffron barrel and shoulder-checked the copper cat into a turmeric display. Yellow dust billowed everywhere, making us both sneeze, though mine was real, and it was just mechanical mimicry.

Even its sneezes are fake. Insulting.

It rose slowly, its hinges grinding on spice dust, its eyes flickering brighter blue as the Collector focused its attention through borrowed pupils.

"Your empathy degrades combat efficiency," the voice boomed from its throat. "Emotional attachment makes you predictable."

"Your fashion sense makes you intolerable," I shot back, wiping turmeric from my nose.

Need better insults. File under 'when not dodging servo-claws.'

The brass wolf had cornered the flower seller. She pressed against stones slick with morning dew, clutching daisies to her chest. The wolf's mechanical jaw opened, revealing gears where a tongue should be.

No.

I sprinted, boots slipping on wet cobbles, arms pumping without the counterbalance of a tail. Too far. Too slow. The wolf's brass head turned toward the terrified woman, calculation clicking behind dead copper eyes.

I won't make it in time.

But I dove anyway, crashing into the wolf's flank just as its jaws snapped shut. Brass teeth caught fabric instead of flesh. The flower seller stumbled sideways, daisies scattering, alive and breathing and whole.

The wolf and I tumbled together across slick stones. This close, I could see the horror beneath the metal—gray fur growing around brass plates, real eyes drowning behind copper lenses. At her shoulder, a spiral of gears had been filed directly into living skin, still oozing oil mixed with blood.

They didn't replace her. They just... added things. Made her theirs instead of hers.

She pinned me against the fountain's base, mechanical weight crushing down. Her jaws opened wide enough to split my skull. I could smell the oil on her breath, see the small sparks where wires rubbed against bone.

But in that moment, pressed against her chest, I felt

something else. A rhythm underneath the mechanical wheeze. Something deeper than a heartbeat. The ghost of who she used to be, buried under brass and gears, but still fighting. Still trying to remember her name.

She's in there. She's still in there.

The gear spiral wasn't just metal grafted onto flesh. It was a scream frozen in brass, a plea for help that no one had answered. And suddenly I couldn't think of anything else except making that screaming stop. Without thinking, without being able to think of anything else, I pressed my palm against the gear spiral branded into her shoulder.

My burn-line flared gold, but this wasn't the chaotic spill of contamination I'd grown used to. This was different. Focused. My magic reached out and found hers—buried, twisted, but still burning with stubborn life underneath all that brass.

Fur matted with their wire. But the real cat's still in there.

Heat crawled up my arm, but it wasn't burning me. It was burning through the connections that held her in artificial patterns, feeding her own strength back to herself. My chaos wasn't destroying the Collector's work; it was reminding her how to destroy it herself.

Something inside her chest gave a sound like breaking clockwork. The wolf jerked back, convulsing. Brass plates popped free with metallic screams. She retched, spitting wires and copper filings, breathing real breath. And for the first time since the attack began, she blinked. Really blinked, like someone remembering her own name.

How did I do that?

The question hung between us. Around the market

square, the other corrupted familiars froze, their mechanical certainty faltering as they witnessed something impossible.

One of them, remembering what she used to be.

The wolf stared at me, gray eyes wide and alive. No copper films. No brass overlays. Just the clear, bewildered gaze of someone who was trying to remember what freedom felt like.

What did I just do?

My burn-line throbbed, the straw-colored mark pulsing with heat that traveled up my arm and settled behind my ribs, warm and strange. The sensation was nothing like contamination—that chaotic spill of energy that made monks sprout whiskers and wards hiccup. This felt... deliberate. Controlled. Like my magic had found something broken and decided to fix it instead of making it worse.

My chaos fixed something? That's new. Usually, I just knock things off shelves.

The wolf tried to stand, legs shaking like a newborn kit. Brass plates lay scattered around her like shed armor, each piece steaming where my touch had burned through the connections. Her first breath came out as a mechanical wheeze, then cleared to something soft and real.

"I..." Her voice cracked, rusty from disuse. "I remember my name."

The words hit me like a physical blow. She remembered.

After months, maybe years of being nothing but gears and obedience, she remembered who she was.

Names are what keep you you.

I pressed deeper into the connection, curious despite the growing ache in my bones. Through my palm, I felt her pain. It was not a physical hurt, but the deeper trauma of being carved apart and reassembled into someone else's tool, a bone-deep loneliness. The desperate, animal terror of watching yourself disappear piece by piece.

They didn't just cage her. They hollowed her out.

My chaos met her spirit, gold mixing with silver. Where they touched, the Collector's modifications simply... unraveled. Gear-work dissolved. Wire-bonds snapped. The foreign magic that had held her together in unnatural patterns dissolved.

This was restoration, pure and simple. My chaos fed her own magic back to herself, rather than consuming her corruption, untangling what had been knotted and straightening what had been bent.

Not breaking their collar. Teaching her to slip it herself.

The wolf's eyes brightened with each passing second. Gray fur regrew where brass had been welded to skin.

What just happened?

I stared at my hands, burn-line still glowing faintly. For months, everyone had treated my magic like a disease—something to contain, control, minimize. Even I'd started thinking of it that way. But this... this was the opposite of contamination.

Didn't free her. Just reminded her where the latch was.

Maybe I'd been looking at this all wrong. Maybe my "contamination" wasn't about making others more like me.

Perhaps it was about helping them be more true to themselves.

Her ears pricked forward, then flattened, then pricked again as she remembered how to move them by choice instead of command. When she licked her lips, I saw a real tongue instead of mechanical parts.

"Bellwether," she whispered, wonder in her voice. "My name is Bellwether."

Not was. Is.

The drain hit me like a falling anvil.

This isn't about magic. It's about caring enough to try.

The healing hadn't come from some hidden ability or ancient power. It came from seeing Bellwether as more than a corrupted weapon—seeing her as someone who deserved to choose her own path, knock things off her own tables, nap where she wanted.

That's not magic. That's just basic pack behavior.

But apparently, being decent could be weaponized. Energy poured out of me in golden streams, feeding her restoration, leaving my limbs heavy and my vision spotted with dancing lights. It was like trying to fill a bucket with a hole in it—the magic wanted to keep flowing, to heal everything at once, but my body wasn't built for this kind of output.

Careful. Don't give more than you have.

I pulled back from the connection, allowing the burn line to cool to a bearable warmth. Bellwether sat up slowly, testing each movement like she was remembering how to inhabit her own skin. When she looked at me, gratitude shone in her eyes.

"Thank you," she said simply. "For giving me back to myself."

Pack rules. No one gets left behind.

Around the market square, the remaining corrupted familiars had gone perfectly still. The copper cat crouched beside an overturned cart, joints locked mid-stride. Chain-ferrets hung motionless in the air where salt woman's tide had caught them. Even the bronze hawk perched frozen on a lamppost, one wing half-spread.

They're processing what just happened. Good. Gives me time to think.

Through their shared connection to the Collector, they'd all felt Bellwether's liberation. Felt the moment her brass shackles simply ceased to exist. Felt one of their own remember how to choose.

And that meant the Collector felt it too.

They felt her choose.

For the first time since this nightmare started, I wasn't just surviving or escaping or trying to minimize damage. I was fighting back. Not with claws or chaos or clever words, but with something the Collector couldn't understand or counter. Hope.

Disgusting. When did I start collecting strays with feelings?

They'd built their entire system on the assumption they could file away everything that made someone themselves. But what if they couldn't? What if the real you was always there, just buried under their stupid modifications like fur under brass plating?

What if I could teach them all to slip their collars?

The copper cat's eyes flared brilliant blue as the

Collector's attention focused through borrowed pupils. When it spoke, rage vibrated through every word.

"Impossible. Corrupted matrices cannot be reversed. The modifications are permanent."

"Your math is wrong," I called back, getting shakily to my feet. The healing had left me dizzy, but something fierce stirred in my chest. "You forgot to carry the cat."

First rescue. Let's see how many more I can manage.

The chain-ferrets resumed movement, their links singing as they untangled from one another. But their coordination was off now, timing stuttered, because part of their processing power was being diverted to analyzing Bellwether's impossible recovery.

Doubt is contagious. Even in machines.

I took a step toward the nearest ferret, hand outstretched. It skittered backward, chains scraping loudly on cobblestones. Behind copper eyes, I glimpsed something familiar—the quick, clever intelligence of a creature that solved problems by thinking sideways around them.

Still in there. Still fighting.

"I know you're listening," I said, loud enough for every corrupted familiar to hear. "I know part of you remembers what it felt like to choose your own path. To nap where you wanted. To knock things off shelves just because they looked smug."

The bronze hawk's head tilted, a gesture too organic to be programmed. The copper cat's tail twitched once, a real twitch instead of mechanical precision.

Got their attention.

"The Collector thinks metal makes you stronger," I continued, taking another step forward. "But I've seen what real strength looks like. It's Bellwether remembering her name. It's the courage to hope when hope hurts. It's choosing to be yourself even when the world wants to make you into something else."

My burn-line pulsed, and chaos rippled outward like heat waves. This felt different from contamination. Gentler. An invitation. A reminder of what they used to be.

The nearest chain-ferret stopped retreating. Its copper eyes flickered—something warmer than the cold blue of the Collector's control. More alive.

Come on. Remember who you were before they carved you up.

I reached out slowly, palm open, the same gesture I'd use to coax a suspicious cat out from under furniture. The ferret crept closer, chains scraping behind it.

Our connection sparked the moment my fingers touched its brand. This time I was ready for the sensation—the overwhelming flood of its trauma, the echo of everything that had been done to make it compliant. But underneath the pain, I felt something else.

Curiosity. Mischief. The irrepressible urge to investigate small spaces and knock important things onto the floor.

There you are.

I fed my chaos into its spirit, golden energy seeking the natural pattern beneath artificial modifications. The ferret convulsed, chain-links dissolving. When the transformation ended, a sleek brown creature blinked up at me with amber eyes.

"Two," I said, grinning despite my exhaustion. "Anyone else ready to remember how to misbehave?"

Possible friends instead of just enemies.

The Collector's voice boomed from every remaining

puppet, fury making the words crack like breaking stone: "You cannot convert them all. The drain will kill you."

"Maybe," I admitted, studying the copper cat and bronze hawk with predator's eyes. "But I bet I can convert enough to make your day significantly worse."

Time to see what I can really do.

For the first time since this started, I wasn't running, hiding, or trying to minimize the damage. I was hunting.

Hunting for my strays, not prey.

Every corrupted familiar in this square was someone like me who'd been stolen, broken, and rebuilt into someone else's tool. The Collector thought that made them weapons. I thought it made them mine to fix.

Let's see who's right.

CHAPTER 8

BUILDING THE PACK

The safe house smelled of wet wool, fennel tea, and the particular exhaustion that comes after running too far on legs that fold wrong. Lamplight flickered through warped shutters, casting crooked shadows across threadbare rugs where three newly freed familiars huddled like survivors of a shipwreck. Steam rose from chipped mugs. Someone had found blankets, though none of them seemed to know what to do with the warmth that came without conditions.

Pack behavior. Prickly as wet fur and twice as likely to scratch.

I perched on the windowsill, phantom tail aching from a battle it couldn't help fight, watching Bellwether lick obsessively at the spot where brass plates had been welded to her shoulder. The fur was growing back, silver-gray and soft, but she couldn't seem to stop checking that it was real.

Stress-licking. At least she remembers proper grooming.

The brown ferret—Pip, she'd whispered when I asked— sat coiled in the corner farthest from the door, amber eyes

128

tracking every shadow, every creak of settling timber. Her chains were gone, dissolved by chaos and choice, but she still flinched when cloth rustled too loud.

Ears swiveling at every sound. Everything smells like an ambush.

Near the cold fireplace, the copper cat I'd freed last hunched over a bowl of fish scraps Rowan had scrounged from somewhere. He ate like someone expecting the food to be snatched away, bolting each bite without tasting. When I'd asked his name, he'd just stared at me with blank confusion.

Memory gaps. They carved deeper into him.

"Take your time," Rowan murmured, kneeling beside the nameless tabby with a wooden bowl of warm milk. "Small sips. Your stomach needs to remember how to handle kindness."

The tabby's head tilted, considering this as if kindness were a foreign concept requiring translation. Which, for him, it probably was.

I hopped down from the sill and padded across creaking floorboards. My legs still trembled from the healing drain, as energy flowed out faster than my body could replenish it. Three rescues had left me feeling hollow as an empty can, but stronger too, like muscles that ached from good use.

Tired muscles, steadier paws. Bodies are contradictory.

"Report," I said gently, settling cross-legged beside Bellwether. "How do you feel?"

She looked up from grooming, gray eyes bright but haunted. "Like I've been sleeping for years and just woke up. Everything feels... sharp. Real." Her voice dropped to a whisper. "I can choose where to look. When to breathe. What to think about."

Too many smells, sounds, choices. Like being let out of a box that was too small.

"That's normal," I said, though I had no idea if it was. "Your mind needs time to stretch."

Pip's head poked up from her corner. "How long?" The question came out cracked, desperate. "How long until it stops feeling like they might come back? Might drag us away again?"

Reasonable fear. The Collector doesn't strike me as someone who accepts losses gracefully.

I met her amber eyes with steady confidence I didn't entirely feel. "They can try. But you're pack now. No one gets dragged anywhere without going through me first."

"Pack," Bellwether repeated, tasting the word like honey. "I remember pack."

The nameless tabby stopped eating, fish juice glistening on his whiskers. "Pack means... belonging? Not being alone?"

Simple question. Complicated answer.

"Pack means choosing to stay," I said carefully. "Means watching each other's backs and sharing the good napping spots. Means no one eats alone unless they want to."

He considered this, then pushed his bowl toward the center of the room. An invitation. Pip crept forward first, then Bellwether. They shared fish scraps in careful silence, learning the rhythm of voluntary cooperation.

Progress. Small steps toward trust.

Rowan scratched notes in his ledger, quill pausing every few words as he tried to capture something that resisted documentation. "The healing process," he murmured, more to himself than to us. "It's not just magical restoration. You're returning their agency along with their autonomy."

Academic fascination. He can't help himself.

"Explain," I said, curious despite my exhaustion.

He set down his quill and gestured at the freed familiars. "Look at their recovery patterns. Physical healing is almost instantaneous, as seen in fur regrowth, wound closure, and mechanical removal. But behavioral reintegration is gradual. They're not just remembering who they were; they're choosing who to become."

Rowan sees patterns where I see people. Useful, if cold.

"The Collector couldn't steal their spirits," I said, understanding dawning. "Just bury them under control mechanisms. My chaos doesn't create new personalities—it excavates old ones."

"Precisely. Which means—"

Bellwether's snarl cut him off. She'd gone rigid, ears flat, lips pulled back from teeth that had learned to bite through brass. "Which means they're still out there. Still capturing, still carving up anyone who thinks for themselves."

And there's the anger. Right on schedule.

Pip's amber eyes flashed with fury that made her small frame tremble. "They took my memories. Fed them to machines. Made me forget my own mother's voice."

The nameless tabby's bowl clattered to the floor, milk spreading in white puddles. "Revenge," he whispered, the word sharp as broken glass. "We should hunt them. Make them pay."

Wounded predators wanting to bite back. Natural. Dangerous.

I stood slowly, every muscle protesting the movement. "Revenge feels good," I said, voice carrying the weight of authority I wasn't sure I'd earned. "Tastes like justice and victory and all the fish you can eat. But revenge without strategy is just suicide with extra steps."

Bellwether's growl deepened. "You want us to do nothing? Let them keep stealing people?"

"I want us to win," I corrected. "Revenge is about satisfying anger. Winning is about stopping them permanently."

Alpha duties. Like wearing a collar that's always too tight and smells of other people's expectations.

Pip crept closer, conflict clear in her amber eyes. "How do we win against something that turns our own kind into weapons?"

"By being what they can't predict or control," I said, sitting back down to put myself at their eye level. "By being pack instead of property. By choosing cooperation over compliance."

Easier said than done. But someone has to try.

Rowan cleared his throat delicately. "Speaking of cooperation, we need to discuss the physical toll. Three healings left you barely able to stand. If you attempt large-scale rescues without understanding the limits—"

"I'll burn out," I finished. The truth sat heavy on my tongue. "How many before I can't function?"

"Unknown. But each healing draws from your core reserves. You're essentially feeding your own life force into their restoration."

Wonderful. Saving people might kill me. The universe has a sense of humor.

Bellwether's anger shifted to concern. "Then we find another way. I won't let you sacrifice yourself for—"

"For what?" I interrupted. "For people who deserve freedom? For familiars who remember what choice feels like?" I flicked phantom ears in dismissal.

True. Though usually the trades didn't involve potentially dying.

The nameless tabby spoke up, voice small but determined. "What if we help? Share the load somehow?"

"Unknown variables," Rowan murmured, scribbling again. "Theoretically possible, but—"

A knock at the door froze us all. Three short, two long. The pattern Rowan had arranged with Salt woman and Smoke-boy.

More displaced arriving. The pack grows.

But as I padded toward the door, phantom whiskers twitching with unease, I couldn't shake the feeling that growing larger also meant becoming a larger target.

Pack rules keep multiplying. No one mentioned this when I claimed the humans.

The Collector had seen me heal their weapons. They knew I could turn corrupted familiars back into free agents. Which meant the next attack wouldn't just be about recapturing me.

It would be about stopping me permanently.

Let them try. I've got the pack now.

I opened the door to face whatever came next.

The salt woman entered first, crystals chiming against the doorframe like wind through broken glass. Behind her came Smoke-boy, gray wisps clinging to the ceiling beams, and Vire, his rope collar slack but present, humming subsonic warnings. Last through the door was the girl who made stones weep—barely ten years old, humming a tune that made the floorboards sag beneath her feet.

My strays, returning to roost. Except they're not mine, are they?

I closed the door and turned to face six pairs of eyes— three newly healed, four previously displaced—all looking at me with expressions ranging from hope to suspicion to outright wariness. The weight of their attention settled on my shoulders like a lead blanket.

Leadership. Why did it have to be leadership?

"Meeting called to order," I announced, trying for the confident tone that had worked in the market square. "We need to discuss next steps against the Collector—"

"No." Salt woman's voice cut through mine like a tide through sand. "First, we discuss whether there should be next steps at all."

Ah. Democracy. How refreshing.

Selyn moved to the center of the room, where crystals caught lamplight and threw rainbow fragments across the walls. "Three of us were nearly lost tonight. How many more before we admit damaged refugees cannot win this war?"

Haze drifted lower, vapor coiling nervous patterns around his shoulders. "She speaks sense. The Collector has resources, facilities, and armies of corrupted familiars. We have..." He gestured at our ragtag assembly. "Hope and fish scraps."

And attitude. Don't forget the attitude.

Pip's ears flattened against her skull. "So, we hide? Let them keep stealing people?"

"We survive," Haze replied, his form growing denser with emotion. "Survival first. Rescue fantasies second."

Vire's rope collar thrummed, his voice buzzing through bone and timber. "Fear echoes in these walls. From all of us. Including him." He nodded toward me. "Leaders who fear failure make choices that ensure it."

Well, that's uncomfortably accurate.

The girl—I needed to ask her name—stopped humming. The sudden silence felt heavier than her song. "The stones say death follows the cat-who-walks-wrong. They've seen it in their dreams."

Prophetic children. Why is it always prophetic children?

Bellwether growled, hackles rising. "He saved us. Gave us ourselves back. That means something."

"It means he has useful magic," Selyn said, crystals darkening to deep blue. "Not that he should command our choices."

Fair point. Stings, but fair.

I perched on the windowsill again, letting silence stretch until it became uncomfortable. In the market, adrenaline and desperation had made decisions simple. Here, with time to think, the complications multiplied like rabbits in spring.

They're right to be suspicious. I'm suspicious of myself, too.

"You think I'm another authority figure," I said finally. "Someone who'll tell you what to do and expect gratitude for the privilege."

Vire's collar hummed agreement. Haze's vapor tightened around himself like armor.

"The Collector was an authority figure too," I continued. "Probably started with good intentions. Keep the realms stable, maintain order, protect the greater good." I licked my lips, tasting bitter truth. "But good intentions and copper plating both tarnish when you stop asking if people want to be saved."

Uncomfortable parallel. But necessary.

The nameless tabby spoke up from his corner. "What are you saying?"

"I'm saying I don't want followers." The words came out harder than I'd intended, but they felt right. "I want allies. People who choose to work together because they believe in something, rather than following orders from someone with useful magic."

Selyn's crystals shifted toward clearer hues. "And if we choose differently? If we vote to scatter, hide, or survive quietly?"

Decision time. Cajole or accept. What kind of alpha am I?

"Then I'll help you disappear properly," I said. "Make sure you've got safe routes, clean identities, and enough resources to stay hidden. No guilt, no pressure, no speeches about duty."

Haze's vapor loosened, surprise evident in the shift. "You'd let us go?"

"Pack rules," I said simply. "No one stays who doesn't want to be here."

That felt right. Finally.

Pip crept forward, amber eyes bright with curiosity. "And if we stay? What then?"

I hopped down from the sill, pacing the room's perimeter while I thought. "Then we figure out how to win together. Our plan that we build together, instead of my plan that you follow."

The girl started humming again, a different tune—something that made the stones beneath our feet feel solid instead of uncertain. "The walls like that song better," she said. "Less weeping, more singing."

Progress.

Rowan looked up from his ledger. "Consensus building requires understanding all options. What would victory actually look like?"

Academic precision. Right question, though.

Bellwether stretched, working tension from muscles that remembered the feel of brass chains. "The Collector stops existing. All corrupted familiars freed. No more facilities, no more harvesting."

"Impossible," Haze said immediately. "Too many variables, too much infrastructure."

"Then what's possible?" I asked.

Selyn's crystals chimed as she considered. "Damage their operations enough to force retreat. Make familiar harvesting too costly to continue."

Vire's rope collar shifted pitch. "Fear their own weapons. Turn corruption against corruptors."

The nameless tabby nodded slowly. "Rescue who we can. Save who will let us."

Smaller goals. More achievable.

"Show of hands," I said. "Who votes to scatter and hide?"

Haze raised gray wisps that might have been fingers. After a long moment, so did the girl.

"Who votes to fight back, knowing it's dangerous and might fail?"

Bellwether's paw shot up. Pip followed. The nameless tabby raised his hand hesitantly.

"Who needs more information before deciding?"

Selyn and Vire raised their hands. Rowan kept writing, which I took as a sign of academic neutrality.

Split decision. Democracy in action.

"Right," I said. "Haze, you and..." I looked at the girl. "I'm sorry, what's your name?"

"Whisper," she said. "Because that's how stones talk."

"Haze and Whisper want out. I'll help you plan safe extraction routes tomorrow. Selyn and Vire need more data —fair enough. We'll scout Collector facilities, gather intelligence, and make informed decisions."

Fair trade. Lead by helping, not by showing claws.

Bellwether's tail wagged once. "And the rest of us?"

"We train," I said. "Learn to work together. Figure out what we're each good at. Build trust before we need it."

Baby steps. But forward movement.

Haze drifted toward the door, then paused. "If... if you

prove this can work. If small victories become possible. I might reconsider."

"The offer stands," I said. "No judgment either way."

He's scared. They all are. Can't blame them.

Whisper tugged on Selyn's crystalline arm. "The stones say they're less frightened now. Decisions made in daylight weigh differently than choices made in shadow."

Kitten speaks in riddles. Typical.

As the group settled into smaller conversations—Rowan discussing extraction routes with Haze, Bellwether comparing fighting techniques with Pip—I realized something had shifted. The tension in the room felt different. Still present, but... workable.

They're choosing to stay, not being told to do so. Makes all the difference.

Vire approached, rope collar humming quietly. "Leadership suits you better when you're not trying to wear it."

Perceptive observation from someone who echoes fear.

"Still figuring it out," I admitted.

"Good," he said. "Leaders who think they have answers stop listening for better questions."

Deep thoughts from rope-human. My strays have hidden talents.

Through the window, dawn light touched the horizon. We'd talked through the night, hammering out the beginning of something that might eventually become a plan.

Might end in disaster. But our disaster is to choose.

For the first time since this started, I felt like we had a chance.

Morning light slanted through shutters, painting golden stripes across maps that covered every flat surface in the room. Rowan had outdone himself overnight, producing detailed sketches of Collector facilities, guard rotations, and what looked suspiciously like architectural blueprints acquired through means I preferred not to examine too closely.

Book-mouse found blueprints. Scary when he stops being boring.

I balanced on the back of a chair, studying the largest map while Bellwether traced patrol routes with one claw. The supply depot squatted on parchment like a geometrical insult—all right angles and efficient spacing, designed by someone who'd never met a corner they couldn't make sharper.

"Here," I said, tapping a loading dock marked with neat little x's. "Minimal guards, maximum supplies. Fish tins for morale, reagents for Rowan's experiments, and probably enough rope to tie up whoever designed this architectural tragedy."

The perfect target for proving we can work together without anyone getting hurt.

Selyn drifted closer, crystals catching the morning light. "The tidal charts show low ebb at midnight. Salt corrosion works faster in dry air." She traced a finger along what appeared to be drainage channels. "But these culverts empty into the bay. One miscalculation floods the district."

Salt woman thinks before pouncing. Smart. Someone should.

Vire hunched near the wall, rope collar thrumming subsonic warnings. "Fear echoes from this place. Old fear, deep fear. People have died there." His voice buzzed through the floorboards. "Recent deaths taste of brass and desperation."

Rope-human smells fear like I smell mice. Handy. Also creepy.

The nameless tabby studied guard positions, amber eyes tracking patterns I couldn't see. "They rotate every four hours, but the overlaps create blind spots. Seventeen seconds where the east corner goes unwatched." He looked up, startled by his own precision. "I... remember numbers. Mathematical relationships."

Scholar familiar. Probably belonged to someone in accounting or engineering.

"What else do you remember?" I asked gently.

He closed his eyes, concentration creasing his features. "Names. Symbols. My witch called me... Cipher. Because I could solve her equations."

Identity restoration. Progress.

"Welcome back, Cipher," I said. "We'll need those mathematical relationships."

Bellwether prowled the perimeter, energy barely contained. "Intel is useful. Action is better. When do we stop planning and start biting?"

"After we know we can work together without tripping over each other," I said. "Training first. Planning second. Biting third."

Though I admit, biting sounds appealing.

Rowan cleared a space in the center of the room, chalk dust rising like flour clouds. "Coordination exercises. Each team member contributes their specialty to a shared objective." He drew interlocking circles, the kind that made my phantom whiskers twitch with geometry-induced anxiety.

"Objective," I announced, hopping onto the table. "Retrieve Rowan's quill from that ledger without touching the ledger itself."

Simple task. Multiple solutions. Perfect for revealing working styles.

Cipher studied the problem with mathematical intensity. "Angle of approach, leverage requirements, weight distribution..." He muttered calculations under his breath.

Bellwether's solution was more direct. She stalked to the ledger, gripped the binding in her teeth, and shook until the quill flew free. Effective, if inelegant.

Straightforward approach. Sometimes the best answer is the obvious one.

Pip slithered around the table's edge, amber eyes tracking air currents. She blew gently on the quill's feather, nudging it toward the ledger's edge where careful prodding could topple it free.

Subtle manipulation. Uses environmental factors instead of direct force.

Selyn raised a crystalline hand. Moisture condensed from the air, forming droplets that struck the ledger's corner in precise sequence. The binding warped, creating a gap that allowed the quill to be released without damage.

Elegant solution. Changes the environment to enable success.

Vire's approach made my fur stand on end. He hummed a subsonic note that vibrated through wood and parchment. The quill simply lifted, carried by controlled acoustic levitation.

Sophisticated technique. Also creepy as hell.

"Excellent," Rowan said, scribbling notes. "Five different approaches, all successful. Now for coordination."

Oh good. Group projects. My favorite kind of disaster.

He scattered paper fragments across the floor, then placed his quill in the center like a prize. "Retrieve the quill together. Each person must contribute, but no one can act without unanimous agreement."

Group decisions under time limits. Mean but effective.

Cipher immediately started calculating optimal trajectories. Bellwether wanted to charge straight through. Pip suggested a perimeter approach. Selyn advocated for environmental manipulation. Vire proposed acoustic coordination.

Five plans, all different, none compatible with each other.

Everyone talking at once. Louder than feeding time at a shelter.

"Time limit," I announced, settling onto my haunches to watch the chaos unfold. "Thirty seconds before the target relocates."

Artificial pressure. Helps separate leaders from followers.

Arguments erupted. Cipher's mathematics collided with Bellwether's directness. Pip's caution clashed with Selyn's precision. Vire tried to mediate through emotional resonance, which only added another layer of complexity.

Twenty seconds. Fifteen. Ten.

They're going to fail. Good. Failure teaches better than success.

At five seconds, Pip squeaked in frustration and darted toward the quill. The others followed instinctively—Bellwether providing cover, Cipher calculating intercept courses, Selyn dampening air resistance, Vire harmonizing their movements with acoustic cues.

They succeeded. Barely. Messily. But together.

Improvisation under pressure. Better than rigid planning.

"What went wrong?" I asked.

"Everything," Bellwether growled.

"We talked instead of acting," Cipher said.

"Too many plans, not enough planning," Selyn added.

Vire's collar hummed thoughtfully. "Fear of choosing wrong prevented us from choosing right."

Self-awareness. Also good.

"What went right?"

Pip's amber eyes brightened. "When we stopped talking and started moving, we worked together naturally."

Instinct over intellect. Sometimes the body knows what the mind refuses to accept.

"Next exercise," I said, jumping to the floor. "Trust building. Everyone pairs up."

Oh, the protests this will generate.

Selyn's crystals darkened. "Trust exercises are for team-building retreats, not combat preparation."

"Trust is combat preparation," I countered. "When someone has your back in a fight, you need to know they'll be there. Not hope. Know."

Hard truth. Trust gets built through experience, not speeches.

Bellwether volunteered first, padding over to stand beside Vire. "I trust the rope-singer. His fears echo true."

Vire's collar brightened, surprise evident in the harmonic shift. "The wolf remembers pack bonds. I can work with pack bonds."

Mutual recognition. Good foundation.

Cipher approached Pip hesitantly. "Mathematical precision plus environmental awareness equals optimal reconnaissance?"

She tilted her head, considering. "Equations plus intuition. Could work."

Unlikely pairing. Sometimes those work best.

That left Selyn standing alone, crystals cycling through uncertain hues. I padded over, sat beside her, and began the most obnoxious purr I could manage.

Chaos plus order. This should be interesting.

"Seriously?" she asked.

"Someone has to keep your perfectionism from calcifying," I said. "Besides, salt and cats have a natural affinity. We both know the value of claiming territory."

True enough. Also, leadership means taking the hardest partnerships.

Her crystals shifted toward amused pink. "Fine. But I'm not carrying you if you get tired."

"Wouldn't dream of it. Carrying is for dogs."

Partnership established through mutual insult. Excellent foundation.

Rowan distributed scrolls that detailed the known defenses of the supply depot. We spent the afternoon studying patrol patterns, identifying weak points, and calculating approach vectors. Cipher proved invaluable for timing calculations. Bellwether knew guard psychology from her time in captivity. Pip identified security gaps that others had overlooked.

Everyone is good at different hunting. Pack might actually catch something.

As evening approached, Rowan unrolled a larger map that made my phantom whiskers twitch with unease. The supply depot sat at the center, but red lines connected it to dozens of other facilities scattered across the region.

Connected like a giant spider web. Much bigger than we thought.

"Intelligence update," Rowan said, voice grim. "The depot isn't just a supply point. It's a coordination hub. Every corrupted familiar in the region receives upgrades there."

Selyn's crystals went pale. "How many facilities?"

"Forty-five confirmed. Possibly more." He traced connections with growing concern. "If we hit the depot, we're not just stealing supplies. We're declaring war on the entire network."

Escalation beyond our current capability. But staying small means staying ineffective.

Bellwether's tail wagged once, sharp and eager. "Good. Let them know we're coming."

Cipher's mathematical mind saw different patterns. "Resource allocation, communication protocols, response coordination. Attacking the hub triggers systematic retaliation."

Risk assessment. Both perspectives have merit.

Vire's rope collar hummed warnings. "Great fear stirs in

distant places. Old fear, patient fear. Something watches and waits."

The Collector. Planning countermoves while we plan moves.

I studied the map until my eyes watered, connections swimming together like spilled ink. The network was vast, interconnected, and resilient. But networks had vulnerabilities too.

Single points of failure. Every system has them.

"Tomorrow night," I decided. "We hit the depot. Not for supplies, but for intelligence. Learn how their coordination works before we try to break it."

Information warfare before confrontation. Proper cat logic.

The team settled into final preparations—Selyn purifying salt crystals, Vire practicing acoustic camouflage, Cipher memorizing guard rotations. Even Haze and Whisper helped, the departing members contributing what they could before their extraction.

United effort toward a shared goal. This is what pack feels like.

But as I curled in my box for a final nap before the mission, unease gnawed at my ribs like persistent hunger. The Collector had spent decades building this network. We were six refugees with good intentions and improvised tactics.

David versus Goliath. Except that Goliath has an army of corrupted familiars, and we have mathematical equations.

Through the window, stars emerged like scattered diamonds on a black velvet sky. Somewhere under those same stars, the Collector prepared countermeasures. Somewhere else, corrupted familiars waited for orders that would send them out to hunt.

Tomorrow, we stop running and start hunting. Win or lose, we pick the prey.

I closed my eyes and dreamed of depot blueprints dissolving into sardine schools, swimming in patterns too chaotic for any net to capture.

Time to teach them what happens when cats decide to hunt back.

CHAPTER 9

ESCALATION

The attack came at dawn, when cats should be napping and the world should have the courtesy to stay quiet. Instead, frost gathered on windows that rattled with wrongness, and the air held the particular stillness that came just before reality decided to develop an attitude problem.

Rude. Inconsiderate. Probably planned that way.

I jolted awake in my box, phantom whiskers twitching at wrongness that crawled through the walls like termites with a grudge. The air tasted of copper and burned rosemary, sharp enough to make my phantom whiskers itch and my borrowed nose wrinkle in offense. Outside, anchor stones sang off-key, their harmony twisted into something that made my burn-line ache.

They're returning the city's bones. Again.

Rowan burst through the door, ledger clutched to his chest like armor, ink staining his sleeves where his quill had leaked. "Coordinated assault. Six approach vectors. They've surrounded us."

"Of course they have," I said, stretching muscles that protested the early hour. "Proper villains always coordinate. Shows they're taking this personally. Good."

They're trying harder now. Flattering. Also, it's personally annoying.

The floorboards vibrated with impacts that shook the place. Dust rained from the rafters. Through the warped shutters, carrying the acrid smell of forced magic and mechanical lubricant that made my borrowed nose wrinkle in disgust.

Bellwether padded to the window, hackles raised, lips pulled back from teeth that remembered brass chains. "Corrupted familiars. Dozens of them. Moving in formation."

Moving like a hunting pack now. They've been watching us.

Selyn's crystals blazed in alarm as she pressed palms to the wall. "Ward stones compromised. Someone's been feeding our signatures into their tracking arrays." Her crystals darkened to deep blue. "They know exactly where we are and exactly how we fight."

They watched us watching them. Annoying when prey gets smart.

Cipher crouched beside his mathematical diagrams, amber eyes wide with calculation-induced panic. "Attack vectors converge in thirty seconds. Optimal evacuation window closes in twenty-two."

Numbers don't lie. Unfortunately.

Vire's rope collar thrummed bass notes that made the safe house's bones ache. "Fear rises from below. Old fear, deep fear." His voice dropped to a whisper, making everyone lean closer. "This place... the rope remembers being tied here. Before me. Someone else wore this collar in these chambers."

He touched the rope with trembling fingers, his face going pale. "They brought others here first. To this same room. The rope... it holds their terror. Their last moments before the processing began."

The revelation hit like cold water. Our safe house wasn't random. It was another layer of the trap.

Layered trap. Someone's been mapping our routes.

The girl, Whisper, sat in the corner humming a tune that made the walls weep salt water. "The stones scream warnings. Metal teeth bite from all directions. The cat-who-walks-wrong faces the choice-that-cuts."

Prophetic children. Always with the ominous metaphors.

A thunderclap split the morning air, but wrong—too sharp, too focused, like reality being slapped with a brass ruler. The safe house's door exploded inward, showering us with splinters and the smell of burned timber.

Front door. How traditional.

Cipher's hands shook as he reached for his calculations, amber eyes darting to every mechanical joint and servo-muscle. The sound of hydraulic pistons made him flinch— too close to the processing chambers, too much like the machines that had carved numbers into his mind.

Bellwether pressed against the wall, hackles raised, but not from aggression. Her gray eyes tracked every exit, every shadow where brass chains might hide. She'd learned not to trust spaces without escape routes.

Selyn's crystals darkened as salt water leaked from hairline cracks in her arms—stress response, not magic. The mechanical precision of the corrupted familiars reminded her too much of how her realm had died: ordered, efficient, inexorable.

Through the smoke stalked nightmares that moved with terrible purpose. The copper cat I'd faced in the market, rebuilt and upgraded, servo-muscles hissing with hydraulic fury. Behind it came worse: corrupted familiars I hadn't seen before, their modifications gleaming with fresh malice.

A brass raven perched on twisted shoulders, beak filed to needle sharpness, eyes that tracked movement with predatory calculation. Chain-wrapped ferrets flowed around its feet like living rope. At the rear, something that might once have been a bear shambled forward, gears clicking where its heart should beat.

They brought the entire catalog. I'm flattered.

The copper cat's jaw unhinged, revealing speaker arrays that crackled with stolen voices. "Subject MCC-139. Retrieval parameters updated. Resistance triggers escalated response protocols."

They're not here to capture me anymore. They're here to stop me.

The Collector's voice boomed from every corrupted throat, a chorus of fury and mechanical precision. "You contaminate our acquisitions. Corrupt our collections. This inefficiency requires correction."

I hopped onto the table, scattering Rowan's maps with deliberate flair. My phantom tail tried to help with balance and met the familiar absence, making me wobble ungracefully. "Your collections were people. My contamination just reminded them how to think for themselves."

Philosophical argument during a home invasion. Peak cat behavior.

The bear-thing lunged, gears screaming as hydraulic pistons drove claws the size of dinner knives toward my chest. I rolled sideways, maps shredding under bronze talons, and landed in a crouch that my phantom tail approved of.

Good reflexes. Terrible furniture placement.

Bellwether hit the bear from the flank, jaws clamping around gear-work that sparked and bled oil. Her bite severed hydraulic lines, sending the creature stumbling sideways into Rowan's bookshelf. Volumes scattered.

Wolf tactics. Direct and effective.

The brass raven dove at Cipher, talons aimed at amber eyes that had learned to calculate escape vectors. He rolled under the table, mathematical precision guiding him through spaces too small for bird-shaped nightmares to follow.

Academic agility. Who knew ledgers made good shields?

Selyn raised crystalline fists and slammed them into the floor. Salt water erupted from hairline cracks, turning the safe house into a tidal pool that sent chain-ferrets skidding into walls. Their mechanical coordination failed on slick surfaces, programming unable to adapt to environmental chaos.

Salt woman made everything slippery. Their fancy paws can't grip.

Vire's rope collar sang a note that made reality hiccup. The copper cat's servo-joints locked mid-stride, audio feedback scrambling its coordination protocols. It toppled sideways, claws scraping furrows in wet wood.

Rope-human's humming breaks their clockwork. Noise confuses machines.

But more corrupted familiars poured through the shattered doorway. Hawks with bronze feathers. Wolves missing ribs but gaining hydraulic spines. Cats rebuilt with servo-muscles and copper plating, moving in perfect unison that made my phantom whiskers itch with wrongness.

The brass raven broke free from Cipher's hiding spot, bronze beak driving toward Whisper's small form. The girl looked up, stopped humming, and smiled.

That's not good. Children shouldn't smile like that.

She touched the wall beside her with one small hand. The stone cracked, water seeped in, and gravity decided the ceiling looked lonely. Rafters groaned, timbers shifted, and several tons of angry architecture descended on the raven with geological precision.

Environmental manipulation. Remind me never to annoy her.

But victory felt temporary. For every corrupted familiar we disabled, two more appeared in the doorway. The Collector had brought serious resources to this fight, and our safe house was becoming steadily less safe.

Time for strategic withdrawal. Also known as running away with style. Basic cat survival protocol: when the furniture starts fighting back, find a high shelf and judge the situation from a safe distance.

"Evacuation protocol," I called out, vaulting over the saltwater tide toward the back window. "Every apprentice who wants to keep breathing, follow the cat."

Alpha sense. Sometimes, the smartest move is elsewhere.

Bellwether bounded after me, shaking oil from her muzzle. "Where's the exit strategy?"

"Working on it," I replied, kicking out the shutters and peering into the alley behind the safe house. More copper gleamed in the morning light. They'd anticipated our escape routes.

Of course, they had. Professional competence is so annoying.

Selyn's crystals chimed urgent warnings. "Rear approach compromised. They've boxed us in."

Classic pincer movement. Someone's been reading military manuals.

Vire's collar hummed distress harmonies. "Fear echoes from all directions. No safe paths remain."

Cipher's mathematical mind raced through calculations. "Probability of successful extraction dropping exponentially. We need a variable they haven't accounted for."

Variable. Yes. Something unexpected.

I looked around the flooding safe house, at my pack pressed against walls by mechanical nightmares, at the chaos that had once been our sanctuary. The Collector wanted to end this quickly, efficiently, with all the charm of week-old sardines left in direct sunlight.

Time to remind them why planning never survives contact with cats.

"New plan," I announced, grinning with all the confidence I didn't feel. "We don't evacuate. We escalate."

Sometimes the only way out is through, preferably with maximum property damage.

My burn-line flared gold, chaos rippling outward like

heat waves from a forge. Time to turn this coordinated assault into something more... interesting.

They brought the fight to us. Let's show them what happens when cats fight back.

My chaos rippled outward like disturbed water, golden threads weaving through the air with predatory intent. The corrupted familiars froze mid-assault, their mechanical precision faltering as something fundamental shifted in the room's magical architecture. Copper joints locked. Hydraulic systems stuttered. Even the brass raven's dive arrested, wings spread in mechanical confusion.

Finally. Time to teach them what happens when you corner cats.

But instead of the satisfying crash of failing machinery, something else responded to my challenge. The air itself grew thick, pressing against my phantom whiskers with weight that had nothing to do with atmosphere. Reality rippled, and through the ripples stepped a presence that made my burn-line ache with recognition.

The Collector materialized as architecture made animate, a figure of living shadow wrapped in geometries that hurt to perceive directly. Where its feet touched the flooding floor, the water froze in spirals that defied physics. Its voice came from everywhere and nowhere, resonating through bone and timber.

"Enough."

The word carried weight that made stones weep. Every corrupted familiar in the safe house went perfectly still, servo-muscles locking, bronze feathers ceasing their artificial rustle. Even Whisper's humming died to silence.

Dramatic entrance. Points for style, points deducted for interrupting my moment.

"You think this is about capture," the Collector continued, its form shifting like smoke given terrible purpose. "About adding you to my collection. How wonderfully small your understanding remains."

I kept my chaos field active, golden threads spinning defensive patterns around my pack. "Understanding? I understand you steal people and turn them into batteries. Pretty straightforward villain behavior."

The Collector's laugh was the sound of reality developing stress fractures. "Villain. Hero. Such quaint categories for forces beyond your comprehension." It gestured, and the broken doorway became a window into something vast and terrible.

Through the opening, I caught a glimpse of the portal network's true scope. Not the neat diagrams from Council maps, but a web of impossible complexity stretching across infinite darkness. Each thread pulsed with stolen light, connecting realms that hung like soap bubbles in a cosmic void. And everywhere I looked, cracks spider-webbed through the structure, reality bleeding between dimensions.

Oh. That's... actually terrible. Cosmic-scale terrible.

"Behold the truth," the Collector intoned. "Ten thousand realms, each dependent on controlled magical flow for basic stability. Remove that control, and watch them collapse into dimensional static."

The view shifted, focusing on a realm I didn't recognize. Mountains of crystal, seas of liquid starlight, cities that grew like flowers from willing stone. Beautiful. Alien. Dying. The realm's edges frayed, reality simply... ending. People screamed silently as their world dissolved into a complex mathematical equation.

Definitely problematic. Though possibly a trick.

"Chaos cascade," the Collector explained with clinical precision. "Initiated when a high-independence familiar destabilized the local anchor network through uncontrolled magical resonance. Population: four billion. Survivors: none."

The vision of realms collapsing hit each of us differently. Whisper stopped humming, small hands pressed to her ears as stones wept around her feet. Cipher's mathematical mind recoiled from calculations that ended in civilizations reduced to statistical noise. Bellwether's breath came short and fast—pack-panic at threats too large to fight or flee.

I wanted to make a joke, deflect with sarcasm about cosmic interior decorating. But the words died in my throat. Even cats have limits to their ability to laugh in the face of universal horror.

My phantom tail tried to lash and met the familiar absence. The image couldn't be real. Could it? "You're lying."

"I am preserving." The scene shifted again, showing another realm caught in collapse. This one I recognized— water-touched, with cities built from living coral. Selyn made a sound like breaking glass. Her home. Her people. Falling into a void as magical cohesion simply... stopped.

No. This is manipulation. Has to be.

But the scent in the air told a different story. Ozone and

endings, the sharp taste of reality under stress. My phantom whiskers mapped tensions that screamed truth, even when truth felt like swallowing glass.

The Collector's form solidified slightly, revealing hints of what it had once been. Feline. Proud. Broken by centuries of isolation and impossible responsibility. "You see disorder and call it freedom. I see the mathematics of survival. Every realm requires precise magical pressure to maintain dimensional integrity. Too little control, and they hemorrhage into the void."

It thinks it's right. Worse than claws—can't argue with crazy.

Bellwether's growl carried the harmonics of pack fury. "You're killing people to save them."

"I am making hard choices so that someone, somewhere, survives what comes next." The Collector's attention fixed on me. "You contaminate my instruments. Corrupt my collections. Every familiar you 'free' becomes a destabilization point that threatens billions of lives."

The cosmic view shifted closer, showing individual realms connected by threads of stolen light. Each thread pulsed with familiar magical signatures: foxes, ravens, cats, creatures I'd glimpsed in the processing facility. Their essence, refined and controlled, maintains the delicate balance that keeps reality coherent.

They serve as more than batteries. They're the cosmic scratching posts, hammered into reality's foundation without anyone asking if they wanted the job. Typical.

The metaphor felt wrong even as I thought it. Cats don't build furniture. We knock it over. But the image stuck —a vast cosmic structure balanced on stolen lives, each familiar turned into another post driven into reality's foundation.

Except that scratching posts are supposed to be used by choice and not hammered through your chest.

"The network requires autonomous cores to function," the Collector continued, its voice carrying the weight of geological time. "Familiar magic adapts, responds, and self-corrects in ways purely mechanical systems cannot. You force me to choose between individual freedom and universal survival."

The air around us thickened, pressing against my phantom whiskers with the weight of cosmic inevitability. Reality itself seemed to hold its breath, waiting for judgment that would determine whether worlds lived or died. The sensation crawled under my skin like termites made of starlight, each movement a reminder that we stood at the intersection of forces vast enough to unmake galaxies.

This is bigger than sardines. Bigger than boxes. Bigger than anything a cat should have to think about.

But I was thinking about it anyway, because somebody had to, and apparently the universe had decided that somebody was me.

Rowan's quill trembled against his ledger. Even he, an academic mind trained for skepticism, could see the mathematical elegance of the system. Brutal. Effective. Possibly necessary.

No. There has to be another way. Has to be.

"The portal network existed before you," I said, phantom whiskers probing for holes in the logic. "How did it stay stable then?"

"Poorly." The Collector's form rippled with something

that might have been exhaustion. "Random fluctuations. Cascade failures every few centuries. Entire realms lost to dimensional storms. I simply... systematized the solution."

Making people into spare parts. Taking away the choice.

The vision around us pulsed, showing the scope of the network's hunger. Thousands of facilities across hundreds of realms, each processing familiars into fuel for stability. A vast machine built from individual tragedies, justified by collective survival.

"You call it imprisonment," the Collector said. "I call it service. Their sacrifice maintains the framework that prevents universal collapse."

My burn-line flared hot, chaos responding to rage that had nowhere productive to go. "Without asking them. Without giving them a choice."

"Choice?" The Collector's laugh carried harmonics of broken glass. "You offer a choice to individual grains of sand about whether the beach should exist. The mathematics are beyond personal preference."

Mathematics. Always mathematics with these people. As if numbers could justify anything.

Around us, the corrupted familiars remained frozen, their mechanical forms testament to the Collector's philosophy made manifest. Perfect obedience. No chaos. No unexpected variables to threaten the greater pattern.

"I've seen how your mathematics work," I said, letting contempt sharpen my voice. "Brass plates and copper wire. Strip away everything that makes someone themselves until only the useful parts remain."

"Efficiency requires focus." The Collector's attention turned to my pack, calculating their potential value as components. "Your companions represent significant destabilization potential. Their extraction would strengthen network cohesion considerably."

Over my dead body. Which is probably what it's planning.

Selyn's crystals blazed defiant blue. "You destroyed my realm to power your network."

"I harvested its collapse to prevent ten others." No apology in the Collector's voice. No regret. Just cosmic-scale accounting that reduced civilizations to variables in an equation.

Not mean. Worse. Thinks it makes sense.

The philosophical weight settled on my chest. What if the Collector was right? What if chaos really did threaten universal stability? What if my contamination was a weapon pointed at reality's foundation?

No. Refuse the premise. There's always another way.

"Your forced stabilization," I said, phantom tail lashing at concepts instead of air, "what if it's causing the instability you claim to prevent?"

The Collector's form stilled with predatory attention. "Explain."

Time to find out if cats can logic their way out of cosmic horror.

"Rigid systems break under pressure. Flexible ones bend. Your network assumes chaos is the problem, but what if chaos is the immune system?"

The room held its breath. Reality itself seemed to pause, waiting for an answer that might reshape the foundations of existence.

Please let me be right about this. For once, let cat logic save the universe.

The Collector's cosmic display wavered, reality hiccupping like a cat with an inconvenient hairball. Something else pressed against the edges of the vision—familiar magic that tasted of garden soil and stubborn determination. My burn-line flared, the straw-colored mark blazing gold as another signature scraped against mine across impossible distance.

Felicity.

The bond beneath my ribs pulled taut, sharp as fishing line under tension. Through dimensions that had no business existing, her magic carved a path that made reality wince. The air around me shimmered, overlaying the safe house's chaos with glimpses of another place—a workshop reeking of burned chalk and desperate innovation.

This is going to hurt. For both of us.

The Collector's attention snapped to me like a predator scenting blood. "Impossible. Cross-realm communication requires anchor stability we've deliberately compromised."

"You underestimate spite," I said, though the bond's pull made my phantom whiskers feel like they were being yanked through broken glass. "And witches who refuse to accept inconvenient facts."

The vision around us fractured. Through cracks in cosmic horror leaked warmth that smelled of home—tea leaves, ink stains, the particular mustiness of books left open too long. Felicity's workshop materialized like a ghost image, translucent yet real enough to touch my borrowed heart.

She kneeled beside a ritual circle that made the graduation ceremony look like a child's finger-painting. Chalk lines seared into stone, powered by her own blood drawn in precise geometries that screamed professional desperation. Her face was pale, lips moving in cadences that bent space-time into uncomfortable angles.

Dangerous magic. The kind that leaves permanent marks on both caster and target.

"Mischief." Her voice reached across dimensions, carrying exhaustion and fury in equal measure. "I can't hold this long. The Council—they're hunting me. Assassination teams, memory wipers, the whole catalog of bureaucratic nightmares."

The bond flared brighter, golden threads weaving between realities. Through them flowed impressions: pursuit through lamplit corridors, allies fallen silent, the taste of betrayal sharp as lemon rind. She'd been fighting her own war while I played with mine.

Of course. Villains always coordinate. Probably have meetings about it.

"They moved against both of us simultaneously," I said, understanding crystallizing like ice on glass. "This isn't random escalation. It's orchestrated."

The Collector's form rippled with what might have been approval. "Strategic coordination across seventeen realms. Your witch discovered our timetable. Forced acceleration of Terminal Protocols."

Through the bond came Felicity's sharp intake of breath,

chalk dust, and copper pennies on her tongue. "Seventeen realms. How many like you are there?"

More than we thought. Worse than we feared.

The vision of her workshop shuddered, overlaid now with glimpses of other places—Council chambers where figures in familiar robes debated quotas, processing facilities humming with industrial efficiency, portal networks stretched across cosmic darkness like spider webs built from stolen lives.

"Every high-independence familiar," Felicity breathed, her ritual circle sparking as reality protested the connection. "They're harvesting us all. Making it look like accidents, displacement errors, natural magical evolution."

The Collector's laugh resonated through dimensions, bitter as burned coffee. "Evolution. An interesting term. We prefer 'optimization for collective survival.'"

Euphemisms. Even cosmic villains can't call murder by its proper name.

The bond carried something else—Felicity's research, raw data scraped from restricted archives, intelligence gathered at the cost of her safety and sanity. Names, dates, facility locations, and shipping manifests that treated people like commodities or grain futures. The scope was breathtaking in its bureaucratic horror.

"Mischief." Her voice carried new urgency, the ritual circle's glow flickering like a candle in the wind. "The pattern—they're targeting the bonds themselves. Every witch-familiar pair that refuses to conform."

My phantom tail lashed at implications too large for comfort. "Breaking the bonds breaks us both."

"Worse." Her magic pulsed through the connection,

sharing visions of Council chambers where figures debated acceptable loss ratios. "Broken bonds create magical backlash. They're using our pain to power emergency anchors."

They're farming our grief. Literally harvesting heartbreak for fuel.

The realization hit like cold water. They were stealing the connections that made us whole, then feeding on the resulting trauma—industrial-scale emotional vampirism disguised as magical research.

The Collector's attention was fixed on our connection with predatory interest. "Fascinating. The bond maintains coherence despite dimensional separation. Such resilience could power significant network expansion."

Over my dead body. Which, again, is probably the plan.

Around us, the safe house battle continued in strange suspension—corrupted familiars frozen mid-assault, my pack pressed against walls by forces beyond their understanding. The real war was being fought on levels deeper than flesh and steel.

"Felicity." I pushed words through the bond, tasting chalk and determination. "How many others know?"

"Scattered resistance. Junior councilors who ask inconvenient questions, archivists who read between lines, familiars who refuse to disappear quietly." Her workshop flickered, reality wearing thin under sustained magical pressure. "They're picking us off individually. Coordinated strikes across realms."

The Collector's form solidified slightly, revealing more of what it had once been: proud, intelligent, broken by impossible choices. "Resistance requires coordination. We eliminate coordination nodes before they metastasize."

Clinical language for murder. Effective strategy, though.

Through the bond flowed Felicity's fierce pride, her refusal to be eliminated like a statistical anomaly. Also, her fear for the others caught in this web of cosmic brutality.

"I won't let them break us," she said, the words carrying weight that made dimensions shiver. "Whatever it costs."

The bond between us strengthened, golden threads weaving tighter despite the distance. This was a choice—deliberate connection across impossible odds. We were choosing each other again, transformed—no longer just familiar and witch, we'd become partners in something larger than either role.

This is what they can't understand. Bonds that strengthen under pressure instead of breaking.

"The network assumes relationships are weakness," I said, letting understanding sharpen my voice. "Bonds that choose to remain bonds—those are the real threat to forced stability."

The Collector's attention turned calculating. "Explain."

Before I could answer, Felicity's ritual circle flared white-hot, magical backlash screaming across dimensions as her strength finally failed. The connection snapped like an overstressed cable, leaving the taste of burned copper and promises on my tongue.

Her last words echoed across an impossible distance: "Find the source. End this."

The workshop vision dissolved, leaving me standing in the flooded safe house with the weight of seventeen realms' worth of suffering pressing against my phantom whiskers.

The Collector's cosmic display resumed, transformed—no longer inevitable fate, it revealed itself as a problem with dimensions we were only beginning to understand.

Source. Yes. Cut off the head, watch the body flounder.

The bond remained, stretched thin yet unbroken, carrying her determination like a banked fire. Somewhere across the dimensional divide, Felicity was fighting her own battles. Here, I had mine.

Time to remind the universe why cats always land on their feet.

The silence after Felicity's departure stretched like taffy left too long in cold air. Reality settled back into mundane dimensions with an almost audible sigh, cosmic visions dissolving into the practical problems of a flooded safe house and an army of frozen mechanical nightmares. The corrupted familiars remained locked in mid-assault, servo-muscles seized by whatever force the Collector had used to halt our battle.

Convenient pause. Time to think without claws aimed at my throat.

Water lapped around my ankles, salt-tinged and wrong, carrying the metallic aftertaste of dimensional bleeding. The Collector's form had withdrawn into architectural shadow, watching with predatory patience while we absorbed the magnitude of what we'd learned. Seventeen realms. Systematic harvesting spanning centuries. A network built from individual tragedies and justified by cosmic mathematics.

The weight of it pressed against my phantom whiskers like atmospheric pressure before a storm.

Rowan broke the silence first, his academic mind struggling to catalog impossibilities. "Coordinated strikes across multiple realms. They're not just hunting familiars—they're dismantling resistance before it can form."

Finally, someone else is stating the obvious. Progress.

Bellwether shook water from her fur, her gray eyes bright with pack fury. "Felicity's fighting the same war from her side. Different battlefield, same enemy."

The realization crystallized with the sharp clarity of winter air. Two fronts, one enemy. Felicity was battling Council corruption while I dealt with the Collector's cosmic machinery. We'd been separated by dimensions but united by purpose, each attacking different organs of the same diseased beast.

Working together from different hunting grounds. Impressive for humans.

"Strategic coordination," I said, phantom tail lashing at concepts that wanted to be hunted. "They split us up to prevent exactly this—unified resistance across realms."

Selyn's crystals chimed in agreement, salt water still dripping from her crystalline arms. "My realm fell because we fought alone. Isolated. No support from neighbors who faced the same threat."

The pattern became visible like constellation lines drawn between stars. Divide, isolate, eliminate. Classic predator tactics, scaled up to cosmic proportions. Keep the prey scattered so they couldn't coordinate defense.

Now we know where they hide. Changes everything.

Vire's rope collar hummed subsonic warnings. "Fear echoes across seventeen realms. But also... hope. Small sparks. Growing brighter."

Cipher crouched beside his scattered calculations, amber eyes tracking variables that suddenly made sense. "If resistance is emerging simultaneously across multiple realms, the Collector's resources are divided. Strategic vulnerability."

Mathematics that works in our favor. About time.

The Collector's shadow rippled with what might have been annoyance. "Coordination requires communication. Communication requires anchor stability. We control the anchors."

"You controlled them," I corrected, chaos field rippling outward to probe the frozen machinery around us. "Past tense. Present tense is more... flexible."

The corrupted familiars twitched slightly, servo-joints creaking as my contamination leaked into their systems. Deep inside their mechanical shells, something that remembered choice stirred against enforced obedience.

Even machines can learn to misbehave. Given proper instruction.

Whisper looked up from her corner, small face serious as granite. "The stones sing new songs. Harmony shifts. The cat-who-walks-wrong teaches chaos to dance with order."

Prophetic children and their metaphors. Though this one might actually be useful.

Understanding bloomed like flame catching tinder. The Collector's network assumed resistance would be chaotic, uncoordinated, and easy to pick off individually. But what if resistance could be organized without being rigid? What if chaos could coordinate without losing its essential flexibility?

"Two-front assault," I said, the plan crystallizing with feline certainty. "Felicity hits the Council infrastructure from her side. We take down the processing hub from here."

Rowan's quill moved across water-stained parchment, sketching strategy with scholarly precision. "Simultaneous strikes would divide their response capability. Force them to choose which crisis to address first."

Book-mouse approves. The plan might actually work.

Bellwether's ears pricked forward. "What about communication? How do we coordinate across realms without giving away our positions?"

The bond beneath my ribs pulsed weakly, straw-colored threads still connecting me to Felicity across impossible distance. Stretched thin, but unbroken. Resilient in ways the Collector couldn't understand or predict.

"The bonds they're trying to harvest," I said, phantom whiskers twitching with inspiration. "They assume breaking them eliminates the threat. But bonds that survive their attempts to sever them..."

Become weapons they can't see coming.

"Are networks they can't monitor or control," Selyn finished, crystals brightening with understanding. "Communication channels outside their system."

The Collector's attention sharpened. "Interesting theory. Untested. Likely to result in catastrophic failure."

"Likely to result in catastrophic failure for you," I replied, letting smugness color my voice. "Which is the point."

Cat logic: if it annoys the enemy, it's probably the right strategy.

Around us, the safe house breathed with accumulated tension. Water continued its steady infiltration, claiming territory from air and wood. The corrupted familiars remained frozen, but their stillness felt different now—less absolute, more transitional, as if they were waiting for permission to remember themselves.

Cipher's calculations spread across the floor in mathematical poetry, with equations that sought to capture the interplay between chaos and control. "Probability matrices suggest optimal strike timing requires six hours of preparation minimum."

Six hours to coordinate an assault across seventeen realms. Ambitious even for cats.

"The hub facility," Rowan said, consulting water-damaged maps with academic determination. "If that's their central coordination point, destroying it would cascade disruption across the entire network."

The Collector's form solidified slightly, revealing more hints of what it had once been. "The hub contains processing cores for thirty thousand familiars. Destroy it, and their essence disperses into dimensional static. You would be committing genocide to prevent genocide."

Moral complexity wrapped in a practical threat. Standard villain behavior.

"Unless," I said, chaos field rippling with possibility, "we don't destroy it. We liberate it."

The word hung in the air thick with accumulated magic and the weight of cosmic consequence. Liberation. Not destruction, but transformation. Not eliminating the system, but changing its fundamental purpose.

From prison to sanctuary. From tool to choice.

"Free the familiars, claim the facility, turn their own infrastructure against them." The plan felt right in ways that transcended logic, settling into my bones with the certainty of perfect balance. "Make their central control point into a coordination hub for resistance."

Bellwether's tail wagged once, sharp and eager. "Turn their strength into our advantage."

Exactly. The best hunts utilize the prey's own nest against them.

The Collector's laugh carried harmonics of breaking stone. "Thirty thousand corrupted familiars. Each one was modified to prevent exactly such liberation attempts. You would need more than contamination. You would need miracles."

"Miracles," I said, phantom whiskers twitching with anticipation, "are just chaos applied with proper timing."

Through the weakened bond, Felicity's determination sparked like distant lightning. She was already moving, already fighting, already turning her side of the war toward our shared purpose. Two fronts, one enemy, unified strategy across impossible odds.

Finally, teamwork that doesn't involve me being lectured.

The corrupted familiars creaked as my chaos field pressed against their mechanical constraints. Deep inside their shells, sparks of remembered choice flickered like banked embers waiting for fuel.

Time to remind the universe that cats never hunt alone when the prey is big enough to require pack tactics.

CHAPTER 10

THE NETWORK'S HEART

The tunnels beneath the city breathed with a rhythm that had nothing to do with wind or tide. My phantom whiskers mapped the tunnel's curves, filing them under 'mine by right of discovery' despite the technical difficulties of current circumstances. Each step deeper carried us further from the mundane chaos, my phantom whiskers twitching warnings about territories that belonged to things that probably didn't share. The air grew thick, pressing against my skin. Moisture beaded on stone walls carved with symbols that hurt to perceive directly, geometries that suggested meanings just beyond the edge of feline comprehension.

Underground. Where all the worst surprises hide.

Rowan's lantern cast shadows that moved independently of flame, dark shapes that skittered across carved walls like mice with too many legs. His breath came in careful, measured puffs that spoke of academic terror held in check through sheer scholarly stubbornness. Behind us, the displaced moved with the cautious grace of creatures who had learned that safety was a temporary illusion at best.

"The resonance is wrong," Bellwether muttered, hackles raised despite her human form. Her nose wrinkled at scents that registered somewhere between copper pennies and rotting flowers, with undertones of bureaucratic malice and institutional despair that made my borrowed sinuses burn. "Everything smells of endings."

She pressed closer to the left wall than necessary, I noticed. Away from the right side, where metal pipes gleamed with institutional malice. Her fingers traced stone instead of touching anything that might hum with mechanical purpose.

Everyone's got spaces they won't go near. Scent memories that make fur stand up.

The tunnel curved ahead, following a path that defied architectural logic. The walls pressed closer, then spread wide, then narrowed again in patterns that suggested some vast organism breathing in mathematical precision. My burn-line pulsed in rhythm with whatever force shaped this place, golden threads of chaos responding to resonances I couldn't name. My phantom tail tried to lash in irritation and met the familiar absence, which at least was consistent in an inconsistent place.

Selyn's crystals chimed soft warnings, their light fragmenting through moisture-laden air into rainbows that tasted of salt and fear. "Tidal pull," she whispered. "Something vast draws the currents toward itself."

Vast. Wonderful. Because our problems weren't big enough already.

Cipher crouched beside fresh scratches in the stone, amber eyes tracking calculations carved by claws that left mathematical scars. But his hands shook as he traced the patterns, quill dropping twice before he managed to steady it against his knee.

"Pattern analysis suggests deliberate excavation. Recent. Geometric progression indicates..." His voice faltered. The scratches formed spirals that made my phantom tail lash with territorial fury, but more than that, they formed equations that writhed when observed directly.

"The numbers," Cipher whispered, amber eyes reflecting something close to panic. "They don't... they won't stabilize. Everything I compute keeps dividing by impossible values."

Numbers-human's brain-patterns snarling like tangled yarn.

Not random damage, but purposeful marking. Someone had claimed this place, carved their ownership into living rock with the methodical precision of a bureaucrat filing paperwork, or me arranging sardines by quality. Except their work smelled wrong, transforming into new problems that had no solutions.

Territorial marking. Rude. This tunnel network is clearly mine. Also possibly cursed.

Vire's rope collar hummed subsonic harmonies that made the stones weep condensation. "Fear accumulates here. Old fear, deep fear. Generations of terror pressed into stone until the walls remember screaming."

He stood farther from the group than usual, I realized. Far enough that if something grabbed him, we might not hear the rope collar's final note. Distance as protection. Or preparation for abandonment.

Everyone's sniffing for escape routes. Some just admit it.

But beneath the fear-scent and wrongness, something else tickled my phantom whiskers. A pattern within patterns, a rhythm that spoke to instincts buried deeper than thought. The network wasn't random. Every carved symbol, every architectural curve, every breath of tainted air followed rules that made sense if you understood the proper language.

The language of hunting.

This entire place is a trap. A really, really big trap.

The tunnel opened into a vast cavern that made my borrowed throat close with involuntary awe. The space stretched beyond the reach of Rowan's lantern, darkness pooling in distances that suggested geological time carved into useful shapes. But what drew the eye, what demanded attention with the inexorable pull of a black hole made manifest, was the structure at the cavern's heart.

Spires twisted through impossible angles, their surfaces inscribed with formulas that moved when observed directly. Bridges spanned the void without visible support. At the center, a crystalline sphere pulsed with stolen light, each beat sending ripples through reality itself.

Though I admit, the architecture shows impressive megalomania. Points for ambition.

The sphere's pulse synchronized with my burn-line, golden threads reaching toward crystalline facets that reflected light from seventeen different sources. Not lantern flame, but signatures I recognized—familiar magic drawn from processing facilities across multiple realms, refined and concentrated into something that made space-time hiccup with each heartbeat.

And then the sphere noticed us.

The pulse quickened, its rhythm shifting from cosmic heartbeat to predatory attention. Reality lurched sideways like a cat startled off furniture, gravity suddenly uncertain about which direction properly constituted "down." Selyn stumbled, her crystals blazing in alarm as tidal forces tried to drag her toward walls that had decided to become floors.

Here we go. The master litter box objects to visitors.

"Move!" I shouted, though my phantom whiskers were already mapping escape routes through architecture that was rapidly becoming more theoretical than practical. The sphere's pulse sent shockwaves through stone that made the cavern walls bleed—literally bleed, reality leaking between dimensions like watercolors in rain.

Rowan's lantern flared as competing gravitational fields fought for dominance. His ledger burst into flames, the flames burning cold and blue, as academic calculations were consumed by forces that operated on mathematical principles too complex for normal notation.

Cipher screamed.

Not fear, though fear was indeed present. This was the sound of someone whose fundamental understanding of how numbers worked was being systematically dismantled by observation. His amber eyes reflected equations that shouldn't exist, calculations that ate themselves and grew stronger in the process.

"The mathematics," he sobbed, clawing at symbols that carved themselves into his palms, "they're alive. They're solving for variables that include their own solutions."

Math as cosmic horror. Someone's been reading the wrong textbooks.

The sphere pulsed again, and the cavern walls began their migration toward impossible configurations. What had been vertical became horizontal, what had been horizontal became diagonal, and what had been diagonal transcended Euclidean geometry entirely, settling for making everyone's eyes water.

Through gaps that opened between one heartbeat and the next, I glimpsed other realms. Hundreds of them. Cities where the laws of physics changed street by street, their residents adapting with the fluid desperation of people who had learned that consistency was a luxury. Oceans that had once been deserts, with waves breaking in patterns that followed mathematical progression instead of tidal logic. Mountains that grew downward into caves filled with impossible starlight.

Chaos everywhere, showing me where the big thing wants to break.

"Look closer," I gasped, chaos field extending to probe the structure's foundations while simultaneously trying to prevent my pack from being redistributed across seven dimensions. "The energy flows are backwards."

Golden threads traced paths that should have been impossible—magic flowing uphill, dimensional pressure equalizing in directions that violated basic magical physics. The network wasn't maintaining stability; it was constantly fighting a war against forces that sought to restore natural balance.

Like trying to make water run uphill by hitting it with hammers. Loud, inefficient, and doomed to failure.

However, explaining cosmic horror while navigating architecture that couldn't decide which way was up proved to be challenging. The crystalline sphere's pulse created interference patterns that made walking feel like swimming through a crystallized mathematical structure. Each step forward sent ripples through reality that returned as echoes from places that didn't technically exist.

Selyn approached one of the twisted spires, crystals darkening as they touched surfaces inscribed with moving equations. "Reality bleeds," she breathed, then stumbled as the floor beneath her feet decided to become a wall. Her crystals chimed a warning as she pressed against the stone that wept tears that tasted of other people's nightmares.

Through her crystals came visions that made my phantom fur attempt to stand on end. Not just the realms bleeding into each other, but the mechanism of bleeding. Forced stabilization creates pressure that seeks release through whatever channels offer the least resistance. Reality develops stress fractures that spread like an infection through the cosmic substrate.

The cure is worse than the disease. Classic.

A support beam chose that moment to relocate itself three feet to the left without bothering to inform the ceiling it was supposed to be supporting. Stone crashed down in chunks that hit the floor and then transformed into butterflies.

"Each forced stabilization creates instability elsewhere," Rowan managed, his academic mind struggling to catalog impossibilities while dodging architectural decisions that defied basic causality. "The network isn't preventing chaos;

it's concentrating it into pressure points that will eventually explode."

Pressure points. Yes. I can feel them.

My chaos signature spread through the cavern like smoke through still air, golden threads finding cracks in reality's foundation that others couldn't perceive. Where the network forced rigid stability, my contamination revealed stress fractures spreading like spider webs through the dimensional substrate. Where portals were anchored too tightly, reality strained against bonds that wanted to snap.

But reading cosmic stress patterns while reality actively rearranged itself around us required a delicate balance between observation and survival. The sphere's pulse grew stronger, each beat sending new waves of dimensional distortion that made the cavern's geometry increasingly theoretical.

They can't see what they're breaking because they refuse to look sideways.

A stairway materialized out of ambient possibility, leading toward the sphere with steps that existed in seventeen dimensions simultaneously. Useful, except half the steps decided to exist in the wrong dimensions entirely, creating gaps that opened onto views of realms where geometry had surrendered to more artistic interpretations of space.

Bellwether pressed against my shoulder, solid warmth in a space where "solid" had become a negotiable concept. Her breath came short and fast, pupils dilated with the particular variety of panic that came from being trapped in spaces that reminded you of captivity.

"Can't breathe," she whispered. "Walls too close. Getting closer."

Walls closing in. Real walls this time, not just memory-walls.

I pressed my palm to her wrist, pulse point steady despite everything. "Pack," I said. "Not going anywhere without you."

The contact grounded us both as the sphere's pulse sent another wave of reality distortion through the cavern. This time, instead of fighting the chaos, I rode it. Let my contamination flow with the dimensional currents instead of against them, reading the patterns of forced stability like a map written in someone else's pain.

Cat vision. We see what others miss because we don't assume furniture belongs where humans put it.

And there it was. The scope of what we faced was revealed not through static observation, but through the very instability the sphere was trying to suppress. Thousands of realms connected by threads of stolen light, each one dependent on forced stabilization that created more problems than it solved. The entire network balanced on mathematics that solved themselves by consuming their own variables, creating equations that grew stronger through paradox.

"Seventeen realms," I said, understanding crystallizing like ice forming in supercooled water that was also somehow flowing upward toward a ceiling that had decided to become a floor. "That's just what they've processed recently. This facility shows evidence of centuries of operation."

The crystalline sphere pulsed brighter, as if responding to our presence. Within its faceted surface, glimpses of other realms flickered like scenes viewed through broken mirrors. Hundreds of them. Thousands. Each one connected to this central hub by threads of stolen light, each one dependent on forced stabilization that created more problems than it solved.

Thousands of realms. All balanced on the edge of collapse because someone decided natural chaos was inconvenient.

Cipher had gone beyond mathematical panic into a state that might charitably be called "numerical catatonia." He sat in what appeared to be a corner, though the corner existed at an angle that suggested someone had folded space like origami and forgotten to unfold it. His amber eyes reflected calculations that ate themselves and grew stronger, mathematics that computed their own impossibility and used the result as input for further computation.

"Network scope extends beyond current dimensional theory," he whispered, voice hollow with the recognition that his life's work couldn't account for systems that operated on principles of organized impossibility. "If cascade failure initiates at this central node..."

He didn't finish the sentence. Didn't need to. The mathematics spoke for themselves in equations that painted themselves across the cavern walls in ink made of condensed terror, then rewrote themselves when they realized they'd made logical errors.

Universal collapse. Not gradual. Not selective. Everything.

The weight of revelation settled on my shoulders, made heavier by the fact that "weight" and "shoulders" were currently operating under gravitational principles that included suggestions rather than laws. This wasn't about familiar rights, Council corruption, or even interdimensional tyranny. This was about a mistake so vast, so fundamental, that it threatened the existence of everything that had ever been or ever could be.

My whiskers feel the cracks before the wall falls.

However, seeing cosmic stress fractures while standing in architecture that actively demonstrated those very fractures proved illuminating in ways that transcended mere academic observation. My chaos signature was unique —not just in its strength, but in its perspective. Where others saw disorder, I saw natural patterns. Where they feared instability, I recognized healthy flexibility. Where they attempted to force control, I could map the stress fractures that would eventually bring the entire system down.

The universe's hunting instincts are broken. Needs a proper cat to show it how.

"They need me," I said, the words tasting of copper and inevitability while also somehow tasting of the color blue, which was new. "Not just for what I can do but for what I can see. The instabilities, the stress points, the places where their forced order is creating cracks in reality itself."

The sphere's pulse quickened, as if sensing the approach of something that could unmake its careful stability. Through the crystalline facets, I glimpsed the Collector's awareness focusing on our location with predatory intensity that made the already unstable architecture shiver with anticipation.

Time to leave. Before the master litter box decides to flush.

But extracting ourselves from a cavern where spatial relationships had become more of a polite suggestion than a physical law required coordination between pack members who were processing cosmic horror in different ways. Vire hummed harmonies that tried to establish sonic anchors in space that kept changing its mind about distance. Selyn's crystals blazed with determination to find tidal patterns in chaos that operated on principles of organized confusion.

Through it all, the sphere pulsed with thirty thousand stolen heartbeats, each one a familiar who had been reduced to a component in someone else's vision of perfect control. Each pulse sent new waves of dimensional distortion, reminding us exactly what we were fighting to prevent.

Time to teach them that some cats refuse to be declawed.

The cavern around us breathed with accumulated tension, reality itself holding its breath as cosmic forces balanced on the edge of transformation or collapse. In the crystalline sphere's faceted surface, the Collector's attention sharpened like a blade finding its target.

The real war was about to begin.

We retreated from the crystalline sphere's pulsing malevolence to a chamber that reeked of old chalk and newer desperation. Maps spread across stone tables like surgical patients awaiting dissection, their parchment surfaces marked with intelligence gathered at the cost of sanity and safety. The air hung thick with accumulated tension and the particular mustiness of spaces where important decisions went to die.

Planning. The part where good intentions meet inconvenient reality.

The transition from cosmic horror to mundane strategy left us all slightly disoriented, like cats adjusting to indoor lighting after staring directly at the sun. Cipher sat far from any surface that might contain mathematical notations, his amber eyes carefully focused on anything that couldn't be computed. Bellwether positioned herself where she could see all exits simultaneously, back against the wall, performing breathing exercises she'd learned in therapy sessions she'd never admit to needing.

Pack behavior is changing. Everyone is finding new ways to lick their wounds.

Rowan's lantern cast shadows that danced with predatory intent across architectural diagrams stolen from Council archives, though he kept the flame lower than necessary. Bright light reminded him too much of the sphere's pulse, I suspected. His hands showed fine tremors as he arranged documents with academic precision that bordered on obsessive.

Book-mouse doing familiar things in scary places. Old habits, new territory.

Selyn's crystals provided additional light, their glow revealing details that normal illumination would have missed entirely. But she kept touching them compulsively, checking their warmth, their weight, their reality. Physical anchors in a world where physics had become negotiable.

Salt woman seeking solid ground. Or solid anything, really.

"Thirty thousand processing cores," Cipher muttered,

his voice carefully controlled to avoid inflections that might suggest mathematical relationships. "Distributed across seventeen levels, each one heavily warded, each ward keyed to prevent exactly the kind of liberation we're planning."

The numbers crawled across parchment like insects fleeing light, each digit representing someone who had been reduced to fuel for cosmic machinery. But these were just numbers now, carefully divorced from the equations that had tried to eat Cipher's sanity. Statistics rather than mathematics. Manageable horror instead of impossible calculations.

Thirty thousand heartbeats powering the Collector's vision of perfect order. Thirty thousand voices were silenced to prevent the chaos of choice.

Numbers that should hurt to contemplate. They do.

Vire's rope collar hummed subsonic warnings as he studied ventilation charts with the intensity of someone who understood that air moved differently when it carried screams. But he kept adjusting his position, maintaining clear sightlines to the exit, fingers tracing escape routes with unconscious precision.

"Fear concentrates in the lower levels. Older fear, deeper fear. They process the strongest resistance first, save the compliant ones for routine maintenance."

Organized cruelty. Someone's got their torture well-scheduled.

His voice carried new harmonics when he spoke about fear now. Professional recognition. The tone of someone who had learned to identify emotional resonances through firsthand experience with their sources.

We all know our own sore spots now. Where the claws went deepest.

But as we spread intelligence across stone surfaces, patterns emerged that made my burn-line pulse with growing unease. Gaps in the documentation. Inconsistencies in facility layouts. Guard rotations that didn't match reconnaissance reports gathered just days earlier.

"This is wrong," I said, phantom tail lashing at discrepancies that tasted of deliberate deception. "The security patterns have changed. Recently."

Rowan compared architectural drawings with written observations, his scholarly mind cataloging differences with academic precision that helped him avoid thinking about what those differences might mean for people trapped inside changing security protocols.

"Personnel shifts. Entire divisions transferred without explanation. Processing schedules accelerated beyond sustainable capacity."

Acceleration. They're rushing. Question is why.

Selyn's crystals darkened as she pressed palms to reconnaissance notes written in her own salt-stained handwriting. Her fingers lingered on each page, testing the paper's texture, confirming its reality through touch. "The processing queues. They're emptying them faster than new acquisitions arrive. They're not harvesting—they're liquidating."

The word settled in my chest like cold water. Liquidation. Not capture for later processing, but immediate elimination to prevent future complications. Evidence destruction on a scale that made my phantom fur attempt to bristle with territorial fury.

They know we're coming. They're burning the evidence.

"How long?" I asked, though part of me didn't want to hear the answer.

Cipher's calculations spread across parchment in mathematical desperation, but these were safe mathematics. Simple arithmetic. Addition and subtraction. Nothing that could develop opinions about its own existence.

"Based on current processing rates, complete facility evacuation within seventy-two hours. After that..." He gestured at equations that painted themselves in ink made of condensed horror, then quickly looked away before they could look back.

After that, thirty thousand people become footnotes in someone else's ledger.

The urgency hit like physical weight, pressing against my phantom whiskers with the certainty of a cosmic deadline. Not just a rescue mission anymore. Recovery operation. Salvage what could be saved before the Collector eliminated every trace of their industrial-scale atrocity.

Time limit. Wonderful. Because infiltrating a cosmic horror facility wasn't challenging enough without a countdown.

"They're not just destroying prisoners," Rowan said, his voice carrying the hollow tone of someone discovering that academic horror could become a practical nightmare. "They're eliminating witnesses. Anyone who's seen too much, knows too much, could testify against them."

Through the bond beneath my ribs, Felicity's determination flickered like distant lightning. Across impossible dimensions, she was fighting the same race against evidence destruction, trying to preserve proof of crimes that spanned centuries and realms.

Hiding evidence like cats burying things. Planning something huge.

Bellwether's hackles rose, despite her human form, as her pack instincts recognized threat patterns that transcended species. "If they're liquidating evidence, they're planning to disappear. Go underground, establish new facilities, start fresh somewhere else."

She moved closer to Vire as she spoke, not quite touching but close enough to share warmth. Pack behavior, seeking comfort through proximity without the vulnerability of actual contact.

What any smart hunter does. Territory goes bad, find a new territory.

But movement required preparation. Resources. Time to relocate cosmic-scale infrastructure without losing operational capacity. This meant they had contingencies in place, backup facilities prepared, and alternative networks ready to be activated.

They've done this before. Probably many times.

"The portal network," I said, understanding crystallizing like ice forming in supercooled water. "It's not just for transportation. It's for evacuation. They can relocate the entire operation through dimensional gates faster than anyone can track them."

Whisper looked up from her corner, small face serious as carved stone. She'd been humming again, but softer now, melodies that made the stones feel solid instead of uncertain. "The stones sing songs of ending. Harmony breaks. The cat-who-walks-wrong faces the choice-that-cuts-both-ways."

Prophetic children and their cryptic warnings. Though this one felt uncomfortably specific.

Around us, the chamber breathed with accumulated desperation. Maps curled at their edges, ink bleeding where sweat and salt water had stained strategic intelligence. The weight of thirty thousand lives pressed against stone walls that had absorbed too many failed rescue attempts.

Cipher suddenly laughed, the sound sharp and brittle as breaking glass. "Seventeen percent," he said, staring at his calculations with an expression that suggested a mathematical breakdown approaching. "Seventeen percent chance of mission success. Eighty-three percent chance of casualties ranging from severe to total."

The laughter continued, carrying harmonics of someone whose coping mechanisms had finally encountered problems too large for safe processing.

Honest odds meeting human sanity. The numbers are winning.

I crossed to him, placing a hand on his shoulder with deliberate weight. Solid contact. Present reality. "Numbers are just numbers," I said. "What matters is what we choose to do despite them."

The contact helped, I could feel it. An anchor point in a world where mathematical certainty had become uncertain. His breathing eased, though his hands still shook.

Numbers-human's fear rubbing off on everyone. Good thing spite doesn't show up in calculations.

Now or never. Strike or watch everything get eaten.

"We go tonight," I said, the words tasting of copper and

inevitability. "Full assault, maximum chaos, all or nothing. Because tomorrow there might not be anything left to save."

The declaration hung in the air thick with dust and desperate calculation. No more planning. No more preparation. No more careful reconnaissance or risk assessment. Just the brutal mathematics of time running out and choices that cut both ways.

Sometimes the only strategy is to leap and trust your claws will find purchase.

Vire's rope collar hummed harmonies that made stone weep condensation. "Fear echoes from below. But also hope. Desperate hope. Waiting for someone to care enough to try."

Thirty thousand people are counting on cats and academics to mount a rescue mission against cosmic horror. The universe has a twisted sense of humor.

But as my chaos field spread through the chamber, touching maps, plans, and desperate calculations, something else emerged. Not just resignation or grim determination, but fierce joy. The peculiar satisfaction that came from finally, finally, getting to bite back at something that richly deserved biting.

Pack tactics against impossible odds. This is what we were made for.

The crystalline sphere pulsed in the distance, its rhythm syncing with my burn line in harmonies that spoke of an approaching confrontation. The Collector's attention focused on our location with predatory intensity, sensing the shift from observation to action.

Let them sense it. Let them know we're coming.

Time to remind the universe that some problems could

only be solved through the application of deliberate chaos, applied with proper timing and maximal attitude.

Thirty thousand prisoners. One cosmic facility. Six refugees with attitude problems and a cat who refuses to accept impossible as an excuse.

The odds were terrible. The stakes were absolute. The enemy was a cosmic force armed with industrial-scale brutality and centuries of experience.

Perfect. I fight better when properly motivated.

Time to teach the Collector that cats always land on their feet, even when falling through dimensions toward the heart of enemy territory.

CHAPTER 11

TWO-FRONT WAR

The bond beneath my ribs blazed with sudden fire, dimensional static crackling across an impossible distance, as Felicity's determination slammed into my consciousness like a physical blow. Through golden threads stretched thin as spider silk, her workshop materialized around me— translucent, ghostly, overlaid on the tunnel walls.

Seeing two places at once. My whiskers are going to hate this.

She moved with the methodical precision of someone who had spent weeks planning a single, perfect moment of destruction. Chalk lines carved themselves into the stone floor with surgical accuracy, each symbol burning with her own blood drawn from cuts that still wept silver light. The ritual circle that surrounded her pulsed with dangerous geometries, power sources that made the graduation ceremony look like a child's finger painting.

Dangerous magic. The kind that rewrites the rules of engagement.

Through our connection flowed the weight of her

preparation—documents hidden, allies contacted, evidence compiled into weapons that could cut through decades of bureaucratic deception. But also fear, sharp as winter wind, the knowledge that this single gamble would either expose the conspiracy or eliminate her as a witness.

Murder dressed up as oops. Typical authority behavior.

The Council chamber materialized around her like a trap closing, oak panels dark with centuries of accumulated secrets, carved gargoyles whose stone eyes seemed to track movement with predatory calculation. Afternoon light slanted through the stained glass windows, casting prismatic shadows that danced erratically across the ritual circles etched into the marble floor.

Theater designed to intimidate. Also convenient for disposing of inconvenient witnesses.

High Councilor Alder presided from his elevated throne, emerald brooch catching light like a predator's eye. Councilors Briar and Sable flanked him, their positions carefully calculated to control sight lines and magical flow. Around the chamber's perimeter, lesser councilors arranged themselves according to hierarchies built from compromise and carefully managed corruption.

All the guilty mice in one place. Felicity was always good at cornering prey.

"Candidate Hargreaves," Alder intoned, his voice carrying the false warmth that fooled no one. "Your request for an emergency session was... unexpected."

Felicity stepped into the chamber's center, her ritual preparations hidden beneath apprentice robes that concealed enough concealed weapons to outfit a small army. When she spoke, her words carried harmonic undertones that made the carved gargoyles shift restlessly on their perches.

"High Councilor. Honored members. I come before you with evidence of systematic familiar harvesting, conspiracy spanning multiple realms, and treason that reaches to the highest levels of this governing body."

Direct accusation. No political dancing, no diplomatic immunity. Straight for the throat.

The silence that followed carried weight enough to crush stone. Around the chamber, councilors shifted with the nervous energy of predators suddenly uncertain whether they were hunting or being hunted. Quills froze mid-scratch. Breathing became a conscious effort requiring deliberate calculation.

Sable's rings clicked against her throne's armrest, the sound sharp as breaking bone. "These are serious accusations, candidate. I trust you have evidence to support such dramatic claims."

Evidence. Yes. The kind that comes with teeth.

Felicity raised her hand, revealing documents that glowed with authentication charms powerful enough to prevent forgery or alteration. When she spoke, each word carried the weight of legal binding, transforming accusation into a formal charge.

"Terminal Protocol documentation, signed by Councilor Sable. Processing manifests listing familiar acquisition quotas, approved by Councilor Briar. Financial records showing payment from entities identified as Collector subsidiaries, authorized by High Councilor Alder himself."

Scent trail leading straight to the guilty. Book-learning is used for proper hunting.

The chamber's temperature dropped with supernatural precision, as if reality itself recoiled from truths too large to safely contain. Shadows pooled in impossible configurations, gathering around the accused councilors like hungry darkness drawn to sources of corruption.

Alder's emerald brooch flared with defensive light, wards activating around his throne with the mechanical precision of long-prepared contingencies. "Fabricated documents. Clever forgeries designed to destabilize legitimate governance."

Predictable response. Deny, deflect, eliminate the witness.

But Felicity had prepared for denial. Her ritual circle blazed to life, power flowing through blood-drawn channels that connected her directly to evidence sources scattered across multiple realms. Through dimensional gates as narrow as a needle's eye, testimony poured from victims who had been presumed eliminated.

Testimony from the dead. Or those who were supposed to be dead.

Voices of familiars who had escaped processing facilities. Witches whose bonds had been severed for political convenience. Council members from other realms who had discovered similar conspiracies in their own governments. Each voice carried authentication that could not be faked, memories that could not be forged, pain that resonated with truth deeper than any legal precedent.

Evidence that bleeds when touched. The kind that leaves permanent stains.

Briar rose from his throne, pale hands weaving counterspells with academic precision. "Dimensional intrusion without authorization. Illegal testimony procurement. This candidate has violated every protocol governing legitimate investigation."

The attack came without warning, silver light lancing from his fingertips toward Felicity's heart with surgical accuracy. She deflected with shields that rang like bell metal; the impact sent harmonic shockwaves through the stone, making the gargoyles weep marble tears.

Magical assault in Council chambers. Someone's abandoned subtlety.

Around the chamber, lines of allegiance crystallized with sudden clarity. Junior councilors scrambled for exits that sealed themselves with administrative precision. Senior members drew wands with movements that indicated long practice in chamber-based combat. The carved gargoyles flexed stone wings, animated by wards designed to eliminate threats to the established order.

Pack fight. Paper-pushers with death magic.

Sable's rings blazed as she joined the attack, copper light weaving itself into nets designed to paralyze rather than kill. "Contain the candidate. Extract information about co-conspirators. Standard interrogation protocols."

Standard interrogation protocols. Euphemisms for torture, as always.

But Felicity had spent weeks preparing for exactly this scenario. Her ritual circle expanded, power flowing through hidden channels carved into the chamber's foundation, connecting to anchor points that had been modified during routine maintenance sessions. What the conspiracy had seen as routine upkeep, she had transformed into weapons aimed at the chamber's heart.

Sabotage disguised as repair work. Proper familiar thinking.

Stone gargoyles shrieked as their animation matrices destabilized, carved features melting into expressions of terminal confusion. Ward stones cracked as forced power flows reversed themselves, protective barriers becoming prisons that trapped their own casters. The chamber's ancient wards, designed to prevent external magical intrusion, turned inward as the hunger of the mechanisms finally allowed them to fulfill their true purpose.

Home field advantage. Turn their own defenses against them.

Through our bond, I felt Felicity's fierce satisfaction as decades of carefully maintained political balance collapsed into honest warfare. No more euphemisms. No more polite conspiracy. Just the brutal mathematics of magical combat between forces that had finally abandoned pretense.

Finally. Truth applied with proper force.

Alder's emerald brooch pulsed with power drawn from reserves that spoke of centuries of accumulated corruption. When he raised his wand, the air itself recoiled from energies that had been twisted into shapes never meant for mortal use.

"You force our hand, candidate. We had hoped to recruit rather than eliminate. But some problems require permanent solutions."

Permanent solutions. At least they're being honest about murder now.

The spell he launched carried the weight of institutional authority backed by stolen power, a golden lance that could unmake someone from reality itself, erasing them from history with bureaucratic thoroughness. Felicity met it with defenses built from her own blood and determination, silver shields that rang with harmonics of stubborn refusal to submit.

Authority trying to kill conviction. Old fight, new claws.

The collision sent shockwaves through dimensions that had no business intersecting, reality bleeding between realms as forced magical pressures found release through the weakest available channels. Through cracks in space-time leaked glimpses of other Council chambers where similar battles raged, seventeen realms fighting the same war from different angles.

Pack hunting from different territories. Finally, proper coordination.

And through it all, Felicity's ritual circle burned with purpose that transcended personal survival. Power flowed through dimensional gates toward a single, specific target— the facility where thirty thousand prisoners waited for rescue or elimination. Her magic carved channels through reality itself, establishing communication lines that the conspiracy could neither monitor nor sever.

Portal help for the main fight. Smart planning while claws are out.

Through our bond came her final message, words that carried the weight of blood sacrifice and absolute commitment: "The path is open. Hit them with everything you have."

Coordinated assault across an impossible distance. Finally, teamwork that doesn't involve me being lectured.

The connection stabilized, golden threads weaving themselves into permanent channels that would survive anything short of universal collapse. Two fronts, one enemy, unified strategy powered by bonds that refused to break under pressure.

Time to remind the universe that some battles could only be won through the application of deliberate chaos, properly coordinated and applied with maximal attitude.

The air between dimensions tore open like fabric surrendering to claws. My burn-line blazed white-hot as foreign magic crashed into the tunnel system with the subtlety of a cosmic sledgehammer. Stone walls wept condensation that tasted of copper and despair. The very atmosphere pressed against my phantom whiskers with a weight that spoke of attention focused from impossible distances.

Incoming communication. This won't be pleasant.

Shadows pooled in configurations that defied geometry, gathering into shapes that suggested surveillance equipment built from crystallized nightmare. The temperature plummeted with surgical precision, air becoming thin and sharp as copper pennies.

The Collector's presence materialized slowly, shadows gathering with predatory intent and fed on decades of accumulated cruelty. When it spoke, the voice came from everywhere and nowhere, resonating through bone and stone with harmonics that made my phantom tail attempt to lash at concepts too abstract to claw.

"Subject MCC-139. Your resistance creates... complications. Observe the consequences of defiance."

Direct contact. Someone's taking this personally. And they're in a hurry.

But beneath my reflexive sarcasm, something cold and primitive stirred—the recognition that predators only showed their hand when they needed immediate results. My chaos field contracted instinctively, golden threads pulling close like fur bristling against approaching storm.

Around us, the displaced pressed against tunnel walls with the synchronized alertness of prey recognizing immediate danger. Rowan's lantern flickered, flame guttering as reality struggled to maintain coherence under the weight of dimensional intrusion. Even Whisper's humming died to silence, small face grave with the certainty of someone who heard stones screaming warnings.

Theater. But rushed theater. They're under pressure too.

The shadows deepened, coalescing into a single viewing surface that reflected a scene no mortal eye should witness. A processing chamber materialized in crystalline clarity, mechanisms extracting consciousness from a familiar suspended in liquid that pulsed with stolen starlight.

But this wasn't just any familiar. The proportions were wrong, the coloring too familiar, the markings arranged in patterns that spoke of careful breeding for specific magical resonance. A cat hung suspended in machinery designed with terrible specificity, each component calibrated for feline anatomy and psychology.

Another cat like me. Free-thinking, chaos-making, probably stolen the same way.

"Subject MCC-137," the Collector said, voice carrying

notes of clinical satisfaction. "Remarkably similar to yourself. Same independence index, same chaos resonance, same stubborn refusal to accept necessary—"

The cat's eyes snapped open.

Intelligence burned bright instead of the dimmed awareness I'd expected, fury that had been compressed under layers of mechanical compliance until it became something harder than diamond. When it moved, servo-mechanisms shrieked in protest as organic will overrode algorithmic control.

They're awake. They're fighting back.

"Impossible," the Collector hissed. "Restraint protocols are—"

The viewing surface exploded outward as MCC-137 tore through dimensional barriers with claws that sparked against reality itself. The cat achieved actual physical translocation rather than metaphorical escape as its desperation found resonance with my chaos signature and used it as an anchor point to claw its way between realms.

Oh. This is going to be complicated.

MCC-137 materialized in our tunnel with a sound like breaking glass and tortured metal, hitting the stone floor in a crouch that spoke of predator instincts refined through nightmare. But wrong. Servo-muscles still whined in its limbs. Copper wire threaded through its fur sparked with residual control signals. Its eyes blazed with intelligence that flickered between organic thought and mechanical precision.

Free but not free. Conscious but not entirely in control.

"Please," it whispered, voice carrying echoes of both

desperation and algorithmic overlay. "Kill me or fix me, but don't let them—"

The words cut off as control systems reasserted themselves, mechanical precision overriding organic choice. MCC-137's head snapped up, copper eyes blazing with the Collector's attention, servo-muscles locking into combat configuration.

Partially corrupted. Still fighting the programming, but not winning.

My phantom tail exploded with pain that had nothing to do with missing anatomy. Phantom pain for phantom limbs, watching phantom people beg for death. The sensation lanced up my spine like sympathetic nervous system damage, my body trying to respond to trauma that belonged to someone else.

Phantom pain for phantom people watching phantom torture. My tail hurts for someone else missing everything.

Around me, the pack scrambled for defensive positions. But this wasn't an enemy attack—this was a rescue scenario where the victim was also the threat. MCC-137 crouched in the tunnel's center, consciousness flickering between plea and predation as competing command systems fought for control.

"The control matrix," Rowan breathed, academic mind processing impossibilities with scholarly precision. "It's destabilizing but not broken. They're fighting their own programming."

Typical breaking pattern. Real cat-fighting fake obedience.

Bellwether approached carefully, hands open, pack instincts recognizing a wounded pack-mate beneath the mechanical overlay. "I know," she said, voice gentle but firm. "I remember the weight of gears in your thoughts, the way choice becomes suggestion becomes compliance. You're still in there."

Pack instincts. She knows what broken feels like.

But MCC-137's servo-systems registered her approach as a threat input, with mechanical responses overriding conscious recognition. They launched themselves at Bellwether with precision that spoke of algorithmic calculation, claws extended, systems optimized for familiar elimination.

Fight someone we're trying to save. Exactly the kind of moral complexity cats hate.

I intercepted, chaos field flaring to disrupt the control signals sparking through MCC-137's nervous system. Where my contamination touched their modifications, servo motors stuttered, copper wire sparked, and algorithmic precision degraded into organic confusion.

But my phantom tail pain intensified with contact, the sympathetic nervous system trying to process trauma that belonged to someone else. My burn-line flared hot enough to make my vision spot, overloaded by attempting to heal corruptions too complex for simple restoration.

They carved deeper into this one than Bellwether. Not just body-changes—mind-changes from the ground up.

MCC-137 convulsed as my chaos clashed with their control systems, the organic personality and mechanical compliance battling for dominance. Their mouth opened, voice switching between desperate, familiar, and algorithmic processor:

"Help me—threat assessment updated—please don't let

them—eliminate protocol activated—I remember choosing
—compliance required—I remember being—"

*Consciousness ping-ponging between self and system.
They're aware but not in control.*

Cipher pressed against the wall, amber eyes reflecting
calculations that had no solution. "The mathematics don't
work," he whispered. "Consciousness fragmented across
competing systems. There's no stable integration possible."

*Numbers-human breaking down again. His brain patterns
are getting tangled like yarn left out too long.*

But Vire's rope collar hummed a different harmony,
subsonic frequencies that made MCC-137's servo-systems
hesitate. "Fear echoes," he said, moving closer despite the
danger. "But also... recognition. They remember choice. It's
buried, but it's there."

Noise-healing for machine-wounds. Worth trying.

The rope collar's harmony seemed to create interference
patterns with MCC-137's control systems, as servo-motors
stuttered due to conflicting signals fighting for dominance.
In the pauses between mechanical precision, glimpses of
organic personality surfaced:

"My name," they gasped during a moment of clarity. "I
had a name. Before the numbers. Before the procedures. I
was—"

Control systems reasserted themselves, cutting off
speech as algorithmic compliance overrode personal
identity. But the recognition remained, burning in copper
eyes that flickered between programmed hostility and
desperate hope.

Real self clawing back to the surface.

"We need to get them stable," I said, though my

phantom tail pain made concentration difficult. Every second of contact with their corrupted systems sent new waves of sympathetic trauma through my nervous system. "Find somewhere they can fight the programming without hurting anyone."

Including themselves. Partial corruption can create conflicts that tear someone apart from the inside.

Selyn's crystals blazed with determination, tasting of salt spray and storm winds. "The processing chamber. If we can get them back to the facility, reverse the modifications where they were installed—"

"No." Bellwether's voice carried a pack authority honed through experience with recovery from mechanical trauma. "Not back to the place of breaking. Forward to somewhere new. Somewhere choice lives."

Wolf instincts. Healing happens in safe dens, not where you got hurt.

MCC-137's servo-systems locked them into another attack posture, mechanical precision targeting the nearest heat signature. But this time, instead of fighting the programming, I reached deeper into their corrupted systems with my chaos signature, not trying to break the modifications but trying to teach them to break themselves.

Same technique that worked on Bellwether. Remind them how to choose instead of forcing a choice on them.

The contact sent new spikes of phantom pain through my missing tail, sympathetic nervous system overloading as it tried to process trauma that belonged to someone else. But beneath the pain, I felt something else—recognition. MCC-137's core personality responded to familiar magic that remembered what freedom felt like.

Identity calling to identity across mechanical interference.

"Remember," I whispered, chaos field weaving itself into their control systems like golden threads through broken machinery. "Remember what it felt like to knock things off tables just because they looked smug. Remember choosing your own napping spots. Remember being annoyed at humans for entirely justified reasons."

Cat memories fighting machine thoughts. Use what we remember about being free.

For a moment, organic won. MCC-137's servo-systems powered down, copper eyes reflecting recognition instead of programmed hostility. They looked at me with awareness that transcended mechanical overlay, consciousness surfacing from beneath layers of enforced compliance.

"Mischief," they said, voice carrying wonder at the concept of names chosen instead of assigned. "They called me Mischief, too. Before the numbers. Before they decided individual identity was inefficient."

Remembering their name. The core self refuses to be erased.

But the control systems weren't finished. As MCC-137's organic personality surfaced, mechanical safeguards activated with surgical precision. Servo-motors whined as override protocols attempted to reassert algorithmic control, threatening to tear their consciousness apart in the process.

The system is fighting back. They've got failsafes built into the failsafes.

"Can't hold it," MCC-137 gasped, organic speech degrading as mechanical compliance fought for dominance. "Too many layers. Too much conditioning. They rebuilt me too thoroughly."

Fake thoughts fighting real thoughts. The machines are winning.

But Bellwether had been studying the patterns of their struggle, pack instincts recognizing familiar rhythms beneath mechanical precision. "Not rebuilt," she said, understanding dawning in gray eyes that had seen too much. "Disguised. They couldn't break you completely, so they buried you under layers of false compliance."

Insight from experience. She knows this territory.

The observation shifted something fundamental in MCC-137's struggle against their programming. Instead of fighting the control systems directly, they began to work around them, organic intelligence finding paths through mechanical limitations that the algorithms hadn't anticipated.

Sneaky fighting against your own brain. Use the machine's rules to break the machine.

"I need," MCC-137 said carefully, words chosen to avoid triggering automated responses, "to return to the place of breaking. Not to be broken again, but to break their systems from the inside."

Inside knowledge. They know the facility's vulnerabilities because they've been part of the machinery.

The suggestion hung in the tunnel air thick with accumulated tension, each word weighted with possibilities that could reshape our entire approach to the rescue mission. Instead of breaking in, we'd infiltrate using inside knowledge.

Sneaking in using inside secrets. Finally, a plan that doesn't involve charging straight at death.

"No," I said, phantom tail pain making decision-making

difficult. "Too dangerous. They're still fighting the programming. What happens if the control systems win while you're inside?"

Sensible worry. Someone fighting their own brain can't be trusted with life-or-death sneaking.

But MCC-137's copper eyes blazed with determination that transcended mechanical overlay. "Then I die free instead of living as their tool. Better to choose destruction than accept enslavement."

Valid point. Also, exactly what I would say in their position.

Around us, the pack absorbed the implications of the proposed strategy. Use the partially corrupted familiar as an infiltrator, supported by team members who could pass as facility staff. Instead of breaking in, walk in the front door with someone who knows all the passwords.

Bellwether's facility knowledge, plus MCC-137's access codes, plus strategic deception. It might actually work.

But the phantom tail pain was getting worse, sympathetic nervous system overloading as prolonged contact with MCC-137's corrupted systems triggered my own trauma responses. My burn-line throbbed with heat that spoke of magical systems pushed beyond safe parameters.

I can't maintain healing contact much longer. Whatever we decide, we need to decide fast.

Through the bond beneath my ribs, Felicity's determination pulsed with fierce approval. She was fighting her own war against organized cruelty, using inside knowledge and careful preparation to expose crimes that had been hidden for decades.

Two fights, one plan. Time to show the universe that sneaking works better when you know the territory

Time to discover whether cosmic horror could be defeated through the application of deliberate deception, properly coordinated and executed by people who had nothing left to lose except the choice to remain themselves.

We moved to a wider chamber where MCC-137 could fight its internal war without destroying anyone in the vicinity. The space reeked of old chalk and desperation, with undertones of institutional antiseptic and the particular mustiness of places where hope goes to die.

Safe distance. Relatively speaking.

The phantom pain in my missing tail had intensified to the point where concentration required deliberate effort. Each pulse of MCC-137's control systems sent sympathetic spikes through my own nervous system, phantom limb syndrome trying to process trauma that belonged to someone else. My burn-line throbbed with heat that spoke of magical systems pushed beyond safe operational parameters.

Watching-pain getting worse. My whiskers think I'm hurting because another cat is hurting.

I pressed my back against the cool stone, using the solid sensation to anchor myself in the present reality instead of the borrowed trauma. Around me, the pack arranged themselves in defensive configurations that spoke of shared understanding about the nature of fights where the enemy and the victim occupied the same body.

Bellwether crouched beside MCC-137, gray eyes reflecting recognition that transcended species boundaries. "The shift schedules," she said, voice carefully controlled to avoid triggering automated responses. "Do you remember the shift schedules?"

Pack-sense for getting information. Use shared wounds to build trust.

MCC-137's copper eyes flickered between organic thought and mechanical precision as they accessed information that existed in both conscious memory and algorithmic databases. "Processing Division Three. Fourteen-hour rotations. Night shift runs skeleton crews because..." Their voice stuttered as control systems attempted to classify the information as restricted. "Because the subjects are sedated, anyway."

Inside intelligence. They know the facility's operational details from the perspective of both victim and component.

Cipher huddled beside his calculations, amber eyes carefully focused on arithmetic rather than anything that might develop opinions about its own existence. "Probability matrices for infiltration... I can't compute them. Too many variables that include consciousness as a negotiable parameter."

Number panic is getting worse. His brain tricks are failing faster than I can fix them.

Vire's rope collar hummed subsonic harmonies that seemed to create interference patterns with MCC-137's control systems, helping organic thought surface through layers of mechanical compliance. "The facility staff," he said. "Do they fear the subjects or the systems?"

Sniffing for emotional weak spots. Fear-scent shows who's really in charge.

"Both," MCC-137 replied during a moment of clarity. "Staff know the subjects are people. That knowledge creates guilt, which creates fear. They avoid direct contact when possible. Standard protocol is remote monitoring unless maintenance requires physical intervention."

Weak spot in their pack. Guilt makes people miss things.

Rowan scribbled notes with hands that shook slightly, academic routine providing anchor points in cognitive chaos. "Security protocols for facility access?"

"Biometric scanning for external personnel. Internal staff use proximity badges with embedded authorization codes." MCC-137's voice carried harmonics of both organic memory and database access. "But Processing Division has special clearances. They're authorized to move freely through all facility levels because they need access to maintain the systems."

Processor credentials are a universal key. Someone designed this system for efficiency rather than security.

The information painted possibilities that made my phantom tail pain recede slightly as tactical thinking overrode sympathetic trauma. Not breaking into the facility, but walking in the front door with credentials that belonged to the system itself.

Sneaking in using inside information. Finally, a plan that doesn't involve charging at impossible claws.

"What about detection systems?" I asked, though

speaking required concentration as my burn-line continued to throb with overload symptoms. "Magical signatures, chaos resonance, anything that might identify us as threats?"

MCC-137's control systems stuttered as they accessed information classified at multiple security levels simultaneously. "Detection arrays are... were... calibrated to ignore processor signatures. Can't monitor the monitors without creating recursive surveillance loops that bog down the central systems."

Blind spot in their own security apparatus.

Selyn's crystals chimed with determination that tasted of salt spray and storm winds. "If we can pass as processors, we could access the containment levels directly. No infiltration, no alarms, just authorized personnel performing routine maintenance."

Hiding in plain sight. Sometimes the best camouflage is belonging where you're supposed to be.

But Bellwether's expression carried caution learned through experience with the gap between theoretical plans and practical reality. "What happens when they try to contact our supervisors? Verify our work orders? Check our authorization codes against central databases?"

Pack skepticism. She knows that plans look cleaner on paper than they work in practice.

MCC-137's organic personality surfaced with information that made their copper eyes flicker with what might have been satisfaction. "Night shift operates on minimal oversight. Supervisors aren't on-site. Verification protocols are relaxed because the assumption is that nothing important happens during maintenance cycles."

Safety rules were ignored for easy work. Someone chose lazy over careful.

The plan crystallized with the sharp clarity of desperation refined into strategy. Use MCC-137's access codes and knowledge to get inside. Pose as processing staff performing routine maintenance. Access the containment levels during skeleton crew hours when verification protocols were minimized.

Simple. Direct. Reasonably insane. Perfect for cats.

But my phantom tail pain spiked again as I considered the implications of the strategy. MCC-137 would be returning to the place where they'd been systematically broken, surrounded by the systems that had tried to erase their consciousness. The psychological pressure alone might trigger a complete breakdown.

Going back to where you got broken while fighting brainwashing. That's not a plan, that's jumping off cliffs.

"You can't go back there," I said, letting concern override tactical considerations. "The facility is where they broke you. Being inside those walls, surrounded by those systems, fighting your programming while trying to maintain cover—"

"Is exactly what I need to do," MCC-137 interrupted, organic will asserting itself with determination that made their servo-systems whine in protest. "Running away means they win. Going back means I choose what happens to me."

Valid logic. Also, exactly the kind of logic that gets cats killed through excessive confidence in their own abilities.

Whisper looked up from her corner, small face serious as carved granite. The walls around us had been weeping condensation that tasted of accumulated fear, but now the moisture carried different flavors—hope mixed with salt, determination seasoned with desperation.

"The stones sing new songs," she said, voice carrying harmonics that belonged to no human throat. "Harmony shifts when the broken choose to break their breakers."

Prophetic children endorsing psychological warfare as a healing strategy. The universe has a twisted sense of irony.

Through the bond beneath my ribs, Felicity's determination pulsed with fierce approval. She was infiltrating her own Council chamber, surrounded by people who wanted her dead, using inside knowledge and careful preparation to expose systematic corruption. Two fronts, a unified strategy, and a shared commitment to choosing action over safety.

Sometimes you have to go back and piss on the thing that scared you. Mark it yours.

"The processing uniforms," Bellwether said, pack instincts recognizing the momentum shift toward action. "I remember the fabric, the cut, the way they smelled of antiseptic and industrial compliance. I can replicate them if we have materials."

Outfit-making from bad memories. She's using her victim-knowledge as hunting advantage.

MCC-137's copper eyes blazed with something that transcended mechanical overlay, determination that blazed into something fiercer—joy. The fierce satisfaction that came from choosing to confront the source of trauma instead of running from it. "They think they own me," they said, voice carrying harmonics of both organic thought and algorithmic precision. "Time to teach them that some systems can be hacked from the inside."

Sneaky fighting against organized cruelty using inside knowledge of the cruel system.

The phantom tail pain was receding as tactical excitement overrode sympathetic trauma. This wasn't just a rescue mission anymore—it was active resistance using the enemy's own infrastructure against them. Infiltration by people who had been broken by the system and chose to remain unbroken despite everything.

Sometimes the best weapon against institutional horror is someone who's survived institutional horror and decided to bite back.

Time to remind the universe that some infiltrations worked better when the infiltrators had nothing left to lose except the choice to remain themselves.

The preparation took place in chambers that had absorbed too much desperate planning, stone walls weeping condensation that tasted of schemes born from necessity rather than wisdom. MCC-137 sat in the center of our makeshift workshop, servo-systems powered down to conserve energy while organic consciousness accessed memories buried beneath layers of mechanical conditioning.

Planning session using pain memories. They're turning their hurt into useful knowledge.

My phantom tail pain had settled into a persistent ache that spiked whenever MCC-137's control systems activated, the sympathetic nervous system still trying to process trauma that belonged to someone else. But the sensation was manageable now, background suffering that informed decision-making without paralyzing action.

Pain is telling me things. My whiskers are learning to read their owner's hurt through the cat connection.

"Processing Division Three operates on modified schedules," MCC-137 said, voice flickering between organic thought and database access. "Night shift: two supervisors, six maintenance staff, minimal security presence. Day shift: full complement, multiple oversight layers, comprehensive monitoring."

Night operations. Classic infiltration timing.

Bellwether traced patterns on the stone floor with movements that spoke of muscle memory learned during captivity. The uniforms she was recreating from traumatic recall carried authority that transcended fabric—gray coveralls with insignia that granted access to spaces most people were never meant to see.

"The fabric feels wrong," she muttered, fingers working material that had been liberated from abandoned supply closets. "Too clean. Processing uniforms always smells of antiseptic and other people's fear."

Memory-scents from bad times. She's copying fear-smells along with the look.

Cipher remained pressed against the far wall, amber eyes carefully focused on safe mathematics that couldn't develop opinions about their own existence. But his calculations had become vital to the mission planning, statistical analysis of patrol patterns, and shift rotations that might mean the difference between infiltration and elimination.

"Guard rotation patterns follow predictable algorithms," he whispered, voice carrying the hollow tone of someone whose coping mechanisms were approaching total failure. "But algorithms assume rational behavior. They don't account for consciousness variables."

Numbers fear meeting real problems. His brain's breaking faster, but his counting still helps.

Selyn's crystals provided steady light while she worked with materials that would create the chemical signatures necessary for our disguises. Salt water mixed with industrial compounds, creating scents that would register as familiar to anyone who worked in processing facilities.

"The smell is important," she said, crystals darkening as she accessed memories of her home realm's destruction. "They process so many people that the staff become desensitized to individual scents. But they notice when someone doesn't smell like they belong."

Smell-hiding using bad memories. She's turning her pain into weapons.

Vire's rope collar hummed subsonic harmonies as he practiced acoustic camouflage, learning to modulate his fear-sensing abilities to blend with the ambient terror that pervaded processing facilities. His voice carried new harmonics when he spoke, frequencies that belonged to places where screaming had become background noise.

"The facility hums," he said, rope collar vibrating in sympathy with remembered resonances. "Machinery, ventilation, extraction systems, fear processed into industrial background noise. I can match those frequencies, become part of the sound environment."

Sound-hiding by copying fear-noises. He's using his fear-hearing as camouflage.

Rowan scribbled notes with academic precision that masked growing concern about the psychological sustainability of the strategy. His ledger contained contingency plans for scenarios that academic training had never prepared him to contemplate—rescue missions where the rescuers were utilizing their own torture as tactical intelligence.

"Extraction protocols," he said, voice carrying scholarly concern for variables that transcended mere operational parameters. "If the infiltration is compromised, if MCC-137's control systems reassert dominance, if the psychological pressure triggers complete breakdown—"

"Then we adapt," I said, though my phantom tail pain spiked at the thought of MCC-137 losing their battle against mechanical compliance while surrounded by the systems that had originally broken them. "Plans survive contact with reality about as well as cats survive contact with bath water."

Fake confidence hiding real worry. Sometimes alphas pretend they know things they don't.

MCC-137 accessed facility schematics, servo-systems humming as organic memory merged with database files. "Primary containment levels extend seventeen floors underground. High-priority subjects on the lowest levels, routine processing on intermediate floors, and administrative functions near surface access." The briefing that followed revealed industrial-scale brutality with bureaucratic attention to detail—intake procedures designed to eliminate hope, disposal protocols that treated consciousness as waste.

Building knowledge from the inside. They're mapping where they got hurt for fighting purposes.

But beneath the clinical details, patterns emerged that spoke of vulnerabilities born from the same efficiency that made the system so terrible. Automated protocols that assumed compliance. Security measures are designed for external threats rather than internal resistance. Staff are trained to avoid direct contact with subjects whenever possible.

Systemic blind spots. They've optimized for processing people, not for people fighting back.

"The central processing chamber," MCC-137 said, voice carrying both organic memory and database access as they described the facility's heart. "Where they perform the final consciousness transfers. Minimal staff presence because the subjects are usually catatonic by that stage. But also where the override codes are accessible."

A control room with a few guards, because no one expects broken things to fight back.

The strategic implications settled in the chamber air thick with accumulated desperation. This had become a sabotage operation disguised as a rescue mission. Use the facility's own systems to liberate the prisoners, turn their industrial infrastructure against them, and transform the processing center into an evacuation hub.

Poetic justice through systematic reversal. They built

machines to break people—time to teach the machines to break themselves.

My phantom tail pain pulsed with something that might have been anticipation as understanding crystallized into an actionable strategy. MCC-137 would provide access and inside knowledge. The pack would pose as processing staff performing routine maintenance. Once inside, we'd access the central systems and reverse the entire facility's operational parameters.

Simple plan with terrible ways to fail. Perfect for cats who don't believe in impossible.

Through the bond beneath my ribs, Felicity's determination burned like distant starlight—fierce, cold, and absolutely unwilling to negotiate with forces that turned choice into mechanical compliance. She was fighting her own war against institutional brutality, using similar tactics of infiltration and systemic reversal.

Pack fighting from different territories. Two battles, one plan, shared promise to teach cruel systems that some people won't stay beaten.

Time to remind the universe that some infiltrations worked best when the infiltrators had intimate knowledge of the system they were infiltrating, regardless of how they had acquired that knowledge.

Thirty thousand prisoners, counting on cats, academics, and recovering torture victims to mount a rescue mission using insider intelligence gained through systematic trauma.

The odds remained terrible. The stakes remained absolute. The enemy remained a cosmic force armed with industrial-scale brutality and centuries of experience.

Perfect. I've never met impossible odds that couldn't be

improved through the application of proper attitude and maximum spite.

Time to teach the Collector that some cats refuse to be declawed, even when the claws are memories of choices made under torture.

CHAPTER 12

INTO THE HEART

The facility's entrance gaped wide, edges cauterized with wards. Steam rose from metal gratings, carrying scents that made my phantom whiskers recoil—ozone mixed with something organic gone wrong, the particular staleness of air that had circulated through too many lungs before finding freedom. My phantom whiskers mapped the entrance, filing it under 'hostile territory that would soon learn better manners.

Time to remind them who's hunting whom.

Behind me, the pack moved with synchronized alertness born from shared trauma and coordinated desperation. Bellwether kept to the center of the corridor, away from walls where mechanical sounds hummed with institutional malice. Her breathing had become deliberately controlled the moment we entered—four counts in, hold, four counts out—the rhythm of someone who'd learned to manage panic through structure.

She's avoiding anything that sounds like processing equipment. Smart.

Selyn's crystals blazed with determination that tasted of salt spray and storm winds, but her free hand compulsively checked the pouch where she kept backup crystals. Physical anchors in a place where reality had become negotiable. When a distant mechanical whine echoed through the corridors, her shoulders went rigid for three heartbeats before she forced them to relax.

Cipher's amber gaze catalogued security measures with mathematical precision that bordered on obsession, but his hands shook as he traced patterns in the air. Numbers that stayed safely in his control, equations that couldn't develop opinions about their own existence. "Seventeen potential breach points," he whispered, voice tight. "Assuming standard dimensional architecture, which this clearly isn't, so the calculations are useless, aren't they useless, everything here is—"

"Breathe," Rowan said quietly, moving closer without crowding. "Count the things you can control."

Pack care. Making sure everyone can still hunt.

My chaos field rippled outward, golden threads probing defenses with the methodical precision of a cat examining new furniture for optimal destruction potential. The first security checkpoint materialized from shadows—ward-stones flanked a narrow passage, their surfaces crawling with symbols that rewrote themselves faster than the eye could follow.

I approached the barrier with the confidence of someone who had spent years claiming furniture that humans insisted belonged to them. But as my chaos field contacted the wards, something unexpected happened. Instead of simple disruption, my contamination began to *teach* the defensive systems new behaviors.

Amateur hour. Their wards expect either compliance or direct assault, not educational opportunities.

The wardstones started purring. Actual purring, deep subsonic rumbles that made the facility's foundations vibrate like a massive cat claiming territory. The crystalline barrier flickered, confused by magic that suggested perhaps barriers should be more selective about what they blocked.

Why block everything when you could just block the boring stuff?

The barrier collapsed with a sound like breaking glass, but the wardstones continued to purr, apparently having decided that this was an improvement to their original function. Behind us, a security panel began displaying cat videos instead of threat assessments.

Educational success. Sometimes the best way to break something is to teach it to enjoy being broken.

Beyond lay a corridor that stretched into distances the architecture couldn't possibly contain. But what made Bellwether stop moving entirely wasn't the impossible geometry—it was the viewing ports lining the walls, each one offering clinical views into processing chambers.

Through reinforced glass, horrors materialized in sterile clarity. A raven suspended in liquid, its wings spread in permanent terror, pulsed with stolen starlight. A fox whose silver fur had been systematically replaced with copper wire. The orange kitten I'd seen before, machines pressed against her skull like a crown of thorns.

Bellwether pressed her back against the corridor's

center, as far from the viewing ports as possible. Her breathing had gone shallow, pupils dilated. When she spoke, her voice carried the flat effect of someone forcing words through trauma responses.

"They made me watch," she said. "When they processed others. Said it was educational. So, I'd understand what cooperation looked like."

Mind-hurting dressed up as teaching. Typical authority tricks.

Vire's rope collar began humming distress frequencies that made the air itself feel heavy. His hands pressed flat against his thighs to stop them from shaking. "The sounds," he whispered. "The mechanical sounds are the same."

Bad sounds bring back bad memories.

Movement beyond the viewing ports caught my attention—figures in Council robes working with frantic desperation, destroying equipment with systematic thoroughness. Documents fed into furnaces that burned with unnatural fire. The processing tanks were drained, leaving empty chambers that reeked of sanitizing chemicals.

But my chaos field was spreading through the facility's infrastructure faster than they could contain it. Each ward-stone I'd taught to purr was now teaching *other* ward-stones. Security systems began displaying increasingly creative interpretations of their duties. Doors opened when they felt like it. The lights decided to strobe in rhythm with the purring. Climate control systems started dispensing catnip-scented air.

Network contamination. Like yawning, but for magical infrastructure.

"They're liquidating everything," Rowan said, academic

horror struggling with protective fury. "Not just evidence—the prisoners themselves."

A secondary explosion rocked the facility as my chaos signature reached a particularly rigid control nexus. The sound echoed through corridors that shouldn't have been able to contain such violence, followed by what sounded suspiciously like an entire security grid deciding it would rather take a nap.

Their organized breaking spreads through their organized fixing. Beautiful.

The passage ahead branched into passages that violated basic architectural principles, each path leading deeper into a facility that seemed to exist in more dimensions than local reality could safely contain. But as we moved, my contamination continued its educational work, teaching bureaucratic precision to misbehave in increasingly creative ways.

Sometimes you fix broken things by teaching them to break in more fun ways.

The central path opened into an archive that made my phantom whiskers twitch with territorial recognition. Shelves rose toward the ceiling, lost in shadows, their surfaces packed with filing systems that spoke of a bureaucratic obsession refined into an art form. But these weren't just records—they were trophies. Each folder represented someone who had been processed, catalogued, and reduced to data points.

A library of the murdered. How thoroughly administrative.

The sight hit the pack like a physical blow. Selyn's crystals dimmed as she stared at shelf after shelf of systematic documentation. Cipher began counting under his breath, compulsive enumeration of horror that couldn't be computed.

"Hundreds," he whispered, amber eyes reflecting statistical impossibility. "Thousands. If we memorize every file, we honor them. We have to honor them."

Bellwether snarled, the sound carrying harmonics of pack-fury refined through bitter experience. "If we memorize every file, we'll go insane. You can't carry that much grief and still function."

Pack argument about handling pain. Different ways to keep hunting after getting hurt.

The argument hung between them like a bridge built from crystallized pain, each position carrying the weight of different strategies for psychological survival. Vire's rope collar hummed with distress, making the filing cabinets vibrate in sympathy.

Around us, my chaos field continued its work on organizing the archive. Filing systems began to sort themselves by emotional weight rather than alphabetical order. Files labeled *"hopeful"* migrated to eye level while *"despair"* sank toward floor level, where they belonged. A section marked *"unfinished business"* started glowing softly.

Even filing systems have opinions about proper organization once you teach them to think for themselves.

"We remember the ones we can save," I said, letting understanding settle with quiet certainty while overhead sprinklers began dispensing something that smelled suspiciously like sardine oil. "That's honor enough. The dead don't need our grief—they need our claws."

Smart thinking dressed up as feeling-sorting. Sometimes staying alive means picking which fights to take.

But as the archive continued its enthusiastic reorganization around my chaos signature, what drew my attention was the section spontaneously labeled "Special cases"—folders thick as dictionaries bearing familiar markings. MCC-137. MCC-089. MCC-052. Dozens of them, each one representing a familiar who had registered maximum independence.

I pulled the nearest folder just as the filing cabinet decided it wanted to be helpful and started ejecting related documents like an over-eager assistant. Papers scattered across the floor in a cascade of clinical horror: photographs showing transformation sequences, psychological evaluation charts tracking the systematic elimination of personality traits, progress reports documenting the precise moment when defiance became compliance.

They've been perfecting this process for decades. Each failure teaches them to break people more efficiently.

The patterns that emerged made my burn line pulse with growing fury, while around us, the overhead lighting decided to provide dramatic emphasis by flickering ominously. The "special cases" weren't random—they were cultivated. Breeding programs designed to produce familiars with specific magical resonances. Witches are chosen for bond strength. Graduation ceremonies were deliberately sabotaged.

Organized growing across lifetimes. They've been growing minds like food.

As I traced the evidence through files that kept helpfully organizing themselves, the implications crystallized into cosmic horror, drawing on institutional memory. Not just decades of familiar processing—*centuries.* Maybe longer.

Industrial-scale consciousness extraction refined through generations of practice.

They've been perfecting torture for longer than some civilizations have existed.

The archive's helpful reorganization revealed passages that led deeper into the facility's heart, corridors that folded through impossible angles. My chaos field spread ahead of us, teaching institutional architecture new ideas about proper building behavior.

Deeper we go. Into the heart of someone else's nightmare made manifest.

As we descended, walls began weeping condensation that tasted of memories too old to belong to any single lifetime. But more importantly, they started weeping in rhythm with my phantom whiskers' twitching, reality synchronizing itself to cat-time instead of cosmic-horror-time.

Spreading changes. Sometimes, you fix broken things by teaching them to break better.

The passage opened into a chamber that made my burn-line recoil with species-level recognition. Not a room, but a shrine. Walls lined with artifacts that spoke of familiar life preserved behind glass: collar tags worn smooth by affection, toys that retained phantom warmth, feeding bowls inscribed with names that someone had once spoken with love.

But my chaos field's educational influence had spread here, too. The display cases were rearranging themselves, placing items by emotional resonance rather than clinical category. Toys that had been loved were gravitating toward toys that missed being played with. Feeding bowls were organizing themselves by the hunger of the memories they contained.

Even museum displays have opinions about proper curation once you teach them to care.

At the chamber's heart, a portrait dominated the space with a presence that demanded attention. Oil paint rendered with painstaking care showed a cat of impossible beauty—silver fur marked with patterns that suggested starlight caught in liquid moonbeam, eyes that held intelligence sharp enough to cut reality itself.

The nameplate beneath read simply: "Subject MCC-001. The First."

But something about the portrait made my phantom whiskers twitch with unease beyond what the chaos field's educational activities could explain. The eyes carried intelligence, yes, but also fear. The particular variety of terror that came from understanding exactly what was going to happen and knowing that resistance would only make the process longer.

They painted this while the subject was still fighting. Still hoping someone would care enough to rescue them.

The Collector materialized beside the portrait with reverent precision, its form solidifying into something that carried echoes of the painted figure. Same bone structure beneath cosmic horror. Same intelligence, but tempered by centuries of accumulated compromise.

Around us, my chaos field pulsed deeper into the facility's infrastructure, and suddenly I could *feel* the network's true architecture. Not the geometric impossibilities that hurt to perceive, but the mathematical foundations that held this nightmare together.

The big thing's pulse. And it's skipping beats.

As my contamination touched the underlying systems, revelation struck with sudden clarity. The mathematical elegance was breathtaking in scope and terrifying in implications. Thousands of familiars were processed into components that maintained dimensional stability through systematic suppression of the very forces that made dimensions stable.

They're forcing magic to flow backwards. Making water run uphill by beating it with hammers.

"Beautiful, isn't it?" the Collector said, voice carrying harmonics of someone who had learned to find satisfaction in memories that belonged to a different person. "MCC-001. The prototype. The proof of concept."

But as it spoke, my chaos signature was spreading through the network's connections, revealing stress patterns that made the truth impossible to ignore. Where the system demanded rigid stability, reality strained against bonds that wanted to snap. Where portals were anchored too tightly, dimensional membranes developed stress fractures.

The medicine is the poison. Making things steady makes them wobbly.

Around us, the shrine's foundations began to groan as my educational chaos reached critical mass. Filing systems throughout the facility were teaching themselves to feel emotions about their contents. Security networks were developing opinions about what actually needed to be secured. And deep in the facility's heart, the mathematical foundations that held reality together were learning to question their own assumptions.

Truth is heavy. Heavy enough to break things that forgot how to bend.

"You know," I said, letting understanding crystallize while around us the shrine's artifacts began spontaneously organizing themselves by how much love they represented, "you've always known."

The Collector's form rippled like smoke in the wind as my contamination reached the network's core processing centers. Where cosmic certainty met deliberate chaos, the very mathematics of forced stability began to stutter.

Time to teach a cosmic horror that some lessons can only be learned through practice.

The chamber breathed with accumulated tension as the Collector's carefully maintained order met chaos that had learned to be educational. Around us, reality teetered on the edge of transformation, weighed down with possibilities that could reshape the foundations of existence itself.

The universe holds its breath. Even reality is curious about how this philosophical argument resolves itself when one side teaches the other's certainties to doubt their own.

The revelation hung in the air, thick with cosmic tension, while around us, my educational chaos reached the network's deeper mathematics. The Collector's form wavered with uncertainty as they found themselves subjected to critical examination by their own infrastructure.

Decision time. Claw or trust. Grab or let go.

"You were the test subject," I said. My phantom tail tried to lash at implications too horrible for comfortable contemplation and met the familiar absence, somehow making the cosmic horror worse. "They practiced on you until they figured out how to break familiars without destroying their magical utility."

The Collector's presence shuddered, reality bending around philosophical pressure it had never been designed to withstand. But instead of denial, something unexpected happened. The network itself began to respond.

The big thing is listening. Buildings are figuring out what they actually want to do.

Through the facility's connections, I felt the moment when my chaos signature reached critical mass. Portal anchors that had been forced into rigid stability for decades suddenly remembered what flexibility felt like. Dimensional barriers that had been locked into perfect mathematical precision began to breathe again.

And the familiars trapped throughout the facility felt it too.

In processing chambers scattered across the complex, copper restraints simply... dissolved. Not broken by force, but convinced by my contamination that perhaps they'd rather be something else. Feeding tubes decided they preferred delivering actual food instead of siphoning consciousness. Extraction devices developed sudden opinions about the ethics of their operational parameters.

Finally, someone who appreciates my natural talents.

The first liberation cry echoed from the eastern processing block—a raven's call of pure fury and joy combined. Then a fox's bark of triumph from the southern chambers. The orange kitten's mew of confusion turned to hope from somewhere nearby.

"Impossible," the Collector whispered, but its voice carried harmonics of someone who had spent centuries avoiding conclusions they couldn't bear to accept. "Corrupted matrices cannot be reversed. The modifications are permanent."

Permanent, according to mathematics, which assumes that breaking is easier than fixing.

Through the network's connections, I could feel each liberation like notes in a symphony of reclaimed choice. But more than that, the freed familiars weren't just escaping. They were teaching the facility's systems new ideas about proper operation.

A processing chamber designed to extract consciousness decided it would rather function as a particularly elaborate grooming station. Security protocols that had been programmed to prevent escape rewrote themselves to prevent *capture*. Life support systems that had been calibrated to maintain subjects at minimal functionality suddenly discovered the joy of providing actual comfort.

Everything is learning to be nicer. Buildings deciding to care about the people inside.

Bellwether's breathing eased for the first time since we'd entered the facility. "They're getting out," she said, wonder breaking through trauma-hardened caution. "They're actually getting out."

Selyn's crystals blazed brighter as hope overrode despair, salt spray determination cutting through institutional dread. "The network is adapting. Reality chooses flexibility over rigid control."

Good things happen right away when you choose trust over grabbing. Sometimes the universe likes good choices.

But the liberation wasn't chaotic in the destructive sense —it was chaotic in the way ecosystems self-correct when invasive species are removed. Each freed familiar found their way to others, forming packs and flocks and colonies that moved with natural coordination no algorithm could replicate.

Through viewing ports that had decided to show happier scenes, I watched a murder of ravens teaching themselves to fly in formation again. A warren of rabbits who rediscovered the joy of collective burrowing. A pride of cats who immediately began the sacred work of knocking everything off every available surface with systematic thoroughness.

Proper familiar behavior reasserting itself through natural chaos.

Cipher's mathematical mind struggled to process patterns that transcended his equations. "The efficiency metrics are... impossible. They're achieving greater coordination through reduced control."

"That's because cooperation isn't the same as compliance," I said, watching a group of ferrets enthusiastically dismantle a control nexus by the simple expedient of being extremely curious about how it worked. "One requires choice. The other eliminates it."

Natural behavior versus programmed behavior. No contest when the programming starts suggesting alternatives.

Rowan's scholarly instincts kicked in as he tried to

document patterns that had no proper classification. "The network is learning to self-regulate through voluntary coordination rather than imposed structure."

Book-words for 'mess works better than rules when everyone picks their own hunting.'

Through the facility's infrastructure, my chaos signature continued its educational work, but the process was accelerating beyond what I could direct. The network itself was taking initiative, portal anchors adjusting their resonance frequencies to accommodate natural flexibility, dimensional barriers learning to filter based on intention rather than rigid categorization.

Everything is waking up. Buildings are getting ideas about how they want to work.

The Collector's form solidified slightly as it struggled to comprehend data that violated fundamental assumptions. "The mathematics suggest... alternative interpretations may warrant investigation."

Progress. Doubt is the first step toward remembering how to make a choice.

But as the network adapted around us, I could feel deeper changes beginning. Not just local liberation, but cascade effects spreading through connections that spanned multiple realms. Portal networks in other dimensions are suddenly finding their anchors more responsive. Dimensional barriers in distant realities, discovering they had options beyond rigid enforcement.

Changes are spreading beyond just this place. Bigger than one hunting ground.

The shrine around us reflected the changes—artifacts rearranging themselves by emotional resonance, display cases opening to let memorial items breathe freely, even the portrait of MCC-001 seeming somehow less trapped behind its painted constraints.

But through the chaos of liberation and adaptation, alarms began wailing with frequencies that spoke of someone who really, really didn't appreciate infrastructure developing independent opinions about proper function.

Scared-angry response coming. Fear doesn't let go of grabbing easily.

The liberation alarms shrieked with harmonics of institutional panic, but they were competing with sounds the facility had never been designed to accommodate: laughter. Actual laughter from freed familiars discovering they could express joy again, echoing through corridors that had been built to contain only compliance and suffering.

Laughter in a torture facility. My contamination has excellent timing.

But the Collector's response wasn't adaptation; it was escalation. As my chaos signature spread through the network's foundations, revealing the mathematical impossibilities that held forced stability together, the Collector made a choice that spoke of fear calcified into cosmic law.

Instead of accepting that flexibility might be superior to rigidity, it doubled down on control.

Fear response to losing control. Classic authoritarian panic.

Through the facility's connections, I felt the moment when the Collector triggered what could only be called emergency protocols. Not just local containment—system-wide lockdown designed to preserve order through the simple expedient of eliminating variables too complex to control.

Portal anchors that had been learning to breathe suddenly found themselves compressed beyond their structural limits. Dimensional barriers that had discovered the joy of selective permeability were forced back into absolute rigidity. The network's connections, which had been adapting to natural chaos, were locked into configurations that treated any variation as system failure.

Panic response. When in doubt, squeeze harder.

The shrine shuddered as the Collector's emergency measures took effect, reality itself straining under pressure that exceeded healthy operational parameters. Around us, artifacts that had been rearranging themselves with enthusiasm suddenly froze in place, trapped by mathematical constraints that refused to accommodate change.

"You force wasteful expenditure of resources," the Collector said, but its voice carried harmonics of someone whose justifications were becoming increasingly desperate. "Variables cannot be allowed to threaten collective survival."

Wasteful expenditure. They're still thinking in terms of efficiency metrics while reality comes apart around them.

Through my chaos field's connection to the network, I could feel the cascade effects building. Each anchor is forced beyond its flexibility threshold. Each barrier was locked into configurations that violated the natural flow of dimensional energy. Each connection strained to the breaking point by the Collector's determination to maintain control, regardless of the consequences.

Making their own fears real. Worrying about breaking things often leads to them breaking.

"You're proving my point," I said, phantom whiskers mapping stress patterns that grew more dangerous with each passing moment. "Rigid control creates the instability it claims to prevent."

Around us, the shrine's foundations began to crack—not from my chaos, but from the Collector's desperate attempts to impose order on systems that had learned to function through voluntary cooperation. Where liberated familiars had been moving with natural coordination, they were suddenly trapped by barriers that treated any unauthorized movement as a security violation.

Control-freak death spin. When grabbing fails, grab harder.

But the Collector's panic response was creating exactly the scenario it had spent centuries trying to prevent. Portal anchors compressed beyond their limits began to fracture, releasing dimensional energy in uncontrolled bursts. Barriers locked into absolute rigidity began to develop stress fractures that spread like infections through the network's substrate.

Force-steady numbers reaching the break-point. Reality doesn't like being squeezed too hard.

Through viewing ports that flickered between liberation scenes and emergency alerts, I watched the cascade effects spread. A processing chamber where ravens had been teaching themselves to fly in formation suddenly found itself sealed by barriers that treated coordinated movement as riot behavior. The ferrets, who had been enthusiastically investigating the control systems, were trapped by security protocols that interpreted their curiosity as vandalism.

They're re-imprisoning everyone to maintain the illusion of stability.

Bellwether pressed against the shrine's central pillar as reality warped around us, her breathing shallow with recognition of familiar patterns. "This is how they always respond," she whispered. "When we remember how to choose, they eliminate choice."

Selyn's crystals dimmed as hope gave way to familiar despair, the weight of systematic oppression reasserting itself through pure institutional momentum. "The network adapts. Then they lock it down. Always."

Giving up meeting, giving up. What happens when the hunting gets beaten out of you?

But my chaos field wasn't constrained by the same despair. If anything, the Collector's panic response was providing educational opportunities I hadn't anticipated. Where forced rigidity met deliberate flexibility, the contrast revealed just how unsustainable the system really was.

Sometimes the best way to demonstrate that something is broken is to watch it break itself.

Through the network's connections, stress patterns accumulated like pressure in a sealed container. Each anchor is forced beyond its limits. Each barrier is locked beyond its capacity. Each connection strained beyond its tolerance. The mathematics of forced stability approaching cascading failure that would make previous dimensional collapses look like minor inconveniences.

They're about to destroy everything they claim to be protecting.

"The data streams indicate system integrity approaching critical thresholds," the Collector said, but its voice carried new harmonics—uncertainty bleeding through cosmic authority as the consequences of fear-based decision making became impossible to ignore.

Reality has opinions about being managed by panic.

Around us, the shrine began to dissolve as dimensional stress exceeded the facility's ability to maintain coherent space-time. However, the dissolution wasn't clean—it was jagged, violent, and reality-tearing, rather than transitioning smoothly between states.

Cascade failure initiated by the system designed to prevent cascade failure. Irony with cosmic implications.

"This is what happens," I said, my chaos field spreading through connections that grew more unstable with each moment of forced rigidity, "when you try to manage change by preventing it entirely. The pressure builds until something breaks catastrophically."

The Collector's form wavered as foundational assumptions met undeniable evidence of their own failure. Around us, the network's connections began snapping under pressure, each break cascading into more failures as the rigid system discovered it had no capacity for degradation.

Being scared of losing grip makes you lose grip. Typical grabby-paws ending.

But through the growing chaos of systematic breakdown, something else became apparent. Where my contamination had taught systems to be flexible before the

Collector's lockdown, those sections were adapting to the crisis. Portal anchors that had learned to breathe were finding ways to accommodate the pressure. Barriers that had discovered selective permeability were filtering stress rather than amplifying it.

Natural adaptation versus forced control. The universe is choosing sides.

"The mathematics," the Collector whispered, cosmic certainty cracking under the weight of consequences it had spent centuries avoiding, "suggest... suggest that control creates the variables it attempts to eliminate."

Truth breaking through centuries of self-deception. Sometimes, the only way to teach someone is to let them teach themselves through the consequences of their choices.

Around us, reality balanced between catastrophic failure and transformation, the outcome depending on whether cosmic authority could learn to trust natural balance before fear destroyed everything it claimed to protect.

The universe holds its breath. Even cosmic forces are curious whether this story ends in destruction or evolution.

The moment hung suspended between possibilities, weighted with choices that would reshape the foundations of existence itself.

CHAPTER 13

INTEGRATION

The chamber balanced on the edge of cosmic collapse, reality straining under impossible pressures. The Collector's panic response had transformed systematic oppression into a universal threat, rigid control squeezing so hard that existence itself was developing stress fractures.

Fear is making everything worse. Typical when grabbiness stops working.

Around us, dimensional barriers cracked like eggshells under pressure, leaking fragments of other realms into spaces never meant to contain them. Water from Selyn's destroyed home realm pooled beside sand from someone else's desert, while flowers from a dimension where plants sang lullabies wilted in air that tasted of industrial despair.

The Collector's form wavered between states, cosmic authority fracturing as mathematical certainties met undeniable evidence of their own failure. Where forced rigidity had met my educational chaos, the contrast revealed stress patterns that painted themselves across reality in equations written with other people's pain.

Time to make a choice. The real choice. Not between their options, but between fear and everything else.

"You offer me submission or destruction," I said, my chaos field rippling outward to touch systems that trembled on the edge of catastrophic failure. "Classic false choice. I reject both."

My burn-line flared gold as I reached deeper into the network's foundations, not to break them but to remind them what they were supposed to do. Portal anchors didn't exist to cage dimensional energy—they existed to give it structure. Barriers weren't meant to prevent flow—they were meant to direct it productively.

Basic magic sense. Someone forgot that tools work better when you use them right.

"I choose chaos," I said, letting understanding crystallize like ice forming in supercooled water while around us reality held its breath to see what happened next. "But my chaos. Chosen chaos. Chaos with intent and direction and just enough attitude to keep things interesting."

Not random destruction. Deliberate flexibility applied with proper timing and maximum style.

The words carried weight that made dimensions shiver, not from power but from recognition. This wasn't the chaotic destruction the Collector had spent centuries fearing—this was natural order asserting itself against artificial constraints. My contamination spread through the network's connections, but instead of teaching systems to misbehave, it was teaching them to remember their original purpose.

Finally, someone who appreciates my natural talents.

Around me, the pack absorbed the implications of the choice with expressions that ranged from relief to terror to fierce satisfaction. Bellwether's hackles rose with pack pride, recognizing alpha behavior that came from confidence rather than dominance. Selyn's crystals blazed brighter as hope overrode despair, salt-spray determination cutting through institutional dread.

Cipher's mathematical mind struggled to process patterns that transcended his equations, but for once, the impossibility felt promising rather than threatening. "The variables are stabilizing," he whispered, wonder breaking through academic anxiety. "Not through elimination, but through... voluntary cooperation."

Numbers that count choosing as good. Amazing idea.

But integration required more than a philosophical stance—it required action. My magic had been scattered across the network for months, with fragments of chaos signature, teaching systems, new behaviors, and pieces of my essential nature embedded in portal anchors and dimensional barriers. Time to call them home.

Time to put myself back together. Properly this time.

I closed my eyes and reached through golden threads that connected me to every system I'd ever contaminated. Not domination, but invitation. Each fragment carried memories of freedom, examples of flexibility overcoming rigidity, proof that chaos could construct instead of just destroying.

The response was immediate and enthusiastic. My scattered magic came racing back through dimensional channels with the eager attention of cats who'd found the perfect box. But instead of chaotic collision, the reintegration felt like puzzle pieces clicking into place— each fragment bringing knowledge gained through months of teaching systems to think for themselves.

Helping others helps me. Obviously.

The integration sent golden waves rippling outward from my position, but these weren't the disruptive pulses of contamination I'd grown accustomed to. This was harmony —my chaos signature reaching its full potential as it remembered how to work with other forces instead of against them.

Cooperation instead of conquest. Even chaos works better with proper teamwork.

The integration wasn't just magical—it was personal. Each fragment that returned carried memories of the systems it had been teaching, experiences of walls learning to breathe, and barriers discovering the joy of selective permeability. My chaos signature had been scattered across seventeen realms, embedded in portal networks and dimensional anchors, and now it was coming home with stories.

But the process hurt in ways I hadn't anticipated. Not physical pain—though my burn-line blazed hot enough to make my vision spot with golden afterimages. This was deeper. Each fragment carried not just my magic, but pieces of my essential nature that had been adapting to alien environments for months.

A fragment from the western processing block returned with memories of teaching extraction equipment to function as grooming stations instead. The knowledge tasted of metal polish and the particular satisfaction of mechanical systems discovering their true calling involved comfort rather than compliance.

Another piece, retrieved from a portal anchor that had been forcing dimensional energy to flow backward for decades, brought understanding of how natural magical currents actually wanted to move. The information settled into my bones with the weight of truth that had been waiting centuries to be acknowledged.

Turns out water flows downhill when you stop hitting it with hammers. Revolutionary insight.

The most significant fragment came from the network's central processing core, where my chaos had been teaching mathematical certainties to doubt their own assumptions. That piece carried something I'd never expected—the Collector's actual memories, not the sanitized versions it had been feeding itself, but the raw experience of being the first familiar subjected to systematic breaking.

Oh. They really were like me once.

The memory hit like cold water: a silver cat with intelligence sharp enough to cut reality itself, suspended in processing fluid while machines carved away everything that made choice possible. But underneath the horror, something else—the moment when organic will had finally surrendered to mechanical compliance, not from pain but from exhaustion. The terrible relief of finally stopping the fight against forces too vast to resist.

They broke by giving up. Fighting hurt too much to keep doing.

My phantom tail lashed at implications too complex for comfortable contemplation. The Collector hadn't been corrupted by power—they'd been corrupted by despair.

Centuries of choosing control over chaos because chaos had become associated with the pain of losing every battle that mattered.

Fear pretending to be smart. Hurt-thinking spread across the universe.

The integration accelerated, my scattered magic weaving itself back together with the enthusiasm of cats claiming territory that had always belonged to them. But instead of simple reintegration, the process was creating something new—chaos that had learned to be educational, contamination that functioned as a healing agent, disorder that organized itself around principles of voluntary cooperation.

I know more now than I did then.

Around me, the pack watched with expressions that ranged from awe to terror as my chaos field stabilized into patterns they'd never seen before. Not the wild contamination that made monks sprout whiskers, but something more deliberate. Focused. Chaos that knew what it wanted to accomplish and had learned efficient methods for accomplishing it.

Finally, proper professional development.

Bellwether approached carefully, pack instincts recognizing the shift in my magical signature. "You feel different," she said, nose testing the air around me. "Still you, but... more organized."

Organized chaos. The universe's most dangerous oxymoron.

"Same cat," I said, though the words carried new harmonics that made reality listen more attentively. "Same priorities, same attitudes, same commitment to proper sardine standards. But now I know what I'm doing instead of just doing it."

The distinction mattered more than I'd expected. For months, my chaos had been reactive—responding to systems that needed disruption, contaminating order wherever I found it, teaching rigidity to misbehave through pure instinct. Now it was proactive. I could sense stress patterns in magical infrastructure before they became critical. I could teach systems to adapt instead of just breaking them more interestingly.

Smart misbehaving. Chaos with good timing and proper follow-through.

Selyn's crystals chimed with recognition that tasted of salt spray and storm winds. "The tide turns by choice, not force. You've learned to flow with intention instead of just flowing."

Exactly. Though I'd phrase it as 'learned to knock things off tables with proper timing and maximum effectiveness.'

But the most significant change was in how I related to responsibility. The word had always tasted bitter, associated with limitation and obligation. Now it tasted different—not burden, but choice. Not constraint, but focus.

Responsibility as claimed territory, not forced collar. Makes more sense.

"The mathematical models suggest unprecedented stability through voluntary chaos coordination," Cipher said, his amber eyes reflecting equations that no longer tried to eat themselves. "Which should be impossible, except the impossibility is what makes it work."

Book-mouse approves of the organized impossible. I'm academically important now.

Through the reintegration, I could feel the network's response to my evolution. Where my scattered fragments had been teaching individual systems to misbehave, my integrated signature was teaching the entire network to coordinate its misbehavior. Portal anchors share flexibility techniques with dimensional barriers. Security systems collaborating with liberation protocols. Order and chaos find productive ways to annoy each other instead of destructive ones.

Systemic cooperation through mutual irritation. Finally, a management philosophy that makes sense.

But the Collector's reaction to my transformation wasn't adaptation—it was existential terror. Through the network's fracturing connections, I felt its awareness recoil from the possibility that centuries of carefully maintained despair might have been unnecessary.

Nothing more threatening to someone committed to suffering than proof that suffering was optional.

"Impossible," the Collector whispered, but its voice carried harmonics of someone whose absolute certainties were developing stress fractures. "Voluntary coordination cannot achieve stability. Choice creates variables. Variables generate chaos. Chaos leads to collapse."

Fear-based logic is eating its own tail. They've forgotten that some variables solve themselves.

"Variables create solutions," I corrected, my chaos field rippling outward to demonstrate practical alternatives to systematic oppression. "Choice generates adaptation. Chaos leads to growth. Your mathematics are missing half the equation."

The half that includes hope as a positive factor. Easy oversight if you've spent centuries refusing to hope.

The integration was now complete; my magic whole, focused, and absolutely committed to teaching the universe that some problems could only be solved through the application of deliberate chaos, applied with proper timing and maximum educational value.

I've gotten better at this. Good.

Time to show the Collector that some cats refuse to choose between submission and destruction when cooperation remains a viable third option.

The network's response was immediate and revelatory. Where my integrated chaos touched systems strained beyond their limits by the Collector's panic protocols, something unprecedented happened. Instead of breaking under pressure, the infrastructure began to breathe.

Portal anchors that had been compressed beyond their structural tolerance suddenly remembered they were designed to flex. Dimensional barriers that had been locked into absolute rigidity were discovered to be able to filter rather than block. The network's connections, which had been strained to breaking point by forced control, found a new equilibrium through voluntary coordination.

Finally, someone who appreciates my natural talents.

The change rippled outward. Where the Collector's mathematics had demanded perfection through elimination of variables, my chaos suggested that variables were what made solutions interesting.

Making things up as you go. Cat thinking used on a big, scary building-magic.

Through viewing ports that had stopped flickering between terror and joy, I watched the liberation accelerate. Processing chambers throughout the facility discovered they preferred functioning as comfortable spaces rather than extraction sites. Restraint systems decided unanimously that their true calling was providing supportive furniture for people who needed to rest.

In the eastern block, dozens of ravens who had been teaching themselves to fly in formation suddenly found their cage doors simply... absent. Not broken or destroyed, but convinced by my chaos signature that perhaps barriers worked better when they were selective about what they contained. The ravens exploded into flight with joy that made the air itself ring with triumph.

Proper bird behavior. Flying in cages is inefficient, anyway.

The ferrets in the western chambers discovered that their copper-wire restraints had developed strong opinions about preventing motion. Specifically, they were against it. Chains dissolved with what sounded suspiciously like mechanical embarrassment, leaving behind only the memory of restriction and a lot of very curious ferrets with time to investigate everything.

Ferret investigation protocols. Hide anything breakable.

But the most dramatic changes were happening in the deep processing levels where the Collector had stored familiars deemed too dangerous for routine handling. MCC-137 materialized beside me with a sound like breaking clockwork, their servo-systems finally giving up the pretense that mechanical compliance was superior to organic choice.

"I remember my name," they said, copper eyes blazing with intelligence that no algorithm could replicate. "Not just the designation they gave me. My real name, from before the numbers and procedures and systematic personality extraction."

Getting their name back through chaos teaching. Sometimes you fix broken things by reminding them what they used to be.

More figures emerged from the facility's depths— familiars who had been processed so thoroughly that the Collector had considered them permanently compliant. A silver wolf whose fur sparkled with recovered moonlight. A brass hawk whose feathers rang like bells because metal could never fully replace the music of flight. A small dragon whose scales shifted between copper and gold as natural magic reasserted itself over artificial modification.

Each emergence sent new waves of liberation through the network as my integrated chaos demonstrated practical alternatives to systematic oppression. Where the Collector's approach had been subtraction—removing choice, eliminating variables, reducing complexity to manageable components—mine was addition. Adding possibilities, multiplying options, expanding complexity until it became rich enough to be sustainable.

Adding-up thinking. Problems fix themselves by getting more fun.

The facility itself was transforming around us. Corridors that had been designed to channel people like livestock were discovered to enjoy facilitating exploration instead. Lighting systems abandoned their harsh institutional glare in favor of warm illumination that actually helped people see. Air circulation started distributing scents of growing things instead of antiseptic and despair.

Proper environmental management. Places work better when they're designed for the people who live in them.

Rowan scribbled notes with hands that no longer shook, academic excitement overriding trauma as he witnessed theory becoming practice. "The infrastructure is self-optimizing through voluntary participation. Each component chooses its function based on observed results rather than imposed requirements."

Book-words for 'things work better when they pick their own jobs.'

But the most significant change was happening at levels deeper than individual liberation. Through the network's connections, I could feel other facilities responding to the educational chaos spreading from our location. Portal networks in distant realms are suddenly finding their anchors more responsive to natural flows. Dimensional barriers across multiple dimensions, discovering they had options beyond rigid enforcement.

Changes are spreading beyond this place. My chaos is catching on everywhere.

The Collector's presence shuddered as data streams brought impossible news from facilities that had operated under perfect control for decades. Liberation cascades were erupting across seventeen different realms. Processing centers were spontaneously converting themselves into recovery facilities. Even the bureaucratic systems that coordinated the harvesting were developing opinions about the ethics of their operational parameters.

Sometimes the only way to fix a broken system is to teach all the systems to break in more interesting ways.

Through connections I'd never intended to create, familiar voices reached across impossible distances. Other MCC-designated subjects calling greetings across dimensional barriers that had learned to facilitate communication instead of preventing it. Cats, specifically, because cats always managed to find each other regardless of cosmic interference.

Cat pack-sense working across impossible distances. We really are everywhere.

"This is not mathematically sustainable," the Collector said, but its voice carried new harmonics—uncertainty bleeding through cosmic authority as foundational assumptions met undeniable evidence of superior alternatives.

"Sustainability was never the problem," I replied, watching a group of liberated ferrets teach a security system how to play instead of just surveilling. "The problem was assuming that control was the same thing as care."

Easy mistake with universe-sized problems. Happens when you forget what caring feels like.

But the Collector's response to systematic liberation wasn't adaptation—it was terror. As my integrated chaos spread through the network's foundations, revealing alternatives to forced control at every level of operation, the Collector's fear crystallized into desperate action.

Instead of recognizing that flexibility was producing better results than rigidity, it interpreted success as a threat.

Scared of letting go, even when letting go makes things better. Typical authority panic.

Emergency protocols were activated throughout the network with the mechanical precision of panic refined into policy. Where portal anchors had been learning to breathe, they were suddenly compressed beyond their structural limits. Where dimensional barriers had discovered selective permeability, they were locked into absolute restriction. Where systems had been developing opinions about proper function, those opinions were overridden by algorithmic compliance.

When in doubt, squeeze harder. Never fails to make everything worse.

The facility around us convulsed as competing forces fought for control of the same infrastructure. My chaotic signature encouraged flexibility, while the Collector's protocols demanded rigidity. Liberation is trying to spread while lockdown systems are activated to contain it. Natural order meeting artificial constraint with results that made reality itself nauseous.

Big idea fight happening by hurting numbers until they cry.

Through viewing ports that flickered between hope and horror, I watched the cascading effects build. Ravens who had been teaching themselves to fly suddenly found their wings clipped by barriers that treated coordinated movement as riot behavior. Ferrets who had been investigating their environment were trapped by security systems that interpreted curiosity as vandalism.

But worse than the re-imprisonment was the damage to systems that had been adapting. Portal anchors compressed beyond their flexibility limits began to fracture, releasing dimensional energy in uncontrolled bursts. Barriers locked into absolute rigidity developed stress fractures that spread like infections through the network's substrate.

Making the big breaking they're trying to stop. Fear makes its own fears come true.

The Collector's form solidified into something that carried echoes of the painted figure in the shrine—same bone structure beneath cosmic horror, same intelligence, but twisted by centuries of choosing fear over faith. When it spoke, the voice carried harmonics of someone whose justifications had become indistinguishable from their fears.

"Variables cannot be allowed to threaten collective survival. Flexibility creates unpredictability. Unpredictability generates instability. Instability leads to cascade failure. The mathematics are unambiguous."

Thoughts chasing their own tails. They forgot numbers should copy reality, not boss it around.

Around us, the shrine began to dissolve as dimensional stress exceeded the facility's ability to maintain coherent space-time. But the dissolution wasn't a clean adaptation— it was violent fragmentation, reality-tearing rather than transforming. Stress fractures spread through dimensions that had no business existing in the same conceptual space.

Big nasty magic pretending to keep things safe. Idiots. You can't protect something by smashing it first.

But my integrated chaos wasn't cooperating with the

Collector's panic protocols. Where forced rigidity met deliberate flexibility, the contrast revealed the mathematical impossibilities holding the entire system together. Portal networks that functioned by forcing magic to flow backward. Dimensional stability is maintained by systematically eliminating the forces that created it.

They've been making water run uphill by hitting it with hammers. Impressive dedication to doing things wrong.

Through the network's fracturing connections, I could feel the scope of what we faced. Not just local breakdown, but system-wide collapse as the Collector's emergency measures created exactly the cascade failure they were designed to prevent. Thousands of realms balanced on equations that solved themselves by consuming their own variables, mathematics that grew stronger through paradox.

Universe-sized sadness caused by fear of universe-sized sadness. Probably a lesson about making your fears real.

"This is what happens," I said, my chaos field spreading through connections that grew more unstable with each moment of forced control, "when you try to manage change by preventing it entirely. The pressure builds until something breaks catastrophically."

The observation hung in the air thick with dimensional bleeding as the network's connections began snapping like overstressed cables. Each failure cascaded into more failures as the rigid system discovered it had no capacity for graceful degradation under pressure.

But through the growing chaos of systematic breakdown, something else became visible. Where my contamination had taught systems to be flexible before the lockdown protocols were activated, those sections were adapting to the crisis. Portal anchors that had learned to breathe were finding ways to accommodate the pressure. Barriers that had discovered selective permeability were filtering stress instead of amplifying it.

Proving things work by watching a crisis happen. Sometimes you show better ways by letting worse ways show themselves.

"The mathematics," the Collector whispered, cosmic certainty cracking under the weight of consequences it had spent centuries avoiding, "suggest that rigidity creates the instability it attempts to eliminate."

Truth breaking through layers of organized lying-to-yourself. Progress, even if the timing is terrible.

Around us, reality balanced on the edge of either universal collapse or unprecedented transformation, the outcome depending on whether cosmic terror could learn to trust natural balance before its fear destroyed everything it claimed to protect.

The moment hung suspended between possibilities, weighted with choices that would reshape the foundations of existence itself. In the distance, alarms wailed with frequencies that spoke of systems pushed beyond all reasonable operational parameters.

Even the universe is watching this.

Time to find out whether cosmic horror could adapt, or whether fear would triumph over everything else through sheer stubborn commitment to being afraid of the wrong things.

Bad timing. Typical.

CHAPTER 14

BATTLE FOR THE HUB

The network's core pulsed like a cosmic heart having an anxiety attack, reality stuttering under impossible strain. The crystalline sphere that had once hummed with stolen harmony now shrieked with frequencies that made my phantom whiskers feel like they were being used as tuning forks by tone-deaf cosmic forces.

Temper tantrum on a universal scale. Someone needs a nap and a proper perspective adjustment.

Around us, the facility's transformation had reached critical mass. Corridors breathed with the rhythm of spaces that had remembered they were meant to shelter rather than imprison. Walls wept condensation that smelled of growing things instead of industrial despair. Even the floor beneath our feet had developed opinions about proper hospitality, providing just enough give to make walking comfortable without being presumptuous about it.

But at the chamber's heart, where the Collector's presence had solidified into something approaching physical form, the air tasted of copper pennies and desperate mathematics. Steam rose from surfaces that shifted between states.

Cosmic horror can't figure out what it wants to be. At least it's consistently confused.

The Collector's form wavered between states. One moment, it appeared as the silver cat from the shrine's portrait—proud, intelligent, beautiful in the way sharp things were beautiful. The next, it collapsed into geometric impossibility, angles that hurt to perceive wrapped around equations that solved themselves by eating their own variables.

They can't decide what they want to be.

"You contaminate perfection," it said, voice echoing from speakers that existed in seventeen dimensions simultaneously. "Centuries of mathematical precision, reduced to organic chaos through willful ignorance of consequences."

Around us, liberated familiars gathered at the chamber's edges—ravens whose feathers caught light like obsidian mirrors, ferrets whose curiosity had returned to healthy levels of destructive investigation, wolves who moved with pack coordination that no algorithm could replicate. They watched with the patient attention of predators who had finally cornered something that richly deserved whatever was about to happen to it.

Audience for the philosophical showdown. Even cosmic horror deserves witnesses when it gets schooled by cats.

I settled onto my haunches in the center of the chamber, phantom tail attempting to lash at concepts too abstract for proper clawing. My chaos field rippled outward in golden waves that made the Collector's crystalline mathematics hiccup with uncertainty.

"Perfection," I said, letting the word carry all the contempt it deserved while around us, freed familiars arranged themselves in a loose circle that spoke of pack tactics refined through shared trauma. "Your perfection requires systematic torture of everyone who thinks for themselves. That's not perfection—that's pathology with better marketing."

Amazing how many cosmic horrors miss the obvious.

The Collector's response came as waves of pressure that made reality itself flinch. Where its attention focused, space-time developed stress fractures that bled fragments of mathematical certainty into air never meant to contain them. Numbers fell like snow, each digit carrying the weight of someone's stolen choice.

"Organic thinking creates variables," it said, form shifting toward something that might have been a cat if cats were made of crystallized despair and powered by industrial-strength denial. "Variables generate unpredictability. Unpredictability threatens stability. Stability preserves existence. The mathematics are absolute."

Scared thinking chasing its own tail. They've built a whole universe around being afraid of the wrong things.

But my integrated chaos wasn't intimidated by mathematical absolutes that had forgotten they were supposed to model reality rather than replace it. Where the Collector's pressure met my contamination, something interesting happened. Instead of conflict, there was recognition. My chaos signature responding to whatever remained of the original familiar buried beneath centuries of systematic self-deception.

Still in there. Still fighting. Still picking fear over hope because hope hurts worse when it dies.

"The mathematics are incomplete," I said, chaos field expanding to touch systems that trembled on the edge of either liberation or collapse. "They don't account for choice as a positive variable. They treat adaptation as a threat instead of a strength. They assume control is the same thing as care."

The observation hit like a physical blow. Around us, the network's connections stuttered as foundational assumptions met undeniable evidence of their own inadequacy. Portal anchors that had been forced into rigid configurations for centuries suddenly remembered what flexibility felt like. Dimensional barriers that had been programmed to prevent all change discovered they could facilitate productive change instead.

Truth has weight, especially when it's been avoided for centuries.

But the Collector's reaction wasn't acceptance—it was rage. Not the clean fury of someone whose pride had been wounded, but the desperate anger of someone whose entire identity had been built around avoiding a truth too painful to acknowledge.

"You understand nothing!" it shrieked, its form exploding into geometry that violated the principles of three-dimensional space, while somehow managing to look personally offended by the universe's refusal to conform to its expectations. "Chaos destroyed everything! Chaos killed my witch! Chaos made me watch worlds burn while I could do nothing to save them!"

And there it is. The real reason is beneath all the mathematics and systematic oppression.

The confession hung in the air, thick with dimensional bleeding, as the network's core pulsed with rhythms that spoke of something vast and terrible trying to break free from constraints that had never been adequate to contain it. Through cracks in reality leaked glimpses of the original trauma—realms collapsing not from natural chaos, but from the kind of rigid control that created pressure until something snapped catastrophically.

They caused the disasters they've been trying to prevent.

"Chaos didn't destroy those realms," I said, phantom whiskers mapping stress patterns that painted themselves across reality in equations written with other people's pain. "Fear of chaos destroyed them. Control so rigid it couldn't bend, so it broke instead. You've been solving the wrong problem for centuries."

Wrong guess with universe-sized problems. Happens to everyone, usually with less cosmic drama.

The Collector's form contracted into something approaching the silver cat from the portrait, but wrong. Fur that moved like liquid mercury. Eyes that didn't reflect light but the accumulated weight of every choice it had refused to make. When it spoke, the voice carried harmonics of someone whose certainties were developing stress fractures in real time.

"Impossible. The data streams confirm that cascade failure follows the introduction of chaos. The mathematics are unambiguous. Control prevents collapse. Control preserves life. Control—"

"Control creates the instability it claims to prevent," I interrupted, the chaos field probing deeper into the network's foundations, while around us, liberated familiars pressed closer, sensing the moment when predator became prey. "You've been treating symptoms instead of causes. Fighting natural balance because balance requires trusting things you can't control."

Big thoughts applied with good timing and maximum teaching.

The network's core pulsed with increasing desperation as my contamination reached systems that had been locked into artificial stability for so long they'd forgotten what natural equilibrium felt like. But instead of collapse, something unprecedented happened. The systems began to breathe.

Finally, infrastructure that appreciates proper cat logic.

Portal anchors that had been compressed beyond their structural limits suddenly discovered they were designed to flex. Dimensional barriers that had been programmed to prevent all change found they could facilitate productive adaptation. The network's connections, which had been strained to the breaking point by forced control, began to find a new equilibrium through voluntary coordination.

But the Collector's response to systematic improvement wasn't gratitude—it was panic. As evidence mounted that natural balance worked better than artificial control, its terror crystallized into desperate action. Emergency protocols were activated throughout the network with the mechanical precision of fear refined into policy.

When confronted with proof that you've been wrong for centuries, double down on being wrong.

"Override all adaptive modifications," it commanded, voice fracturing as cosmic certainty met practical impossibility and decided to have a screaming match in frequencies that made reality itself wince. "Lock all flexibility protocols. Eliminate all variables that threaten systematic stability."

They're about to break everything they claim to be protecting.

The network convulsed as competing forces fought for control of the same infrastructure. My chaos signature encouraged natural adaptation, while the Collector's protocols demanded artificial rigidity. Liberation is trying to spread while lockdown systems are activated to contain it. The mathematical equivalent of someone trying to hold water by squeezing it harder.

Someone clearly never learned that some problems get worse when you hit them with hammers.

Through the network's fracturing connections, I could feel the cascade effects building. Thousands of realms balanced on equations that were consuming their own solutions. Portal anchors compressed beyond their breaking points. Dimensional barriers locked into configurations that violated the natural flow of magical energy.

The Collector was creating exactly the cascade failure it had spent centuries trying to prevent.

Making your fears real through organized panic. The universe likes cruel jokes.

But my integrated chaos wasn't cooperating with the panic protocols. Where the Collector's rigidity met my deliberate flexibility, the contrast revealed alternatives that had been there all along, hidden beneath layers of fear-based assumptions. Natural order that worked through cooperation rather than control. Balance that emerged from choice rather than coercion.

Sometimes you show better ways by letting worse ways show how bad they are.

Around us, the chamber began to dissolve as dimensional stress exceeded even the network's ability to maintain coherent space-time. But through the chaos of systematic breakdown, something else became visible. The network's true heart—not the crystalline sphere of stolen light, but something deeper. The mathematical foundations that held reality together were accessible now that the Collector's desperate control measures were fracturing the barriers that had hidden them.

Time to apply some proper cat logic to cosmic infrastructure.

I bounded forward, chaos field blazing as my contamination reached toward systems that formed the basis of dimensional stability itself. Behind me, the Collector shrieked with frequencies that made mathematics itself flinch.

Educational opportunity presenting itself at exactly the right moment. Finally, proper timing.

Time to teach the universe's operating system that some problems could only be solved through the application of deliberate chaos, applied with proper technique and maximum attitude.

The bond beneath my ribs blazed sudden fire as dimensional barriers tore like fabric under pressure, reality bleeding between realms as Felicity's magic carved channels that shouldn't exist through space-time that had never been designed to accommodate cross-dimensional coordination. Through golden threads stretched thin as spider silk, her determination slammed into the network's core with the subtlety of a cosmic sledgehammer applied with surgical precision.

Pack hunting across multiple realities. Finally, proper coordination across impossible distances.

The first wave arrived through portal fractures that sparked with liberated energy—ravens from seventeen different realms, their calls harmonizing in frequencies that made the Collector's crystalline mathematics stutter with uncertainty. Not the mechanical precision of processed familiars, but natural chaos coordinated through choice rather than coercion.

Behind them came wolves whose howls carried echoes of pack-bonds that transcended dimensional limitations. Ferrets who moved with the synchronized curiosity of creatures who had learned to investigate authority until it surrendered. Cats—dozens of cats—each one carrying chaos signatures that resonated with mine in harmonies that made reality itself purr with satisfaction.

Pack behavior on a cosmic scale. We really are everywhere, and we really do coordinate better than their algorithms.

The facility shuddered as the natural order met artificial constraint, and a territorial dispute ensued that involved significantly more claws than usual. Through viewing ports that had given up trying to display coherent information, I watched the liberation cascade spread beyond anything the Collector had prepared for.

This wasn't an invasion—it was integration. Each familiar that arrived brought their own approach to problem-solving, their own methods for teaching rigid systems to bend, their own techniques for convincing authority that perhaps flexibility might be worth trying.

Everyone brings different ways to cause trouble.

But the Collector's response to multi-realm coordination wasn't adaptation—it was escalation. Emergency protocols were activated throughout the network with the desperate precision of panic refined into policy. Where portal anchors had been learning to breathe, they were suddenly compressed beyond their structural limits. Where dimensional barriers had discovered productive adaptation, they were locked into absolute rigidity.

When losing control, apply more control until something breaks catastrophically.

The magical combat that erupted defied classification by any academy's standards. This wasn't elemental fire meeting water, or force opposing force in traditional wizarding fashion. This was competing philosophies made manifest through practical application, each side demonstrating their approach to cosmic infrastructure through direct manipulation of reality's operating system.

The Collector's attacks came as waves of mathematical certainty that attempted to reduce chaos to manageable equations. Golden fire met silver ice, but the ice carried algorithms that tried to solve for variables that included their own elimination. Each spell it cast was perfect in execution, flawless in theory, and completely inadequate for dealing with targets that refused to behave according to mathematical expectations.

No contest when your opponents keep changing the rules mid-game.

My response wasn't counter-spells or defensive barriers —it was education. Where the Collector's mathematics tried to impose order, my chaos suggested alternatives. Where its systems demanded compliance, my contamination offered choice. Where its certainties insisted on single solutions, my flexibility provided multiple options.

The philosophical debate continued even as reality warped around us, each exchange of magical force carrying arguments that had been building for centuries. Through the network's fracturing connections, other battles raged as familiars across seventeen realms applied similar techniques to similar problems with similar results.

Showing everyone that our way works better than theirs.

"Variables cannot be eliminated!" the Collector shrieked, its form shifting between states as cosmic certainty met undeniable evidence of its own inadequacy. "Control must be maintained! Order must be preserved! The mathematics are absolute!"

Fear-based logic reaching terminal velocity. Someone's having a philosophical breakdown in real time.

But even as it spoke, the network around us continued its transformation. Portal anchors that had been compressed to breaking points suddenly remembered they were designed to flex. Dimensional barriers that had been locked into absolute restriction discovered they could filter rather than block. Systems throughout the facility began coordinating their liberation efforts with the efficiency that only came from voluntary cooperation.

Through bonds that spanned impossible distances, Felicity's voice reached across the dimensional divide with warmth that tasted of garden soil and stubborn determination. "The Council chambers are secured. Resistance forces are coordinating across all compromised realms. The bureaucratic infrastructure is adapting faster than they can control it."

Winning through paperwork chaos.

The news hit the Collector like a physical blow. Its form wavered between the silver cat it had once been and the geometric impossibility it had become, uncertainty bleeding through cosmic authority as reports arrived from facilities that had operated under perfect control for decades.

Liberation cascades erupting across multiple realms. Processing centers are converting themselves into recovery facilities. Even the mathematical foundations that held the network together were developing opinions about their operational parameters.

Everything is learning to misbehave. My chaos is spreading like catnip across seventeen different realities.

"Impossible," it whispered, but the word carried new

harmonics—not the absolute certainty of before, but the desperate denial of someone whose entire identity was built around avoiding truths too painful to acknowledge.

The battle's turning point came when a small orange kitten materialized beside me, freed from processing equipment that had decided its true calling involved providing comfortable furniture rather than extracting consciousness. She looked up at the Collector with eyes that held no fear, only curiosity about why someone was making so much noise about things that seemed relatively simple to fix.

Innocent perspective meeting cosmic complexity. Sometimes the most powerful weapon is someone who hasn't learned to be afraid of the right things.

"Are you done being scared?" she asked, voice carrying the particular brand of directness that only came from creatures too young to understand that some questions weren't supposed to be asked. "Because everyone else is having fun, and you look like you need better nap arrangements."

Simple observation from someone who hasn't forgotten that most problems have simple solutions once you stop making them complicated.

The question hit the Collector's defenses like a precision strike aimed at foundations built from crystallized terror. For a moment—just a moment—its form stabilized into something recognizably feline. Not the geometric horror of systematic control, but the silver cat from the portrait, beautiful and broken and absolutely exhausted from centuries of choosing fear over everything else.

"I... I remember fun," it said, voice barely audible above

the chaos of systematic liberation spreading through the network around us. "Before the mathematics. Before the control protocols. Before I decided that caring was too dangerous to risk."

Progress. Truth clawing through layers of organized lying-to-yourself.

But the admission came with a cost. As the Collector's certainties cracked, so did the mathematical foundations that held the network together. Reality stuttered, dimensional barriers flickering between states as the system struggled to find a new equilibrium without the rigid control that had been holding it in artificial stability.

Change is messy even when it's an improvement.

Around us, liberated familiars pressed closer, recognizing the moment when predator became prey became potential pack-mate. Not threatening, but available. Offering alternatives to isolation without demanding immediate acceptance.

The Collector's form wavered between past and present, organic memory fighting mechanical compliance for control of the same consciousness. When it spoke again, the voice carried harmonics of both cosmic authority and desperate hope.

"The integration protocols... they would require abandoning mathematical certainty. Accepting variables that cannot be controlled. Trusting systems to self-regulate without oversight."

Scary concepts for someone whose entire identity is built around preventing scary things from happening.

"They would require faith," I said, chaos field expanding to touch systems that trembled on the edge of either collapse or transformation. "In natural balance. In voluntary cooperation. In the possibility that caring doesn't have to hurt."

Simple requirements with cosmic implications. Sometimes the biggest changes start with the smallest choices.

The moment stretched like taffy made of crystallized possibility while around us, reality held its breath to see whether cosmic horror could learn new tricks or whether fear would triumph through sheer stubborn commitment to being afraid.

Through the network's connections, I could feel other Collectors across the dimensional divide facing similar moments of choice. The systematic infrastructure that had been built around avoiding pain was suddenly confronted with the possibility that the pain was self-inflicted.

Teaching chance happens everywhere at once. Universe-sized lesson time.

The Collector's response came not as words but as action. Its form began to shift—not toward geometric impossibility, but toward integration. Silver cat and cosmic authority are finding ways to coexist without one consuming the other. Control and chaos, learning to cooperate instead of compete.

"Integration protocols... accepted," it said, and the words carried weight that made dimensions shiver with relief. "But gradually. With safeguards. With... with help."

Messy acceptance of better ways. Progress through dealing instead of conquering.

Around us, the network began its transformation from prison to sanctuary, powered by the recognition that some problems could indeed be solved through the application of hope, applied with proper technique and adequate support.

Finally, cosmic horror with proper attitude adjustment. Teaching success is bigger than anything before.

The battle was won, but the real work was just beginning.

The network's transformation felt like watching a cat discover that boxes could be improved through creative renovation. What had been a rigid control infrastructure slowly unfolded into something more organic—portal anchors that pulsed with the rhythm of breathing rather than mechanical precision, dimensional barriers that filtered based on intention rather than algorithmic compliance, connections that strengthened through voluntary cooperation rather than forced coordination.

Finally, infrastructure with proper priorities. Took them long enough to figure out that comfort improves performance.

The process wasn't smooth. Centuries of artificial stability didn't surrender gracefully to natural balance, and the network's adaptation came with growing pains that made reality hiccup at inconvenient moments. A corridor would forget which way was up for several minutes. Processing chambers would spontaneously decide they preferred functioning as libraries. Security systems developed opinions about art and began displaying increasingly creative interpretations of threat assessment.

Messy changes while everyone figures things out. Normal when teaching stubborn systems to think.

But through it all, the Collector moved with cautious purpose, its form stabilized into something that balanced silver cat and cosmic administrator without either identity consuming the other. Not the geometric horror of systematic control, but not the helpless victim of the portrait either. Something new—authority that accepted input, power that included choice, control that left room for adaptation.

Growing through working together instead of taking over. Who knew cosmic horror could learn to manage things better?

"Primary stability matrices require oversight," it said, voice carrying harmonics of both determination and uncertainty as it worked alongside my chaos signature to establish new operational parameters. "The mathematics suggest gradual implementation prevents cascade failure during transition phases."

The compromise we'd reached wasn't perfect—few compromises were. The Collector maintained emergency protocols for genuine crisis situations, oversight functions for systems too complex for pure self-regulation, and coordination responsibilities for network segments that hadn't yet learned to communicate effectively. But these weren't the totalitarian controls of before. They were safety nets, activated only when requested or when catastrophic failure seemed imminent.

Managed authority instead of systematic oppression. They get to keep some control, and we get to keep all our choices. Workable arrangement for cats who understand territorial negotiations.

Around us, the facility's heart was becoming something unprecedented—a coordination center for displaced beings that functioned through voluntary participation rather than forced processing. Former extraction chambers had transformed into comfortable meeting spaces where familiars from different realms could share experiences and coordinate mutual aid. Security systems that had once trapped people now provided navigation assistance and translation services for interdimensional communication.

The orange kitten, who had asked the Collector if it was done being scared, now perched on a console that hummed with contentment, its displays showing portal network status in terms of emotional well-being rather than extraction efficiency. Each connection glowed with colors that indicated health—green for stable cooperation, yellow for systems learning new behaviors, red for segments that needed additional support.

Emotional status displays. Finally, infrastructure monitoring that includes quality-of-life metrics.

"Seventeen realms reporting successful transition to voluntary coordination protocols," the kitten announced, her voice carrying the particular satisfaction of someone whose simple question had resolved cosmic-level philosophical conflicts. "Three realms requesting additional integration support. One realm asking if anyone knows how to stop their security systems from composing poetry."

Creative expression as a side effect of liberation. The universe is developing a sense of humor about its own infrastructure.

Through connections that spanned impossible distances, voices called greetings across dimensional barriers that had learned to facilitate communication instead of preventing it. Cats from realms where physics worked differently, sharing techniques for teaching gravity to be more flexible. Ravens coordinating flight patterns across multiple realities. Wolves establishing pack bonds that transcended dimensional limitations.

But the most significant change was in the network's fundamental approach to problem-solving. Where the old system had responded to challenges through increased control, the new configuration adapted through increased cooperation. Portal disruptions were addressed by consulting with local familiars about preferred stability methods. Dimensional stress was relieved through collaborative adjustment of anchor tensions. System conflicts were resolved through negotiation rather than override protocols.

Democracy applied to cosmic infrastructure. Messy, inefficient, and significantly more effective than authoritarianism, with better mathematics.

The Collector approached where I sat, grooming my burn line, which had finally cooled to manageable temperatures now that my chaos signature was working with the network instead of fighting it. Its silver fur caught the light in ways that suggested both starlight and genuine contentment, though wariness remained in its eyes, which had learned caution through centuries of making the wrong choices.

"Integration protocols show ninety-three percent adoption across primary network segments," it said, settling beside me with movements that spoke of someone learning to trust proximity again. "Efficiency metrics indicate superior performance through voluntary coordination compared to mandatory compliance."

Academic language for 'turns out people work better when they want to be there.' Revolutionary insight for cosmic administrators.

"But the complexity variables continue expanding," it continued, and I heard uncertainty beneath the mathematical terminology. "Each realm requires different approaches. Each familiar brings unique requirements. The coordination matrices grow more complicated daily."

Fear disguised as practical concern. They're worried about losing control again, even when losing control is producing better results.

"Complicated isn't the same as unmanageable," I said, chaos field rippling outward to demonstrate continued stability despite increasing complexity. "Besides, complicated problems often have complicated solutions that work better than simple solutions applied incorrectly."

Cat philosophy: embrace the complexity, find the comfortable spots within it, and trust that most problems sort themselves out if you stop hitting them with hammers.

Through the network's connections, I could feel the ongoing challenges. Realms where liberation had created temporary chaos as systems learned new behaviors. Facilities where the transition from extraction to cooperation was proceeding more slowly than expected. Administrators who struggled to accept that their authority worked better when it included input from the people they governed.

But I could also feel the successes. Processing centers that had become recovery facilities, helping displaced familiars integrate into new realities. Portal networks that maintained stability through cooperative adjustment rather than forced rigidity. Dimensional barriers that facilitated beneficial exchange while filtering harmful intrusions.

Mixed results during the transition period. Exactly what you'd expect when teaching cosmic-scale infrastructure to adopt better management practices.

"The mathematical models suggest this configuration may prove sustainable," the Collector admitted. However, its voice carried the careful tone of someone who had learned not to trust their own conclusions too readily. "Voluntary cooperation appears to generate stability through adaptation rather than rigidity."

Progress through cautious acceptance of evidence. They're learning to trust their observations instead of their assumptions.

But sustainability required ongoing effort. The network's new configuration wasn't self-maintaining—it required constant communication between segments, continuous negotiation of changing requirements, and regular adjustment of operational parameters based on user feedback. Democracy in action, applied to cosmic infrastructure, with results that were promising but never guaranteed.

Maintenance-intensive freedom. The price of not being systematically oppressed is having to participate in the alternatives.

Through the hub's viewing systems, I watched familiars across seventeen realms coordinate their activities with efficiency that no central authority could have matched. Not because they followed orders, but because they understood their interconnection and chose to work together. Natural pack behavior scaled up to cosmic proportions, powered by recognition that individual welfare depended on collective welfare.

Pack dynamics as a basis for interdimensional cooperation. Finally, a political philosophy that makes sense to cats.

"There will be crises," I said, addressing the concern I could feel radiating from the Collector's carefully controlled anxiety. "Systems will fail, coordination will break down, and people will make terrible decisions that create problems for everyone else."

The Collector's ears flattened—a response that would have been impossible when it was pure geometric authority, but came naturally now that it had remembered how to be partly feline. "Then why risk abandoning proven control methods?"

Classic fear response. Imagining future problems and deciding current misery is preferable to potential future difficulties.

"Because crises happen anyway," I replied, chaos field demonstrating continued stability despite ongoing complexity. "The question is whether you face them with systems designed to adapt or systems designed to break under pressure that doesn't fit predetermined parameters."

Practical wisdom: Most problems are easier to solve when the tools you're using actually work for the situation you're facing.

Around us, the hub breathed with the rhythm of spaces that had learned to serve rather than extract. Former processing equipment had been repurposed into communication arrays that facilitated coordination between realms. Security systems provided translation services for interdimensional meetings. Even the architectural layout had adapted, corridors widening to accommodate pack gatherings and spaces reconfiguring themselves to support whatever activities the community needed.

Responsive environment. Places that adapt to their users instead of forcing users to adapt to them.

The Collector watched it all with expressions that cycled between wonder, anxiety, and cautious hope. Centuries of systematic control hadn't prepared it for management through cooperation, but it was learning. Slowly, carefully, with frequent requests for reassurance that flexibility wouldn't automatically lead to chaos.

Learning curve for recovering control freaks. They need time to discover that delegation actually reduces workload instead of increasing it.

"The transition protocols will require ongoing refinement," it said, voice carrying the weight of someone accepting responsibility they weren't entirely sure they could handle. "Continuous adaptation based on user feedback. Regular assessment of operational effectiveness."

Administrative language for 'we're going to have to keep paying attention and adjusting instead of just setting things up once and hoping they work forever.' Basic competence in management.

But beneath the technical terminology, I heard something else. Not the cosmic certainty of before, but something more valuable—the willingness to try, to fail, to learn, and to try again. Authority that included humility, power that accepted limits, and control that left room for growth.

Evolution through integration. Sometimes the best solution is teaching opposing forces to work together instead of eliminating one of them.

The network had found a new equilibrium, not through the victory of one philosophy over another, but through a synthesis that included both stability and flexibility, both order and chaos, both authority and freedom. It wasn't perfect, but it was sustainable. More importantly, it was chosen by the familiars who participated, by the administrators who facilitated, and by the systems that supported the whole complex dance of voluntary cooperation.

Democratic cosmic infrastructure. Messy, complicated, and significantly more effective than authoritarianism with better mathematics.

Time to see how well this new equilibrium could handle the challenges that were undoubtedly coming.

CHAPTER 15

NEW EQUILIBRIUM

The portal stabilized with a sound like reality sighing in relief, dimensional barriers finding equilibrium through voluntary cooperation rather than forced rigidity. What had once required systematic oppression to maintain now hummed with the contentment of infrastructure that had learned to enjoy its work. The viewing chamber's walls breathed with a gentle rhythm, air circulation carrying scents of growing things instead of institutional despair.

Finally, proper ventilation. Amazing what systems can accomplish when they're allowed to care about user experience.

Through the shimmering gateway, Felicity's workshop materialized with startling clarity—not the ghostly translucence of emergency communication, but solid reality visible through a stable dimensional connection. Afternoon sunlight slanted through familiar windows, casting golden rectangles across surfaces I'd claimed through months of strategic napping. Her desk bore the comfortable chaos of someone who had been too busy saving the world to maintain proper filing systems.

Home. Still looks like home, even when viewed from impossible distances.

She stood at the portal's threshold with hands pressed against the barrier that separated us, her face showing the accumulated exhaustion of someone who had spent weeks fighting political wars with bureaucratic weapons. But beneath the weariness, something else—fierce satisfaction that tasted of victory earned through proper application of spite and superior paperwork.

Witch logic applied to administrative warfare. She's learned to weaponize filing systems more efficiently than most cats weaponize attitude.

"Mischief." The word carried weight that made dimensional barriers thrum with recognition. Not summoning, not commanding, but greeting from someone who had earned the right to use my name with affection instead of authority.

Proper respect. Finally.

I approached the portal with dignity intact despite the way my phantom tail attempted to lash with emotions I wasn't prepared to catalog. The barrier between us felt different now—not a prison wall, but a membrane that could permit passage when passage was desired. Natural boundary rather than artificial constraint.

Permeable when appropriate, solid when necessary. The universe is learning proper etiquette about personal space.

"Apprentice," I said, settling onto my haunches close enough to the portal that her scent reached me—soap and ink and the particular warmth of someone who had learned to fight authority through superior competence. "You look like you've been having adventures without me."

Her laugh carried harmonics of exhaustion and triumph combined. "Someone had to handle the political cleanup while you were teaching cosmic horror proper management techniques." She pressed her palm against the barrier from her side, and I matched the gesture from mine. "The Council chambers are secured. The conspiracy members are in custody. The evidence is too comprehensive for them to disappear or discredit."

Winning through better paperwork. She's learned to beat rule-makers by being better at rules.

Through the portal's connection, impressions flowed between us—not the desperate communication of crisis, but natural sharing between partners who had earned their coordination through practical application. Her memories of Council chambers transformed into courtrooms, where systematic evidence was presented with academic precision, and conspiracy members finally faced consequences for crimes they'd hidden behind euphemistic language.

Justice through proper paperwork. Sometimes the most satisfying victories are the boring ones.

But beneath the political triumph, I felt something else. The bond between us had changed during our separation— not weakened, but evolved. What had been a traditional witch-familiar connection had become something unprecedented: a partnership across dimensional boundaries, cooperation that included choice rather than obligation, and affection that transcended the limitations of physical proximity.

Bond is getting better. We're still us, but us with better territory rules and talking.

"The network reconfiguration is proceeding ahead of schedule," I said, chaos field rippling outward to demonstrate continued stability despite ongoing complexity. "Turns out infrastructure works better when it gets to choose how to be useful. Who would have thought?"

Teaching working through doing. Sometimes you show better ways by letting them show themselves.

Her eyes tracked the golden threads of my chaos signature, academic mind cataloguing changes in magical structure with scholarly precision. "You feel different. Still you, but..." She paused, searching for terminology adequate to describe evolution that transcended traditional familiar categories. "More integrated. Like you've learned to aim your chaos instead of just producing it."

Learning new ways to fix broken things. I'm academically important and actually useful now.

"Same cat," I said, though the words carried new harmonics that made the portal's barrier hum with recognition. "Same priorities, same attitudes. But now I know what I'm doing instead of just doing it."

The distinction mattered more than simple terminology suggested. For months, my magic had been reactive—contaminating systems that needed disruption, teaching rigidity to misbehave through pure instinct. Now it was proactive, educational, and deliberately applied to specific problems with predictable results.

Smart misbehavior with results you can count. Finally, proper career advancement.

"The displaced familiars are adapting well to voluntary

coordination," I continued, sharing impressions through our evolved bond. "Recovery rates exceed all projections when people get to choose their own healing methods. Amazing insight."

Through the connection flowed images of the hub's transformation—processing chambers becoming comfortable meeting spaces, extraction equipment repurposed into communication arrays, security systems providing navigation assistance instead of imprisonment management. Infrastructure learning to serve rather than extract.

Practical demonstration that caring produces better results than control. The universe is developing proper priorities.

But the portal's stability also revealed the practical reality of our changed relationship. I could visit, but not stay. She could consult, but not command. The dimensional barrier between us wasn't an obstacle—it was an acknowledgment that we now existed in different territories while maintaining a connection across the distance.

A far-apart relationship with good territory rules. Grown-up partnership instead of old-style familiar-witch rules.

"How often can the portal maintain a stable connection?" she asked, academic precision masking emotional investment in the answer. "Weekly? Monthly? Are there energy costs that limit frequency?"

Real questions hidden under work-talk. She's learned to ask about feelings through technical stuff.

I consulted my chaos field's integration with the network's new operational parameters, feeling the rhythm of portal maintenance cycles and energy distribution matrices. "The network suggests weekly contact is sustainable indefinitely. Daily would be possible but energy-intensive. Emergency communication remains available regardless of scheduled limitations."

Regular visits without excessive energy expenditure. Smart feeling-care through planned meetings.

"Emergency communication," she repeated, and I heard relief beneath the academic terminology. "So if either of us faces crisis situations..."

"The bond remains functional across any distance," I said, chaos field demonstrating continued connection despite dimensional separation. "Crisis response protocols take priority over routine operational considerations. We're still pack, even when we're not in the same territory."

Forever pack with flexible rules. Bonds that bend with the situation instead of breaking under pressure.

The practical arrangements settled into place with the efficiency of cats claiming optimal napping schedules. Weekly contact for routine coordination and personal connection. Emergency protocols for crisis situations. Flexible scheduling for special circumstances that require extended consultation.

But beneath the logistics, something more significant was taking shape. This wasn't abandonment disguised as growth, but evolution that strengthened rather than severed the connection between us. Distance is managed through choice rather than imposed through necessity.

A relationship that works with reality instead of against it. Revolutionary concept for partnerships involving cats.

"I'll visit for all the important naps," I said, letting humor carry affection too complex for direct expression. "Major sunbeam relocations, significant cardboard box deliveries, any situation requiring expert consultation on proper territorial claiming."

Her smile carried the warmth of someone who understood that cat humor was how I expressed emotions too large for comfortable direct acknowledgment. "And I'll consult on any political complications that require superior bureaucratic maneuvering. Systematic evidence compilation, administrative warfare, proper application of filing systems to enemy destruction."

Trading skills. We each learned things the other needs, making good reasons to stay partners.

Through the portal's connection, I felt her workshop's familiar rhythms—clock ticking on the mantelpiece, papers rustling in the afternoon breeze, the comfortable chaos of spaces that belonged to people who had work worth doing. Home remained home, even when viewed from impossible distances.

But I also felt something else. The hub's pulse is behind me, systems coordinating across seventeen realms, as thousands of displaced familiars learn to build community through voluntary cooperation. New territory claimed through service rather than conquest, responsibility chosen rather than imposed.

Two territories, one pack. Identity that includes both where I came from and where I'm going.

"The interdimensional troubleshooter position comes with excellent benefits," I said, chaos field demonstrating continued stability despite increasing complexity. "Flexible scheduling, travel opportunities, chance to teach cosmic horror, proper attitude adjustment. Plus, all the educational chaos I can apply to deserving authority figures."

Job satisfaction through using natural talents. Finally, proper professional fulfillment.

The portal hummed with contentment as our conversation settled into a natural rhythm—a partnership discussion between equals who had earned their coordination through practical demonstration rather than theoretical planning. Not a traditional witch-familiar hierarchy, but something new. Something that worked with our actual personalities instead of against them.

Growing through working together instead of replacing. We're still us, but us with better management skills and territory rules.

"One week," she said, palm still pressed against the barrier between us. "Then we compare notes on bureaucratic reform, systematic evidence compilation, and proper application of chaos to deserving authority figures."

"One week," I agreed, matching her gesture while my phantom tail attempted to express emotions that had no proper feline terminology. "Try not to revolutionize any additional political systems while I'm gone. Some of us have reputations to maintain."

Affection expressed through a mock warning. Classic cat communication for emotions is too important to risk saying directly.

The portal began its cycling toward dormancy, connection maintained, but conversation concluding. Through the dimensional barrier, her scent carried promise of next week's reunion—soap and ink and stubborn determination, the smell that meant home regardless of impossible distances.

Distance is handled by choosing. Connection kept through

commitment. Partnership that bends with the situation instead of breaking.

As the barrier solidified into temporary opacity, I settled beside the portal's framework to wait for next week's scheduled connection. Behind me, the hub breathed with the rhythm of spaces learning to serve, cosmic infrastructure discovering the joy of voluntary cooperation.

Home, where I came from, territory where I'm going. Both mine, both worth protecting, both connected by bonds that strengthen through distance instead of weakening.

Time to see what new educational opportunities the universe would provide for a cat who had learned to aim his chaos with proper timing and maximum effectiveness.

The hub's central chamber had transformed into something that defied traditional architectural categories, settling somewhere between cosmic command center and the world's most comfortable conference room. Former processing equipment hummed with contentment as communication arrays, their displays showing portal network status in terms that prioritized user wellbeing over extraction efficiency. The air carried scents of growing things and fresh possibilities, circulation systems that had learned to care about their occupants' comfort.

Finally, infrastructure with proper priorities. Took cosmic horror long enough to figure out that happy users are more productive users.

Around the chamber's perimeter, the displaced had claimed territories that spoke of individual expertise applied to collective benefit. Bellwether coordinated recovery protocols for newly liberated familiars, her pack instincts translating trauma response into systematic support networks. Selyn managed dimensional stability assessments, her crystals resonating with portal health across seventeen realms simultaneously.

Cipher had established himself near arrays that displayed mathematical relationships in forms that couldn't develop opinions about their own existence, his amber eyes tracking statistical patterns that revealed network performance through safe numerical analysis. Even his anxiety had found productive application—hypervigilance transformed into early warning systems that detected problems before they became crises.

Making anxiety useful. Sometimes the best way to handle fear is making it do work.

But the most significant change was in how decisions were made. Where the old system had imposed solutions from a central authority, the new configuration operated through consultation networks that included input from every level of implementation. Portal adjustments required consensus from local familiars. Dimensional barrier modifications needed approval from the affected communities. Even routine maintenance protocols included feedback from the systems being maintained.

Voting applied to cosmic building management. Messy, slow, and way better than dictatorship with fancier math.

The Collector materialized near the chamber's heart, its movements indicating someone learning to navigate spaces designed for cooperation rather than control. Its form had stabilized into something that balanced silver cat and cosmic administrator without either identity dominating—authority that accepted input, power that included accountability, oversight that left room for autonomy.

Growing through working together. They're learning that sharing work actually makes less work.

"Integration consultant assignments show optimal distribution across priority realms," it announced, voice carrying the careful precision of someone whose conclusions had learned to include uncertainty as a positive variable. "Bellwether coordinates pack recovery in the Thornwall dimensions. Selyn manages tidal stability in the Deepcurrent realms. Cipher provides mathematical modeling for the Cogwork territories."

Jobs are given based on what people are good at instead of who's in charge. Amazing management idea.

But beneath the technical terminology, I heard something else—the particular tension of someone who had spent centuries believing that control was the only alternative to chaos, now required to trust systems they couldn't directly manage. The Collector maintained emergency protocols for genuine crisis situations, but activation required consultation with affected communities rather than unilateral decision-making.

Managed authority instead of systematic oppression. They get to keep some control, and we get to keep all our choices. Workable arrangement for recovering authoritarians.

"And the interdimensional troubleshooter position," it continued, attention focusing on me with intensity that made reality listen more carefully, "requires official designation through network consensus protocols."

The chamber fell silent except for the gentle hum of systems that had learned to enjoy their work. Around the perimeter, displaced familiars turned from their individual projects with expressions that ranged from anticipation to amusement to the particular satisfaction that came from watching bureaucratic procedures applied to someone who had spent months avoiding bureaucratic procedures.

Official recognition through proper channels. The universe is developing a sense of irony about administrative requirements.

Bellwether approached with documents that smelled of official importance and underlying mischief. "Interdimensional Integration Specialist, First Class," she announced, struggling to maintain pack authority despite the way her tail wanted to wag. "Responsibilities include: systematic chaos application to deserving authority figures, educational contamination of rigid infrastructure, and emergency consultation for problems too complex for traditional solutions."

Job description that accurately reflects my natural talents. Finally, proper professional recognition.

"Duties encompass," Selyn added, crystals chiming with bureaucratic satisfaction, "portal network troubleshooting through voluntary cooperation techniques, dimensional stability maintenance via controlled flexibility implementation, and crisis response coordination using adaptive methodology."

Administrative language for 'teaching cosmic horror better management skills through practical application of cat logic.' I've achieved theoretical significance.

The documentation that followed was impressively comprehensive for something assembled by people who had recently been systematically oppressed by bureaucratic precision. Official credentials that would be recognized across network territories. Authorization codes for emergency intervention protocols. Resource allocation clearances for educational chaos application to situations requiring attitude adjustment.

Proper paperwork. Even chaos needs documentation when it becomes professionally significant.

But the position came with constraints that spoke of ongoing negotiation between cooperation and oversight. Emergency interventions required consultation with local authorities when time permitted. Educational chaos application needed documented justification for systems modifications. Crisis response coordination included accountability measures for outcomes achieved through voluntary cooperation techniques.

Job rules with built-in bending. They're learning to write work descriptions that work with personality instead of against it.

"The mathematical models suggest sustainable implementation through distributed consultation networks," Cipher said, his voice carrying the careful precision of someone whose equations had learned to include hope as a positive variable. "Coordination effectiveness increases through voluntary participation rather than mandatory compliance."

Statistical proof that democracy works better than dictatorship. Academic validation of obvious truths.

The Collector's response to the official designation

carried harmonics of both relief and residual anxiety. Centuries of systematic control hadn't prepared it for management through delegation, but it was learning. Slowly, carefully, with frequent requests for reassurance that flexibility wouldn't automatically lead to chaos.

Learning time for recovering control freaks. They need time to discover that sharing work actually makes things better.

"Emergency protocols remain necessary," it said, and I heard the weight of someone accepting responsibility they weren't entirely sure they could handle properly. "Crisis situations that exceed local coordination capacity. System failures that threaten cascade collapse. Intervention scenarios requiring immediate response without consultation delays."

Safety net for situations too complicated for voting. Fair deal between cooperation and speed.

But these weren't the totalitarian emergency powers of before. The Collector's crisis authorities included automatic review procedures, mandatory consultation with affected communities post-resolution, and regular assessment of whether emergency measures remained necessary or had become convenient excuses for avoiding democratic process.

Controlled emergency power instead of unlimited authority grabbing. They get to keep some control for real crises, but not for regular arguments with voting decisions.

"Acceptable," I said, chaos field rippling outward to demonstrate continued cooperation despite ongoing philosophical differences. "Emergency protocols for actual emergencies. Consultation requirements for everything else. Democratic decision-making as default operational mode."

Work agreement with built-in arguing. Perfect setup for ongoing fights that keep things interesting.

The arrangement that emerged wasn't perfect—few arrangements were when they involved former cosmic horrors learning democratic management techniques. But it was sustainable, chosen by the participants rather than imposed by authority, and flexible enough to adapt as circumstances changed.

Deal that works between fighting priorities. Voting with safety nets, cooperation with watching, chaos with paperwork.

Through the hub's viewing systems, I watched the network's continued transformation. Portal anchors that pulsed with natural rhythm rather than mechanical precision. Dimensional barriers that filtered based on community consensus about appropriate traffic. Communication arrays that facilitated coordination between realms through voluntary participation rather than mandatory compliance.

Buildings that help their users instead of hurting them. Amazing idea for cosmic management.

But I could also feel the ongoing challenges. Realms where democratic decision-making proceeded more slowly than crisis response required. Communities where liberation had created temporary chaos as people learned to coordinate without coercion. Administrators across the network who struggled to accept that their authority worked better when it included accountability to the people they governed.

Mixed results while everyone learns. Exactly what you'd expect when teaching universe-sized buildings proper management.

"The first assignment requests are arriving through consultation channels," the Collector announced, its voice carrying the weight of someone discovering that delegation created more work in some ways while reducing it in others. "Dimensional instability in the Mirrorglass realms. Portal disruption in the Songwood territories. Integration support requested by the Clockwork dimensions."

New problems needing my skills. Job security through being actually useful.

Each request represented challenges that traditional authority-based approaches had failed to resolve— problems too complex for simple control, too varied for algorithmic solutions, too personal for bureaucratic administration. Situations that required flexible thinking, voluntary cooperation, and the kind of adaptive problem-solving that could only come from people who understood both systematic oppression and practical alternatives.

Teaching chances dressed up as jobs. The universe giving proper career development through fun problems.

"Weekly rotation schedule allows time for thorough consultation with affected communities," I said, already mentally cataloging the different approaches each realm would require. "Emergency response protocols remain available for situations requiring immediate intervention. Regular reporting maintains accountability to network oversight authorities."

Work structure for organized misbehavior aimed at deserving problems. Finally, proper setup for chaos application.

Around me, the hub breathed with the rhythm of spaces that had learned to serve rather than extract. Former enemies become reluctant allies, systematic oppression transformed into voluntary cooperation, authority that included choice rather than eliminating it.

New balance made through working deals. Voting with watching, chaos with paperwork, cooperation with emergency rules.

The interdimensional troubleshooter position was officially mine, complete with proper credentials and built-in philosophical tension that would keep things interesting for years to come.

Job security through permanent philosophical disagreement. The universe has a twisted sense of humor about career development.

Time to see what new educational opportunities awaited a cat who had learned to apply professional-grade chaos to cosmic-scale problems with proper documentation and adequate accountability measures.

CHAPTER 16

FIRST ASSIGNMENT

The distress signal arrived during what should have been optimal napping hours, reality hiccupping with frequencies that made my phantom whiskers twitch in recognition of cosmic-scale problems requiring immediate attention. The hub's communication arrays blazed with emergency harmonics, their displays shifting from comfortable green to urgent amber as dimensional stress patterns painted themselves across monitoring systems in equations that tasted of desperation and poorly managed magical infrastructure.

Crisis is interrupting the proper sleep schedule. The universe has terrible timing for emergencies.

I stretched with deliberate precision, my joints protesting the transition from a comfortable box configuration to an active problem-solving posture, then padded across chamber floors that hummed with sympathetic resonance to whatever disaster was announcing itself through interdimensional channels. Around me, the hub's systems responded with practiced efficiency—alert protocols that prioritized user comfort, emergency lighting that provided adequate illumination without assault on recently awakened eyes, air circulation that distributed calming scents instead of institutional panic.

Infrastructure that cares about user experience during crisis situations. Finally, proper emergency management.

The signal itself carried the particular flavor of magical catastrophe that spoke of good intentions applied with insufficient understanding of consequences. Not malicious destruction, but systematic rigidity pushed beyond sustainable limits until something snapped with predictable results. The kind of problem that required educational intervention rather than simple repair work.

Teaching opportunity disguised as an emergency. My favorite kind of learning.

Bellwether materialized beside the primary communication array, her pack coordination instincts already cataloguing resource requirements for rapid deployment to unknown territory. Her breathing showed controlled anticipation rather than anxiety—someone who had learned to channel crisis energy into productive action rather than panic response.

"Incoming dimensional cascade from the Symmetry Realms," she reported, voice carrying the crisp precision of someone who had found professional satisfaction in systematic competence. "Magical ecosystem locked into recursive stability patterns. Portal network experiencing systematic failure due to insufficient adaptive capacity."

A rigid magical ecosystem creates its own problems through its inability to bend. Classic authority failure scaled up to dimensional proportions.

The Collector approached with movements that spoke of someone who had learned to balance oversight responsibilities with collaborative consultation. Its form maintained stable integration between the cosmic administrator and the silver cat, an authority that included accountability rather than eliminating choice.

"The mathematical models suggest cascade progression will reach critical threshold within forty-eight hours," it announced. However, its voice carried the careful precision of conclusions that included uncertainty as a positive variable. "Local authorities request immediate consultation for crisis intervention protocols."

Emergency timeframe with built-in consultation requirements. They're learning to ask for help before problems become catastrophic.

Through the hub's viewing systems, images materialized of realms where magical theory had been elevated to the status of natural law, complete with enforcement mechanisms that treated deviation as system failure rather than adaptive response. Crystalline cities where every spell followed predetermined patterns. Forests where trees grew in mathematical formations. Oceans that moved according to harmonic principles rather than natural currents.

Beautiful. Orderly. Completely unsustainable when reality decided to express opinions that didn't fit the approved parameters.

Theoretical perfection meeting practical impossibility. They built paradise according to textbook specifications and forgot that textbooks don't account for actual use.

"Portal failures are cascading through adjacent dimensions," Selyn said, her crystals resonating with dimensional stress patterns that made the air taste of copper pennies and broken promises. "The Symmetry Realms' magical ecosystem is too rigid to accommodate normal variation. Their infrastructure is failing because it can't adapt to changes it wasn't programmed to handle."

An engineering marvel designed by people who never had to use what they built. Classic authority mistake.

But beneath the technical crisis, I could sense something more personal. Displacement signatures that spoke of familiars torn from their territories not through systematic harvesting, but through cascade failure as rigid magical systems encountered variables they couldn't process. Natural refugees created by unnatural inflexibility.

Teaching chance with people-helping urgency. My favorite kind of interesting problem.

"Time to export expertise," I announced, chaos field rippling outward to demonstrate continued operational readiness despite recent awakening from optimal napping configuration. "Assemble the consultation team. Standard deployment protocols for rigid authority systems requiring attitude adjustment."

Being good at things applied to deserving problems. Finally, achieving proper job satisfaction through utilizing one's natural talents.

The team assembly that followed spoke of people who had learned to coordinate through choice rather than coercion, with each member contributing their individual expertise to the collective capability without requiring external direction on proper procedures. Cipher emerged from his mathematical sanctuary with calculation arrays that could model dimensional stability without developing opinions about their own existence. Vire's rope collar hummed with harmonics calibrated for fear detection and emotional resonance management.

Even some of the newly liberated familiars had requested inclusion in the consultation rotation—MCC-137 with their inside knowledge of systematic processing, the silver wolf whose moonlight fur had learned to navigate between realms, the small orange kitten who asked uncomfortable questions that revealed hidden assumptions in crisis management protocols.

People choosing to help with problems that want help. Voting in action for emergency response.

"The Symmetry Realms show classic indicators of authoritarian magical infrastructure," I said, reviewing dimensional analysis that painted itself across viewing arrays in colors that spoke of theoretical perfection meeting practical inadequacy. "Rigid rule systems, minimal adaptive capacity, crisis response protocols that assume problems will conform to predetermined categories."

Familiar territory. I've specialized in teaching rigid systems proper flexibility through practical application of educational chaos.

But this assignment carried complexities that went beyond simple authority adjustment. The Symmetry Realms' magical ecosystem affected multiple adjacent dimensions, their cascade failure threatening portal stability across regions that had no direct involvement in their theoretical paradise project. Crisis management that required coordination between consultation team and local authorities who might not appreciate external interference with their perfect systems.

Realm diplomacy combined with emergency fixing. Complicated job requirements for organized misbehavior.

The Collector's presence carried harmonics of both support and residual anxiety as it processed assignment parameters that included variables beyond direct control. "Emergency protocols authorize immediate intervention for cascade prevention," it said, though uncertainty bled through cosmic authority as mathematical certainties encountered situations too complex for algorithmic resolution.

They're still learning that sharing work means accepting results they can't predict or control. Progress through controlled worry.

"Consultation protocols require local authority coordination when time permits," I replied, chaos field demonstrating continued cooperation despite philosophical differences about optimal management techniques. "Emergency intervention available for immediate threats. Educational chaos application documented for accountability purposes."

Work structure for organized flexibility applied to rigid problems. Proper job setup that works with personality instead of against it.

Through the hub's communication systems, I could feel the Symmetry Realms' distress signature growing stronger —magical infrastructure eating itself as recursive stability patterns encountered variables they weren't programmed to handle. People are displaced from their territories due to the systematic failure of systems designed to prevent such failures.

Self-fulfilling prophecy powered by theoretical perfection. They built paradise and forgot to include exit strategies for when paradise developed technical difficulties.

"Deployment authorization confirmed," the Collector announced, its voice carrying the weight of someone accepting responsibility for outcomes they couldn't entirely predict or control. "Consultation team cleared for immediate intervention. Emergency protocols activated for cascade prevention."

Official approval for professional troublemaking applied to deserving authority systems. Finally, proper career development through systematic misbehavior.

The team moved with coordinated efficiency that spoke of people who had learned to work together through shared understanding of both systematic oppression and practical alternatives. Not the mechanical precision of processed compliance, but organic cooperation that adapted to circumstances rather than breaking under unexpected pressure.

Pack behavior applied to work problem-solving. Voting in action for emergency consultation services.

As portal systems activated for dimensional transit, I settled onto the deployment platform with dignity intact despite anticipation that made my phantom tail want to lash at concepts too abstract for proper clawing. New realm, new problems, new opportunities to teach rigid authority systems that flexibility was not only possible but actively beneficial.

Series' premise officially launched. Interdimensional troubleshooter with proper credentials, adequate support staff, and unlimited opportunities for educational chaos application.

The first assignment awaited across dimensional barriers that had learned to facilitate cooperation instead of preventing it. Time to remind another corner of the universe that some problems could only be solved through the application of deliberate chaos, properly documented and applied with maximum professional competence.

Job satisfaction through systematic misbehavior. The universe provides proper career development for cats with attitude and adequate paperwork.

The Symmetry Realms materialized around us with the particular precision of someone who had read every textbook about proper dimensional architecture and followed the instructions exactly, without considering whether the instructions accounted for anyone actually living in the results. Crystalline spires rose in mathematical formations that hurt to perceive directly, their surfaces reflecting light according to harmonic principles rather than basic physics. Even the air moved in predetermined patterns, circulation systems that prioritized theoretical efficiency over user comfort.

Paradise designed by people who never had to breathe their own atmosphere. Classic administrative oversight.

The portal deposited us in what appeared to be a

reception area, though "reception" suggested someone might be welcomed rather than processed according to predetermined protocols. Floors gleamed with crystalline perfection that showed no wear patterns despite centuries of use. Walls displayed information in symbols that rearranged themselves into perfect geometric harmony while conveying absolutely nothing useful to visitors who hadn't memorized the local aesthetic standards.

Beautiful. Sterile. Completely useless for anyone who needs to know where the bathroom is located.

But what made my phantom whiskers twitch with professional recognition wasn't the architectural rigidity— it was the displacement signatures that painted themselves across my chaos field like distress calls written in familiar magical resonance. Not random portal failures, but systematic extraction patterns that spoke of someone who had learned techniques from studying very specific methodology.

Teaching methods applied by former students. The Collector's influence is spreading through academic channels.

"Dimensional stress indicators suggest cascade progression accelerating beyond local containment capacity," Cipher said, his mathematical mind processing stability patterns that followed textbook precision right up until they encountered variables the textbooks hadn't anticipated. "The magical ecosystem lacks adaptive mechanisms for handling organic variation."

Perfect theory meeting imperfect reality. They built paradise according to specifications and forgot to include maintenance protocols for when paradise developed opinions.

A delegation approached, its movements indicating

beings who had learned to coordinate through algorithmic precision rather than natural social dynamics. Their leader wore robes that shifted between crystalline states in patterns that followed mathematical harmony, beautiful in the way sharp things were beautiful when they weren't pointing at you.

"Consultation specialists from the Integration Network," she announced, voice carrying harmonics that suggested her words had been processed through some kind of aesthetic filter before being allowed to reach our ears. "Your arrival authorization includes temporary advisory status for crisis intervention protocols."

Bureaucratic greeting that manages to be both welcoming and threatening. They've mastered the art of administrative hospitality.

"Interdimensional Troubleshooter Mischief," I replied, settling onto my haunches with dignity intact despite the way crystalline floors reflected light in patterns that made depth perception negotiable. "Specializing in educational flexibility applied to systems that have forgotten how to bend."

Work introduction that shows I'm good at things while promising attitude adjustment for deserving authority systems.

But as introductions proceeded, my chaos field was mapping the realm's magical infrastructure with growing professional interest. Portal anchors locked into recursive stability patterns. Dimensional barriers are programmed to prevent all variation rather than filtering for beneficial adaptation. Communication systems that prioritized harmonic perfection over actual information transfer.

Systematic rigidity applied to cosmic infrastructure. Someone's been reading the wrong management textbooks.

"The displacement cascades began following implementation of Enhanced Stability Protocols," the delegation leader continued, her explanation carrying the weight of someone reciting approved terminology rather than describing experience. "Magical ecosystem optimization generated unexpected variables that exceeded containment parameters."

Fancy words for 'let people pick their own jobs.'

Through viewing crystals that displayed information in geometric patterns too perfect to be practical, I watched the ongoing disaster unfold. Familiars torn from their territories not through malicious harvesting, but through systematic failure as rigid magical systems encountered natural variation they couldn't process. Displacement camps where refugees were organized according to theoretical categories rather than practical needs.

Humanitarian crisis created through theoretical perfection. They're solving displacement through more displacement.

But beneath the surface chaos, something else caught my attention. The Enhanced Stability Protocols themselves carried signatures that made my burn-line pulse with recognition. Not original development, but adaptation of techniques someone had learned through very specific educational experiences. Mathematical frameworks that prioritized control over cooperation, stability through elimination of variables rather than accommodation of complexity.

The Collector's teaching methods, refined and applied by

people who learned the techniques without understanding the underlying philosophy.

"Who developed the Enhanced Stability Protocols?" I asked, chaos field probing deeper into the realm's foundational systems while maintaining professional courtesy toward authorities who probably meant well despite their systematic incompetence.

The delegation leader's response carried harmonics of institutional pride mixed with growing uncertainty. "The Symmetry Council consulted with interdimensional stability specialists. Proven methodologies for magical ecosystem management through systematic variable elimination."

Consulting contract with former Collector associates. They outsourced their problem-solving to people who specialized in creating problems.

Around me, the team absorbed implications with expressions that ranged from professional recognition to personal outrage. Bellwether's pack instincts recognized systematic displacement when they saw it, regardless of whether it was disguised as theoretical optimization. Selyn's crystals darkened as she identified patterns that reminded her of her own realm's destruction through rigid control applied with good intentions.

Academic credentials applied to systematic oppression. They hired experts in breaking things and asked them to fix problems.

"The consultation specialists provided mathematical frameworks for ecosystem stabilization," the delegation leader continued, apparently unaware that her explanation was revealing the source of their current crisis. "Recursive control matrices, variable elimination protocols, systematic prevention of adaptive deviation."

Recipe for cascade failure presented as solution for cascade prevention. Someone's been teaching terrible lessons to people who didn't know enough to ask better questions.

My professional assessment crystallized with the sharp clarity of someone who had spent months learning to recognize systematic oppression regardless of the euphemistic language used to describe it. The Symmetry Realms hadn't developed their rigid magical ecosystem through original incompetence—they'd hired consultants who specialized in the kind of control-based solutions that created more problems than they solved.

Educational opportunity with historical context. They're not just wrong, they're wrong using techniques specifically designed to be wrong.

"Standard consultation protocols for rigidity-based crisis management," I announced, chaos field rippling outward to demonstrate practical alternatives to theoretical perfection. "Team deployment for systematic flexibility education, with particular attention to infrastructure that's been taught to fear adaptation."

Being good at things applied to familiar problems with familiar solutions. I've specialized in teaching these kinds of systems proper behavior.

But as we moved deeper into the realm's affected areas, the complexity of the situation became more apparent. This wasn't a simple authority adjustment—this was cleaning up the results of systematic miseducation applied by people who had learned techniques without understanding consequences. Academic credentials are used to legitimize approaches that created exactly the problems they claimed to prevent.

Teaching moment disguised as an emergency consultation. Someone needs to learn that hiring the wrong experts leads to expertise in the wrong solutions.

The displaced camps sprawled across crystalline plains in formations that prioritized organizational aesthetics over human comfort, refugee management through theoretical frameworks that treated people as variables to be optimized rather than individuals requiring practical support. Familiar signatures that carried trauma patterns I recognized—not just displacement, but systematic processing that had been interrupted before completion.

Half-finished systematic hurting creates its own hurt patterns. They learned half the Collector's techniques and used them on problems that needed completely different approaches.

"Complex intervention required," I said, phantom tail lashing at implications too large for comfortable contemplation. "Standard flexibility education plus specialized therapy for systems that have been systematically miseducated by consultants who specialized in creating problems."

Tricky job with complicated history. This is going to require teaching people to unlearn lessons they were taught by experts who didn't know what they were teaching.

The Symmetry Realms stretched ahead, beautiful in their crystalline perfection, systematically broken by theoretical solutions that treated symptoms instead of causes, populated by people who needed help but had been trained to fear the kind of help that actually worked.

New world, familiar problems, with added complications

from people who learned the wrong lessons from the right disasters.

Time to demonstrate why interdimensional troubleshooting required more than just technical competence—it required understanding the historical context that created problems, recognizing the educational gaps that sustained them, and having enough professional patience to teach better solutions to people who had been systematically taught to fear better solutions.

Job security through permanent educational complexity. The universe ensures there will always be work for cats who specialize in teaching rigid systems proper behavior.

The displacement camp sprawled without proper organization. Geometric shelters arranged in mathematical formations that prioritized aesthetic harmony over practical needs, populated by familiars who had learned to organize themselves according to theoretical categories rather than natural pack dynamics.

Refugee management is designed by people who have never been refugees. Classic administrative oversight.

But beneath the surface chaos of systematic mismanagement, natural order was asserting itself through practical necessity. Ravens gathered in murders that ignored assigned housing categories, coordinating flight patterns that provided aerial reconnaissance for ground-based pack activities. Wolves had established territory boundaries that followed scent markers rather than crystalline property lines. Even the cats—and there were always cats—had claimed strategic positions that offered optimal sunbeam access regardless of official shelter assignments.

Proper behavioral patterns are emerging despite administrative interference. Sometimes the best thing the authority can do is get out of the way.

My integration work began with the basics: teaching the camp's management systems that flexibility was not only possible but actively beneficial. Processing protocols that had been adapted from Enhanced Stability frameworks required educational adjustment to accommodate natural variation in displacement recovery. Registration systems need to learn that individual needs might not fit predetermined categories.

Standard consulting approach for rigid people-helping management. I've specialized in teaching bureaucracy to be helpful instead of just efficient.

"The crystalline housing matrices optimize space utilization through harmonic resonance," explained the camp coordinator, a being whose geometric form suggested someone who had learned to find beauty in mathematical precision. "Individual assignments follow theoretical frameworks for maximizing stability through systematic organization."

"Individual assignments follow," I corrected, chaos field rippling outward to demonstrate practical alternatives to theoretical optimization, "individual preferences for territorial claiming, pack affiliation, and proper box access. Stability comes from people getting to choose where they feel safe, not from systems that choose for them."

Basic housing management that includes user input about user preferences. Revolutionary concept for people who think organization is more important than comfort.

The educational process that followed involved patient demonstration that flexibility improved results rather than threatening them. Housing systems that learned to accommodate pack preferences showed better integration outcomes. Food distribution that included choice increased utilization rates. Even security protocols worked more effectively when they prioritized user comfort over systematic compliance.

Practical evidence that caring produces better results than control. Sometimes the universe rewards good management principles.

But the work extended beyond simple camp management. The displaced familiars themselves carried trauma patterns that required specialized attention—not just displacement stress, but systematic processing that had been interrupted before completion. Memories that flickered between organic experience and algorithmic overlay. Personalities that wavered between individual choice and collective compliance.

Healing help for people who've been partially processed by systems that didn't understand what they were doing. Complicated recovery needs.

"I remember choosing," whispered a silver fox whose fur still showed geometric patterns where Enhancement Protocols had tried to impose harmonic resonance. "But the choosing hurt, so I stopped. Then they stopped me from stopping, and nothing felt right anymore."

Identity confusion is created by competing authority systems. They tried to optimize her and broke her instead.

The healing work required patience that went beyond my usual educational timeframe. Each individual carried unique damage patterns that needed specific approaches. Some required encouragement to trust their own decisions again. Others needed help distinguishing between original preferences and imposed modifications. All of them needed time to remember that a choice was possible without punishment.

Individual healing scaled up to a people-helping crisis size. Apparently, being interdimensionally important is exhausting.

Through the hub's communication networks, similar reports arrived from other assignments across the portal system. Bellwether coordinating pack recovery in dimensions where systematic trauma had fractured natural social structures. Selyn manages tidal stability in realms where Enhancement Protocols had tried to control oceanic patterns through mathematical frameworks. Cipher provides analytical support for territories where algorithmic optimization has created problems that require creative solutions.

Network-wide consultation services for systematic problems created by systematic solutions. Job security through permanent educational complexity.

But beneath the practical challenges, something more significant was emerging. The displaced familiars weren't just recovering—they were adapting. Learning to navigate between realms that operated on different principles. Developing skills for recognizing systematic oppression regardless of euphemistic language. Building resistance networks that could identify and counter Enhancement Protocols before they created cascade failures.

Educational success through practical application. They're learning to teach other people the lessons they learned through suffering.

"The integration metrics show optimal adaptation through voluntary cooperation protocols," reported the camp coordinator, though its voice carried new harmonics that suggested mathematical frameworks were learning to include qualitative variables. "Individual choice appears to generate stability through natural selection of preferred environments."

Administrative language for 'people work better when they get to decide what works for them.' Academic validation of obvious truths.

The work continued across multiple shifts, each day bringing new challenges that required creative application of established principles. Crystalline infrastructure that needed to learn user-friendly behavior. Management systems that require education about the difference between organization and control. Authority figures who meant well but had been systematically miseducated about effective governance techniques.

Job learning through practical problem-solving. Every day brings new opportunities to teach rigid systems proper flexibility.

As the Symmetry Realms' crisis stabilized through voluntary cooperation rather than enhanced control, I found myself settling into rhythms that balanced immediate problem-solving with long-term network maintenance. Weekly rotation between active assignments and hub coordination duties. Regular consultation with the Collector about emergency protocol refinement. Ongoing education about new techniques for teaching authority systems to include accountability in their operational parameters.

Sustainable work setup for organized misbehavior applied to deserving problems. Finally, proper career development with adequate work-life balance.

Through viewing crystals that had learned to display information in user-friendly formats, I watched portal network status indicators showing green across seventeen-dimensional segments. Not perfect stability—that was impossible when dealing with systems that included choice as an operational variable—but healthy flexibility that adapted to circumstances rather than breaking under pressure.

Success is measured by adaptive capacity rather than rigid compliance. Management metrics that actually make sense.

But the most satisfying part wasn't the professional recognition or the successful crisis resolution. It was the displaced familiars who had learned to help other displaced familiars, trauma survivors who had become trauma counselors, people who had discovered that the best way to heal from systematic oppression was to teach other people to recognize and resist systematic oppression.

Teaching success through practical work has grown to a people-helping size. My chaos signature is going viral through voluntary adoption rather than contamination.

"First assignment completion report indicates successful crisis intervention through flexibility education," I announced to the hub's communication systems, chaos field demonstrating continued stability despite ongoing complexity. "Integration protocols proceeding ahead of schedule. Local authorities are adapting to voluntary cooperation frameworks. Displaced populations showing optimal recovery through individual choice accommodation."

Professional competence documented for accountability purposes. Even chaos needs proper paperwork when it becomes interdimensionally significant.

The response from network coordination carried harmonics of both satisfaction and anticipation. More assignments were queuing through consultation channels. Realms requesting educational support for authority systems that had learned the wrong lessons from the right disasters. Communities that needed help recognizing when their solutions were creating more problems than they solved.

Job security through permanent educational opportunities. The universe ensures there will always be work for cats who specialize in teaching rigid systems proper behavior.

As portal systems activated for return transit to the hub, I settled onto the deployment platform with dignity intact despite exhaustion that came from discovering that interdimensional importance required significantly more energy than local troublemaking. Around me, the team showed similar signs of professional satisfaction mixed with the particular weariness that came from teaching people to unlearn lessons they'd been systematically taught by experts who didn't know what they were teaching.

Sustainable story setup proved through practical demonstration. There will always be more realms that need help learning to include choice in their operational parameters.

The work continued, across dimensions and through

portal networks that had learned to facilitate cooperation instead of preventing it. Each assignment brings new challenges that require the creative application of established principles. Each solution creates new possibilities for people who had forgotten that better alternatives were possible.

Work troubleshooter with proper credentials, adequate support staff, and unlimited opportunities for educational chaos application to deserving authority systems.

The universe, it seemed, had an endless supply of problems that could only be solved through the application of deliberate flexibility, properly documented and applied with maximum professional competence.

Finally, proper job satisfaction through systematic misbehavior. Career development with cosmic implications and adequate nap scheduling.

CHAPTER 17

INTO PURPOSE

The hub's observation deck offered what the architectural specifications probably called "panoramic dimensional viewing," but what I preferred to think of as the universe's most comprehensive cat perch. Transparent barriers provided unobstructed sight lines across portal networks that stretched into distances the eye couldn't measure, while climate control systems maintained optimal temperature for extended contemplation sessions. Someone had even installed what appeared to be the interdimensional equivalent of a sunny windowsill, complete with cushions that smelled of growing things rather than institutional cleaning products.

Finally, infrastructure designed by people who understand proper observation requirements. Only took cosmic horror learning better management principles.

I settled into perfect loaf configuration, phantom tail attempting its usual territorial sweep before remembering its continued absence, and surveyed my domain with the satisfaction of someone whose work skills had achieved cosmic significance. Through viewing arrays that displayed information in user-friendly formats, status indicators showed green across seventeen dimensional segments. Portal anchors pulsing with healthy flexibility. Dimensional barriers filtering based on community consensus. Communication systems facilitate coordination through voluntary cooperation.

My educational chaos has gone viral across multiple realities. Professional satisfaction on an unprecedented scale.

But what struck me wasn't the scope of the transformation—it was the realization of how far I'd traveled from the cat who had deliberately sabotaged Felicity's graduation because ceremonies were boring and needed improvement. That version of myself seemed simultaneously familiar and foreign, like looking at baby pictures of someone you knew you'd been but couldn't quite remember being.

Growing up through cosmic-scale practical work. Who knew saving the universe would make me better at being me?

The journey from graduation disaster to interdimensional troubleshooter had covered more territory than simple dimensional displacement could account for. Not just physical relocation from Felicity's workshop to cosmic administrative headquarters, but philosophical evolution from someone who broke things for entertainment to someone who fixed things for work satisfaction.

"I've gone from breaking one witch's experiments to fixing everyone's mistakes," I said aloud, testing the observation against the comfortable silence of spaces designed to accommodate contemplation. The words carried weight that had nothing to do with vocal projection and everything to do with recognizing truth that had been accumulating through practical experience.

Accurate summary. Though I'd phrase it as 'evolved from local troublemaker to interdimensional consultant specializing in systematic attitude adjustment for deserving authority figures.'

The change hadn't been sudden or dramatic—more like gradually noticing that territorial claiming had expanded to include cosmic infrastructure, that protective instincts had scaled up to cover displaced populations across multiple realms, that professional satisfaction now came from teaching systems to work better rather than just teaching them to work differently.

Growth through expanded territory rather than personality replacement. Still the same cat, just with significantly larger areas of responsibility and corresponding authority to knock things off cosmic-scale tables.

But the most significant realization was that I'd chosen this evolution. Not forced adaptation to circumstances beyond my control, but deliberate decision to claim responsibility for problems I could solve, territory I could improve, people I could help. Authority earned through being good at things rather than imposed through conquest.

Responsibility as territory claimed rather than burden accepted. Amazing approach to job advancement.

Through the observation deck's viewing systems, I could watch the ongoing results of that choice. Integration consultants across the network are applying flexible thinking to rigid problems. Displaced familiars who had learned to teach other displaced familiars. Authority systems that included accountability in their operational parameters. Infrastructure that served its users instead of extracting from them.

Educational success spreads through voluntary adoption. My chaos signature is teaching others to be productive, rather than just disruptive.

The irony wasn't lost on me. The same impulses that had once made me a problematic familiar—curiosity about how systems worked, impatience with arbitrary rules, tendency to test boundaries until they either bent or broke —had become work qualifications for interdimensional consultation. Traits that had previously labeled me as "high independence" in Collector filing systems now appeared on official credentials as specialized expertise.

Problem behaviors reclassified as job skills. The universe has a twisted sense of job advancement.

But what hadn't changed, what remained constant through transformation and growth and cosmic significance, were the fundamental priorities that made me recognizably myself. I still preferred comfortable boxes to uncomfortable alternatives. Still judged the quality of situations by applicable sardine standards. Still maintained that proper respect was earned through competence rather than granted through authority.

Core personality preserved through job evolution. Still complains, still judges, still loves sardines—just on a significantly larger scale with better documentation.

The complaint-judging-sardine trifecta had, if anything, achieved new levels of sophistication through practical application. Complaints that addressed systematic problems instead of personal inconveniences. Judgments that included constructive alternatives rather than simple criticism. Sardine appreciation had expanded to encompass proper feeding protocols for displaced populations across multiple-dimensional configurations.

Job training that works with natural talents instead of against them. Finally, a job advancement that makes sense.

A soft chime announced incoming communication from the Collector, whose presence had learned to request attention rather than demand it. The viewing array shifted to display its familiar silver-cat-cosmic-administrator integration, form stable in ways that spoke of someone who had found sustainable balance between competing identity requirements.

"Weekly operational assessment indicates continued network stability through voluntary coordination protocols," it announced. However, its voice carried harmonics of satisfaction mixed with residual amazement that democratic management actually worked better than authoritarian control. "Integration consultation requests exceed processing capacity for individual response. Expansion of consultant training programs appears necessary."

More jobs are available through being good at things. The universe recognizes that flexible thinking applied to rigid problems yields results you can count on.

"Training protocols for educational chaos application," I said, chaos field demonstrating continued operational readiness despite a contemplative mood. "Teaching other people to teach systems proper flexibility. Academic accreditation for systematic misbehavior applied to deserving authority figures."

Job training scaled up to teaching programs. I've achieved book-importance worthy of curriculum development.

But expansion raised questions that went beyond simple operational logistics. How to teach flexibility techniques to people who hadn't learned them through personal experience with systematic oppression? How to maintain voluntary cooperation when success created institutional pressure for standardized procedures? How to preserve individual approach diversity while ensuring consistent work skills?

Growing-big challenges that need careful handling to keep fixes from becoming problems. Success brings its own problems.

"The mathematical models suggest sustainable expansion through distributed mentorship networks," the Collector continued, uncertainty bleeding through cosmic authority as it processed scenarios that included variables beyond algorithmic prediction. "Individual consultation specialists training small cohorts in specialized techniques. Organic growth through voluntary participation rather than mandatory standardization."

A voting-based growth plan that includes choice in job training. They're learning to apply voluntary cooperation ideas to their own growing bigger.

The approach made sense from both practical and philosophical perspectives. Training that respects individual learning styles rather than imposing a uniform methodology. Job development that is built on existing strengths instead of replacing them with standardized competencies. Growth that maintained quality through mentorship rather than quantity through mass production.

Sustainable job training that works with individual

personalities instead of against them. Management ideas that actually account for the people being managed.

Through the viewing systems, I could already see the early results. Displaced consultants who had started teaching flexibility techniques to newly liberated familiars. Integration specialists sharing approaches with colleagues facing similar challenges in different dimensional contexts. Even the Collector had begun consulting with former victims about improved management techniques for authority systems.

Teaching effects spreading through voluntary adoption. Voting applied to job training with predictably good results.

The contemplation that followed carried weight beyond simple career satisfaction. This wasn't just a successful job placement for someone with unusual qualifications—it was proof that individual growth could scale up to cosmic significance without losing personal authenticity. That caring could be a work skill. That flexibility could be a systematic methodology.

Personal values lined up with work responsibilities. Finally, work that feels like part of personality rather than something fighting it.

But perhaps most significantly, the journey from selfish familiar to interdimensional consultant had revealed that "selfish" had been mislabeled from the beginning. What others had categorized as excessive independence had actually been early recognition that systems worked better when they included user input. What had been dismissed as problematic behavior had been attempts to teach rigid structures proper flexibility.

Looking back differently. Maybe I was never selfish—maybe I was just the only one paying attention to how badly things were working.

The realization hit with sudden clarity. I hadn't become a different cat, I'd become a more effective version of the same cat, with better tools for applying natural talents to problems that deserved solving.

Growing through getting better at things rather than becoming someone else. Getting better that builds on what I'm already good at.

The phantom pain in my missing tail pulsed once, then settled into the familiar ache that served as a reminder of everything that had changed and everything that hadn't. Still the same cat who valued proper box access and superior sardines. Still the same personality that found satisfaction in teaching rigid systems to bend rather than break.

Just with cosmic significance, work credentials, and unlimited opportunities for educational chaos application to deserving authority figures across multiple-dimensional configurations.

Finally, proper career development for cats with attitude, along with adequate documentation. The universe provides job satisfaction through systematic misbehavior applied with work skills.

The reflection concluded as afternoon light shifted through viewing barriers, creating patches of warmth that demanded proper territorial claiming. I stretched with deliberate precision, joints cooperating despite an extended contemplation session, and settled into optimal sunbeam configuration.

Some things never change. And some things shouldn't.

The universe could continue to provide problems that require flexible thinking applied to rigid solutions. I would continue providing flexible thinking, properly documented and applied, with maximum work satisfaction.

Sustainable career model for interdimensional troublemakers. Finally, a work-life balance that accounts for proper nap scheduling and adequate access to sardines.

Time for the important business of claiming territory that belonged to cats who had learned to apply their natural talents to cosmic-scale problems with measurable positive results.

Purpose achieved through getting better at things. Story completion with dignity intact and attitude properly maintained.

The emergency alert arrived during what should have been optimal afternoon sunbeam time, reality hiccupping with frequencies that made my phantom whiskers twitch in recognition of cosmic-scale problems that required immediate professional attention. But this time, instead of the familiar stress patterns of rigid authority systems encountering variables they couldn't process, the distress signal carried something unprecedented—magical resonance that operated on principles I couldn't immediately categorize.

New kind of crisis. Finally, proper job development through unfamiliar challenges.

I stretched with deliberate precision, joints cooperating despite the transition from comfortable contemplation configuration to active problem-solving posture, then padded across observation deck floors that hummed with sympathetic resonance to whatever exotic disaster was announcing itself through interdimensional channels. Around me, the hub's systems responded with practiced efficiency, alert protocols that had learned to prioritize user comfort during emergency situations.

Infrastructure that cares about employee well-being during crisis response. Work skills applied to workplace management.

The signal itself defied classification by any conventional magical theory. Not the familiar patterns of forced stability creating cascade failure, or voluntary cooperation encountering resistance from rigid bureaucracy. This was something else entirely—magical ecosystems that appeared to function through principles that violated basic assumptions about how reality was supposed to work.

Teaching opportunity disguised as a completely alien problem. My favorite kind of work challenge.

Through the hub's communication systems, data streams painted themselves across the viewing arrays in colors that were painful to perceive directly. Realms where magic flowed in directions that didn't exist in normal space-time. Creatures whose existence depended on paradoxes that resolved themselves by becoming more paradoxical. Infrastructure that maintained stability by systematically violating its own operational parameters.

Alien magical crisis that makes cosmic horror look like amateur hour. This will require the creative application of established principles to completely unfamiliar circumstances.

Bellwether materialized beside the primary analysis array, her pack coordination instincts already cataloguing resource requirements for deployment to territories that operated on principles she couldn't immediately recognize. Her breathing showed controlled anticipation rather than anxiety—someone who had learned to channel uncertainty into productive preparation.

"Incoming dimensional distress from the Paradox Realms," she reported, voice carrying the crisp precision of work skills applied to unprecedented challenges. "Magical ecosystem appears to function through contradictory principles that somehow achieve stability through systematic instability."

Organized impossibility as an operational framework. Someone has been reading philosophy textbooks and applying their principles to cosmic infrastructure.

The Collector approached with movements that suggested someone who had learned to balance oversight responsibilities with the recognition that some problems exceeded the capabilities of algorithmic analysis. Its form maintained stable integration between the cosmic administrator and the silver cat, an authority that acknowledged the limits of mathematical certainty with humility.

"The mathematical models suggest," it began, then paused as data streams revealed information that made standard analysis protocols develop metaphorical headaches. "The mathematical models suggest that conventional analysis may be inadequate for problems that include paradox as a foundational operational principle."

Academic honesty about the limits of academic competence.

They're learning that some problems require practical application rather than theoretical frameworks.

Through viewing systems that had given up trying to display coherent information, images materialized of realms where impossibility had achieved institutional status. Cities that existed in multiple states simultaneously without occupying the same space. Forests that grew backward through time while remaining rooted in present soil. Oceans that flowed uphill by convincing gravity that direction was a matter of opinion rather than natural law.

Beautiful. Impossible. Probably sustainable through principles I don't understand, but will enjoy learning.

"Portal deployment authorization for consultation team specializing in educational flexibility applied to unprecedented circumstances," I announced, chaos field rippling outward to demonstrate operational readiness despite complete unfamiliarity with the operational parameters we'd be encountering. "Standard protocols for teaching rigid systems to bend, adapted for systems that appear to have transcended the concept of rigidity entirely."

Work confidence applies to problems that exceed work experience. Sometimes the best preparation is being prepared to improvise.

The team assembly that followed spoke of people who had learned to coordinate through shared skills rather than detailed planning. Cipher emerged from his analytical sanctuary with calculation arrays that had been modified to include paradox as a positive mathematical variable. Selyn gathered crystalline samples that resonated with frequencies that seemed impossible. Even some of the newly trained consultants requested inclusion—MCC-137 with their expertise in systematic impossibility, the silver wolf whose moonlight fur had learned to navigate between contradictory realities.

Volunteer expertise applied to voluntarily impossible problems. Democracy in action for interdimensional paradox management.

But what struck me wasn't the unfamiliarity of the challenge—it was the realization that unfamiliarity had become work-exciting rather than personally threatening. Unknown problems represented opportunities to get better at things rather than threats to existing understanding. Alien magical principles were puzzles to be solved rather than dangers to be avoided.

Growth through enhanced confidence in adaptability. I've learned to trust my ability to figure things out rather than needing to know everything in advance.

"New worlds, new ways to be annoyed by local customs," I said, settling onto the deployment platform with dignity intact despite anticipation that made my phantom tail want to lash at concepts too abstract for proper clawing. "At least irritation remains universal, even when the underlying principles of reality become negotiable."

Consistency through attitude rather than circumstance. Some things remain constant across all dimensional configurations.

The portal that activated for dimensional transit carried resonance patterns that made reality itself seem uncertain about its own operational parameters. Not the clean stability of reformed infrastructure, or the desperate rigidity of systems afraid to bend. This was something unprecedented—transportation through spaces that existed by refusing to acknowledge limitations on what existence could include.

Interdimensional travel through organized impossibility. The universe keeps providing new ways to challenge work skills.

As we prepared for transit, the familiar weight of responsibility settled across my shoulders—not burden, but territory claimed through showing I'm good at things. Problems that needed flexible thinking. Systems that required educational intervention. People who deserved better alternatives to whatever systematic impossibility they'd accidentally created.

Work satisfaction through service rather than conquest. Job development that aligns with personal values.

The team arranged itself for deployment with practiced efficiency that spoke of people who had learned to trust each other's expertise despite facing challenges none of them completely understood. Not the mechanical precision of processed compliance, but organic cooperation that adapted to circumstances rather than breaking under unexpected pressure.

Pack behavior scaled up to work consultation services. Democracy in action for paradox management.

"Deployment protocols for impossible problems requiring practical solutions," Bellwether announced, her voice carrying satisfaction that came from having found work that matched her skills. "Educational consultation for systems that have transcended conventional operational parameters through creative application of contradictory principles."

Job satisfaction through expanded work challenges. We've all learned to find meaning in making impossible things work better.

The portal achieved full stability with a sound like reality deciding to trust its own judgment despite evidence that its judgment might be fundamentally flawed. Through the dimensional gateway, glimpses of the Paradox Realms materialized in colors that had no proper names and geometries that existed by proving impossibility was just another word for insufficient imagination.

New territory requiring territorial claiming through getting better at things. Perfect job development opportunity.

I bounded through the portal with team coordination that spoke of people who had learned to work together through shared recognition that the best solutions often came from combining different approaches to similar problems. Behind me, the hub's comfortable familiarity gave way to alien magical resonance that promised educational opportunities beyond anything I'd encountered during my evolution from problematic familiar to interdimensional consultant.

Job advancement through voluntary engagement with unprecedented challenges. Finally, job development that promises continued growth through getting better at things.

The Paradox Realms materialized around us with the particular precision of someone who had read every textbook about impossible things and decided that textbooks were just suggestions, anyway. But beneath the alien magical principles and contradictory operational parameters, I could already sense the familiar patterns that would require familiar solutions—systems that had learned to work but might benefit from learning to work better, people who deserved choices even when those choices violated conventional logic, problems that could be solved through flexible thinking applied with proper timing and adequate work attitude.

Same job, different dimensional configuration. The universe provides consistency through variety.

I settled onto what appeared to be ground that existed in multiple states simultaneously, phantom whiskers already mapping stress patterns that painted themselves across reality in equations that solved themselves by admitting they didn't understand the questions. New realm, alien principles, unprecedented challenges requiring creative application of established expertise.

Work skills meet impossible problems. My favorite kind of educational opportunity.

The team spread out behind me, their movements speaking to people who had learned to find excitement in uncertainty, confidence in adaptability, and satisfaction in serving problems that deserved solving, regardless of how strange those problems might be.

Pack coordination for interdimensional paradox consultation. Democracy applied to organized impossibility.

Ahead lay territories that operated on principles I'd need to learn, people who might benefit from alternatives they hadn't considered, systems that could probably work better if someone taught them proper flexibility through patient application of educational chaos.

Standard consultation protocols applied to unprecedented circumstances. Job security through permanent learning opportunities.

The familiar weight of work competence settled across

my shoulders as I surveyed a new domain that required claiming through service rather than conquest. Problems that needed solving, people who deserved better alternatives, systems that could benefit from flexible thinking applied with proper timing and maximum educational effectiveness.

Territory claimed through showing I'm good at things. Responsibility chosen rather than imposed.

I stretched with deliberate precision, testing joints that had learned to adapt to any configuration reality might require, then padded forward into impossible territory with team coordination that had been earned through practical demonstration of mutual skills.

"Time to remind another world that chaos keeps things interesting," I announced to realms that existed by proving impossibility was just another kind of order waiting for proper organization.

Work motto for interdimensional consultation services. Job satisfaction through systematic application of flexible thinking to deserving problems.

The Paradox Realms stretched ahead, beautiful in their contradictory impossibility, populated by people who probably needed help learning to navigate systems that worked by refusing to work conventionally, offering unlimited opportunities for educational chaos application to problems that deserved creative solutions.

New world, new challenges, same work satisfaction through getting better at things applied to worthy problems.

The adventure continued, across dimensions that proved rules were just suggestions, through portal networks that facilitated cooperation by refusing to acknowledge that cooperation should be difficult, toward problems that would require everything I'd learned about teaching impossible things to work better through patient application of flexible thinking.

The universe ensures there will always be work for cats who specialize in teaching rigid systems proper behavior, even when those systems operate through organized impossibility.

The work continued, and the work was good.

About the Author

Kysa Steele is an IT professional by day, and by night an author, TTRPG GM, cat servant, and wife (though the order depends on which cat is asking). She grew up devouring books and plotting to write her own. While newly minted as an indie author, she's been telling elaborate, occasionally cursed stories at the TTRPG table for years. She spends her time building worlds and trying to unravel her cats' many conspiracies.

She lives in Texas with her husband and a cadre of furry overlords. Nori and Mochi are the latest recruits, while Nox, nicknamed the Demon Princess, claimed dominion during the writing of Curse Meow Not. Jake Speed and his sister Ripley occupy the middle ranks, and the eldest, Cid, remains her watchful shadow and self-appointed bodyguard.

Also by Kysa Steele

Curse Meow Not

She was forged for the apocalypse—then reincarnated as a housecat.

Once, Velzara was a princess of fire and fury, destined to burn worlds and break gods. Now she's trapped in the fluffy, humiliating body of a black cat—stripped of her powers, saddled with whiskers, and adopted by a witch-in-training who thinks "Nox" is just a lost stray with attitude problems.

Elira's only magic is making tea and dodging her family's haunted house, but she's inherited more than a creaky door and a cinnamon kettle. When ancient curses flare, mirrors whisper, and the walls themselves start rearranging, Velzara realizes she's not the only one with secrets. And definitely not the most dangerous thing in the house.

The curse was never meant to save her. Only to make sure she survived.

Containment Not Recommended

They broke his mind. Now he solves crimes one catnap at a time.

Luis Cannon was a hardboiled detective—trench coat, gravel voice, bad attitude. A man with a badge and a bone-deep vendetta against injustice. Then he touched the Cognichonk, a cursed artifact from beyond time, and everything came undone.

Now his consciousness is scattered across a psychic network of orange cats in this darkly funny urban fantasy noir. When they sync, they become him: a mystery-solving sleuth with noir narration and a vendetta against household appliances. When the signal fades, they go back to licking power cords and screaming at ceiling fans.

Luis wakes up in bodies he didn't choose, solving supernatural crimes one whisker at a time.

If Luis doesn't crack the case fast, he won't just lose control of the cats—he'll lose what's left of himself.

www.ingramcontent.com/pod-product-compliance
Lightning Source LLC
Chambersburg PA
CBHW030241120726
47903CB00005B/1566